NICHOLAS BLAKE

The Sad Variety

VINTAGE BOOKS
London

Published by Vintage 2012

2 4 6 8 10 9 7 5 3 1

First published in Great Britain in 1964 by Collins

Vintage
Random House, 20 Vauxhall Bridge Road,
London SW1V 2SA

www.vintage-books.co.uk

Addresses for companies within The Random House Group Limited
can be found at: www.randomhouse.co.uk/offices.htm

The Random House Group Limited Reg. No. 954009

A CIP catalogue record for this book
is available from the British Library

ISBN 9780099565628

The Random House Group Limited supports The Forest Stewardship
Council (FSC®), the leading international forest certification
organisation. Our books carrying the FSC label are printed on FSC®
certified paper. FSC is the only forest certification scheme endorsed
by the leading environmental organisations, including Greenpeace.
Our paper procurement policy can be found at:
www.randomhouse.co.uk/environment

Printed and bound in Great Britain by Clays Ltd, St Ives plc

CONTENTS

CHAPTER 1

A Prelude in W.3

'But I can't understand why——'

'Why what?' said the man called Petrov repressively.

Paul Cunningham blinked at him, as if he had picked up a leaf and found it was a scorpion. He was more accustomed to imposing discipline than to being disciplined. 'Why kids have to be brought into it. Surely the obvious thing would be to——?'

'To deal direct with the principal?' Petrov gave his jolly laugh. 'My dear Mr Cunningham, I have explained it to you—the Professor is a very tough nut to crack. Even supposing we could smuggle him out of the country, there's no saying how long it would take to break him down, efficient though our methods are. And speed is essential. No, he's a tough nut, but the nut has one soft spot.' He beamed at Paul Cunningham. 'We know your feeling for the young, dear sir. But personal feelings are not important when——'

'I still don't like it.'

'I'm afraid you haven't very much choice in the matter.'

Paul flushed. It was like being in the grip of a boa-constrictor. Almost a loving embrace at first, then the coils gradually tightening. No, a bear's grip: Petrov resembled a bear—the bulky body and sloping shoulders. Paul felt the breath squeezed out of him.

'Another cup of coffee, comrade?' said Annie Stott. She was a sallow woman of thirty-eight, thin-lipped, skimpy-haired, with the pebble eyes of a fanatic. Paul had not met her till tonight: the preliminary approaches had not included her. He put her down as an old-guard Party member, in whose mind even the Hungarian rising had not caused the slightest deviation. All he knew about her was that she occupied this flatlet in Acton and worked in a commercial electronic-apparatus firm near by.

'I suppose she's going as my political commissar,' he said to Petrov's broad back.

'Miss Stott is an intelligent and resourceful woman,' replied Petrov, not turning round from his scrutiny of Annie Stott's bookcase. 'She'll keep you in order . . . All the right books. Marx,

Engels, Lenin, Palme Dutt; Jack London for relaxation. An earnest type . . . And here's a darker patch on the wall. Once occupied by the late lamented Joseph Stalin. Splendid!' Petrov gave another bellow of hearty laughter.

'Curious way to conceal your political affiliations.' Paul's present humiliation and prospective danger made a sour taste on his tongue.

'There's cover and cover, my friend. Ah, here's the coffee.' Petrov drank, smacked his lips. 'Delicious.'

'For you?' Annie Stott ungraciously plunked down a cup in front of Paul.

'No thanks, comrade. I can't bear Instant anything.'

She looked at him contemptuously. 'What d'you want? Best Brazil? Do you realise that last year 20,000 tons of coffee were thrown into the sea, by order of the bosses?'

'Well, don't blame me. I'm not a capitalist.'

Petrov clapped his large hands. 'Well done! Just like brother and sister. A bossy sister and her sulky younger brother. I see you don't need teaching your parts.'

So the odious Miss Stott was to masquerade as his sister, thought Paul. Two or three weeks of it, in an isolated West-country cottage: it would be insupportable. He looked round at the flat. Everything in it was commonplace, drab, ostentatiously austere. How different from his comfortable room in the staff quarters at the training college, let alone the more exotic hide-out in Pimlico. He glared at a filing cupboard beside the wretched little gas fire, and shivered: in its utilitarian ugliness it bore a close resemblance to its owner. The room smelt of dust, cyclostyle ink, leaflets and the closed mind.

'How fortunate we are', said Petrov expansively, placing his palms on his fat thighs, 'that Mr Cunningham is so respectable . . . Long may it last.'

'Are you referring to that posh place he teaches at?' Miss Stott disagreeably asked.

'I am referring particularly to his contacts with the mighty. It's quite a stroke of luck that he should know the head of an Oxford college well enough to rent his cottage for the Christmas vacation. Nice and handy to the scene of operations. Yes, really a godsend.'

'Be careful. Miss Stott is wincing. She doesn't believe in God.'

'It was a figure of speech, Paul. And since she is your sister,

2

you'd better start calling her Annie . . . I said, you'd better start calling her Annie.'

Paul flushed again. 'Very well.'

'Let me recapitulate. You will pick up the equipment here and drive down to Smugglers' Cottage on 18th December. You will bring the necessary provisions. There's a farm a hundred yards down the hill, where you can get milk and butter. Your excellent sister will arrive by train, with the child, on the 21st: you will meet them at Longport station, on the 6.23 p.m. Before she arrives, establish your presence there and your ostensible reason. You need quiet to start a book. What book,' continued Petrov, his rumbling tones quite unaltered, 'are you writing?'

'I—well, I haven't——'

'Come, come, Paul, this will never do. A little more attention to detail, please. You must not only decide what you're going to write, but start writing it. One weak spot, and a cover story can be ripped open.'

'Oh God! I think all this absurd cloak-and-dagger stuff——'

'The comrade is not interested in what you think,' said the woman.

'You may call it absurd, but your life—and more important things than your life—will depend upon it. You and Annie must establish, in the minds of any neighbours you may meet, a firm impression of brother and sister holidaying together with another sister's child—one who has recently been ill and needs the country air. Before you go down there, Annie will coach you in all the necessary facts about her family, upbringing, career, and so on. Don't forget people in the country are extremely curious about strangers. There must be no discrepancies to cause gossip or suspicion.'

In the stuffy room Paul Cunningham heard Petrov's voice rumbling hypnotically on. Perhaps it felt like this to be brainwashed . . . The telephone at the cottage must not be used, after the coup, except in an extreme emergency. There was a public call-box half a mile down the hill, in the village of Eggarswell . . . London would put through the calls to the target, Annie would do the collecting . . . The preliminary coup at the Guest House five miles away would be carried out by the pair of them . . . How long it would take to soften up the subject was uncertain——

3

'But he'll call in the police at once,' protested Paul, 'and then we're sunk.'

'We shall make it clear to him that this would be inadvisable. He dotes on the child. He wouldn't want anything unpleasant to happen.'

'But even suppose he does cough up, the child will tell where we—I had to rent the cottage in my own name.'

'The child will be taken there in the dark. The view from the back windows could hardly be identified later by a——'

'The fact is, you don't care a damn what happens to me afterwards,' Paul shouted. 'I suppose you and Annie will have skipped out of the country.'

'You are taking a risk. We're taking a bigger one. You just have to remember that, if you won't gamble, you'll certainly be ruined. We've had all this out before.' Petrov stretched his powerful arms above his head, yawning. 'Besides, the child is expendable.'

The gas-fire creaked and popped. The fusty little room seemed to contract round Paul. 'Look, you can't mean——?' His voice dried up.

Annie Stott sniffed. 'Paul still seems to think we're playing kiss-in-the-ring. My poor dear brother, no one is asking *you* to be an executioner.' She rapped on the baize-covered table. 'Will you try to get it into your head that great issues are at stake? Wragby has made a major break-through which could put the Western powers five years ahead of us in the anti-missile field. If we fail, the imperialists can count on that period of immunity. Do you suppose the Pentagon wouldn't yield to the temptation to attack Russia? And that would mean the death of hundreds of thousands of children, not one.'

'I simply don't agree that——'

'We're wasting time,' broke in Petrov. 'If Mr Cunningham proposes to back out, he can sub-let the cottage to you, Annie, and we'll find you another assistant. But you know the consequences, my friend. You're in the thing too deep already.'

Paul knew all too well. He thought of his own childhood with an impoverished widow mother, his congenial job, his comforts, and the austere South African uncle who would leave him a fortune if—if Paul were not involved in a scandal. All this could be swept away by one movement of Petrov's hand.

mental world was one of abstractions, slogans, diagram
where everything—even the kidnapping of a child—b
personalised. She would not have accepted this, no.
understand it was a reason why she had been chosen for t
woman was essential to it, but a woman who would not be ...ened
by the pleadings of a child.

'Well, is there anything else?' she inquired briskly.

Paul came out of his daze. Ever since they had shown him the
ruinous evidence, a miasma of fear and unreality had hung over his
life: though he tried to pretend to himself that, because there was
no attempt at blackmail, the whole horrid business had somehow
ceased to exist, the uneasiness persisted. This evening it had come
to a head. He vaguely heard a brief conversation between Petrov
and Annie, and its commonplace detail heightened the sense of
unreality, as though it was not words but ectoplasm that was
coming out of their mouths, swirling into the dingy room like a fog,
reaching for him, wrapping him round in a cocoon.

'Well, Paul, I'll be seeing you.' Petrov's voice, with its faint
American accent, broke into the nightmare.

'Just a word,' said Paul, 'I must have a word with you alone.'

'No microphones fixed on your stairs, Annie?' Petrov guffawed,
took Paul's upper arm in a ferocious grip, and led him out. The
staircase was dark. The hall smelt of tomcats and carbolic.

'Well?'

'The photographs. When do I get them back?'

'You can have them now.' Petrov produced an envelope from the
pocket of his voluminous overcoat. 'Go on. You can look at them, if
you don't believe me. They're the right ones, aren't they?'

Hurriedly, shamefacedly, in the yellowish hall gaslight, Paul
glanced at the photographs. Petrov peered over his shoulder.
'Really, what antics!'

Licking his lips, Paul said: 'What about the negatives?'

'They'll be returned after the operation. We could hardly——'

'No, of course not. But how do I *know* I'll get them back?'

The big man kneaded Paul's arm painfully. 'You don't. Or you
might get *them*, but there could be copy negatives. You'll just have
to trust your old Petrov. After all, we're trusting you. Nah, nah,
don't worry so, we'll see you all right. You're a good fellow. I've got
to quite like you.'

7

The father-figure went out, light-footed, into the street. Dismally Paul climbed the stairs again. Annie Stott was sitting at the table in the same attitude. The gas-fire popped and creaked.

'You're supposed to start briefing me. We'd better get on with it. My train goes at 9.50.'

The woman sat quite silent. Paul had a sudden fantasy that Petrov, after ushering him out of the door, had turned and shot her dead with a silent gun.

'Are you all right? Annie?' His voice quavered a little.

'Of course I'm all right. I was just thinking. Now then, Paul, the first thing you've got to remember is to bring a jar of French mustard amongst the provisions. I can't abide English.'

CHAPTER 2

The Guest House

DECEMBER 27

It was the Thursday after Christmas. Lucy Wragby was the first of the visitors to wake up at the Guest House. She liked waking early, for no day was long enough to contain all the things she wanted to do. On the mantel-shelf, the clock which for a second hand had a clown endlessly pulling himself over a horizontal bar, said 7.10. Other Christmas presents littered the small room: the blue anorak her father had given her, and a pair of black tights from Elena, were draped over a chair: a handsome doll in Edwardian skating costume lay face-down on the window-sill—Lucy's interest in dolls had died an unnatural death a year ago, when she was seven and started riding lessons. On the bedside table lay a box of oil crayons, a pile of Puffins, and an exercise book containing the first few chapters of a new novel she was writing.

Lucy shook her long dark hair loose about her shoulders and got quickly out of bed. Switching on the electric fire, she drew the curtains. Outside it was beginning to get light. The elms beyond the lawn chattered drowsily with invisible rooks, and between their trunks showed a few lights from the awakening village beyond. The lawn itself looked as if moonlit: it took Lucy a few seconds to realise that it was snow. Oh glory! she thought: tobogganing: the schedule for today must be drastically revised.

Her impulse was to rush into the next room, tell her parents the glad news, and set her father to work buying or making a toboggan. But she realised that, even on holiday, certain grown-up regulations must be respected.

It was cold by the window. Lucy turned on the overhead light, and glanced at herself in the mirror on the way back to bed. The face was familiar. A thin face, pale-skinned, grey eyes set well apart, long dark lashes. 'Hallo, you,' she said: then, 'Why, the child is quite a beauty,'—repeating what she'd overheard the old Admiral say the day after they'd arrived. It had been slightly embarrassing when the Admiral went on, 'takes after her mother, eh?' and Elena had to explain that she was only Lucy's stepmother.

Elena was certainly a super stepmother—not a bit like the ones in fairy-tales—and Lucy boasted about her a good deal to her school friends: Elena had been a famous actress in Hungary, and done something very brave when there was a rebellion there, and then she had managed to escape from the country and come to England, and a few years later Father had married her. Lucy remembered another thing she had overheard, at the wedding. One of the guests said to another, 'She's got quite a look of Caroline, hasn't she?' And the other replied, 'Yes, I dare say that's why Alfred's married her. He was so devoted to poor Carol.' Caroline, Lucy's mother, had died when the child was three years old.

Back in her warm bed, Lucy meditated on all this. As far as she was concerned, Elena had never put a foot wrong. She had not tried to suck up, or fished for compliments, or been cold and snubbing; she had never tried to extract confidences from Lucy about her own mother or her father. Of course, Elena could be moody. Lucy had learnt to respect these black moods and keep out of the way. Father had explained that they were partly because of Elena's actress temperament and partly because of some awful things that happened to her in Hungary.

It was nice, too, that she and Papa got on so well. Elena could be

9

marvellously gay when she was in form: she had quite drawn Papa out, as Lucy said to herself in her best grown-up manner. Papa could be awfully stern, or remote, even unfair: men were like that: but Lucy felt how much he loved her, and never resented for long his occasional outbreaks of temper. What she could not bear was grown-ups quarrelling. Papa and Elena almost never did, as far as she knew, which had made it all the worse when, two months ago, they'd had a scene she burst into the middle of by accident. A silly scene about a framed photograph of Lucy's mother which Papa always kept on his desk. Elena wanted to put it away. You could see her point: no second wife likes to have the first one glaring at her whenever she goes into her husband's room. On the other hand, it was strange that Elena should have waited all this time before asking him to put it away. The photograph was not on the desk now, and Lucy had hidden the anger and tears of the scene as deep in her mind as she could.

But she was vaguely aware that things, in some mysterious way, hadn't been quite so good since then. She knew her father was working very hard at the establishment, and guessed from his touchiness and absence of mind that he must be struggling with some crucial problem. But Elena's dark moods seemed to last longer now; and there was something lacking, not whole-hearted—Lucy had sensed—in Elena's response when Papa came home one day with a light of triumph on his face.

Lucy switched her mind away from such thoughts, and began to plan a new chapter of her serial novel, in which the heroine (herself) should be snowed up in a Guest House with a number of sinister characters, escape by toboggan, and lead the police back to capture the whole gang.

In the next room, Elena Wragby stirred from an uneasy sleep and buried her head in her husband's shoulder as if to shut out the light of the early morning. There were a few minutes of forgetfulness, while he made love to her, then her thoughts started again flowing through the hideous channel they had grooved for themselves—flowing unstaunchably.

Alfred Wragby lay back, his mind crystal clear, savouring once again the triumph he and his team had achieved. During the week immediately after the break-through, he had felt total exhaustion and a sense of dull anti-climax. Now he was himself again. There would be other problems in the future; but for a week or so he could concentrate on giving little Lucy the perfect holiday.

Lance Atterson awoke by the side of Cherry, who appeared as 'Mrs Atterson' in the Guest House register. Pushing back the fringe over his forehead, he dabbled his beard in the girl's face. She remained unconscious. Lance squinted at his guitar lying on a pile of Cherry's clothes on the floor, and debated whether he should wake her with a sharp burst of music. He decided not to—the less attention they called to themselves in this dump, the better. It occurred to him that it was the first time in his twenty-five years, as far as he knew, that he'd woken up beside an heiress. He raised himself to look down on the phenomenon. Puffy eyelids; round, dead-white face, with a streak of green under each eye; a mess of lank yellowish hair; the lips pale as a codfish. She was certainly no Bardot. He pulled down the bedclothes, scrutinising the wide breasts that looked to him like puddings which hadn't risen properly.

The trouble was, she looked so innocent. She was young enough, but not as young as all that, for God's sake. Like an overdeveloped child. No relation between the woman's body and the child face. Not that she wasn't a tolerable performer in the sack. Well, thought Lance, I couldn't help it if she chucked herself into my lap. Who am I to deprive her of the kicks?

'Come on, my old-age pension, wake up!' He shook the girl's puppy-fat shoulders. 'Rise and shine, dumpling.'

Admiral ffrench-Sullivan reached out to the bedside table and put in his false teeth. In the other bed, his wife Muriel snored. What could be seen of her face above the bedclothes and beneath the face-pack resembled that of an irritable pug. The Admiral did not look at it. He opened the book by an Indian mystic upon which he was engaged, but the serenity of soul it should have communicated failed to possess him. 'Worldly goods', enunciated the sage, 'are but shadows of the eternal.' No doubt, thought the Admiral, but I could do with some more of those shadows. When his wife awoke, she'd start up again about the servant problem, the cost of living, the need to keep up appearances, and the disastrous speculations

11

which had lost the Admiral all his money except for the half-pay pension. She was a born grumbler and nagger: the Admiral suffered daily from it, and yet he was fond of her. She had been such a gay spark once. Flinging the wisdom of the East on to the floor, he began to speculate once again on ways and means, and particularly upon the hints thrown out by that queer fellow his wife insisted on calling 'the mystery man'.

In a room next to the Wragbys', which he had been lucky to obtain at rather short notice, Mr Justin Leake sat up, arms behind his head, congratulating himself on his perspicacity. It was now simply a matter of when and how the pressure could best be applied. Lightness of touch was desirable at first, so as not to panic the victim into inappropriate courses, then an increasing firmness. Of course, the present one differed from his usual cases. Really not his line at all, to be concerned with a person below the age of consent. And this time he was not entirely his own master.

Nigel Strangeways left Clare Massinger dressing, and went out on the lawn for a turn before breakfast. The east wind that had blown for days was bitter as ever. The light coating of snow might come in useful, thought Nigel, though it was hardly conceivable that his own talents would be called upon.

The security department for which he had done one or two jobs in the past had summoned him a few weeks ago. It was simply a matter of keeping an eye on Professor Alfred Wragby while he was on holiday at Downcombe. At the Professor's own establishment, they provided ample protection. But Wragby's head contained an important secret, which the other side would be glad to get hold of. The department, being short-handed and run to death just now, could not easily spare a man for surveillance. Purely a routine matter: Wragby was an absolutely reliable chap, unlike some of those boffins, and used to looking after himself—on Special Operations during the war: just a nice free holiday for Mr Strangeways.

'But do it tactfully, old boy,' the head of the department said. 'Wragby's a bit hot-tempered, and he wouldn't like having a nursemaid in attendance. No need to reveal your squalid identity. Unless, of course——'

'What about his family?' Nigel had asked.

'Wife—his second wife. Daughter of eight.'

'What's the wife like?'

'Ex-actress. Rather intense. Naturalised British.'

'And before?'

'Hungarian.'

'Good God in heaven!'

'Now, Nigel, don't get worked up. We've satisfied ourselves about her. She fought against the government in the rising—I mean *fought*, on the barricades with a tommy gun. Managed to get across the Austrian frontier after the Russians moved in.'

'But hasn't she any family there still?'

'Father and mother dead now. No brothers or sisters. There was a baby—by her first husband, who was killed in the fighting. Tragic business. In the confusion at the frontier, the baby got separated from her. She gave it to a companion, a man, to carry in the dash across no-man's-land. They were shot at. When she reached safety she looked back and saw the man's body lying on the ground. He was dead. With the baby beside him. Her party had to restrain her forcibly—she wanted to run back and pick up the baby. Poor girl nearly went off her head. She heard later that the infant had died too—a month afterwards.'

'Well, that seems all right.'

'Don't fuss, Nigel. We've checked and double-checked her . . .'

Nigel remembered this conversation now, as he paced the lawn. The Guest House, in the cold sunny light, looked an emblem of security—an eighteenth-century manor, which had gracefully stepped down from being the residence of many generations of village squires to its present status. Its eight bedrooms were generally occupied—by the 'right sort of people', whom the proprietor seemed able to select infallibly by some kind of osmosis. He had slipped up, thought Nigel, on young Atterson and that absurd beat girl who accompanied him; or perhaps it was not a slip-up—Cherry had a certain air of breeding which she could not quite conceal, hard though she tried, behind her gauche manner and outrageous conversation.

At breakfast, Nigel looked across to the table where she was sitting, with Lance Atterson and Justin Leake. The Guest House kept up the U standards of the manor by using a long table for luncheon and dinner, but tempered them with separate tables for breakfast, when the majority of guests would not wish to fraternise. Cherry's corpse-white face surmounted a huge black sweater with the C.N.D. badge pinned to it.

'Oh, but I'm rotten to the core. I shall become a psychopath,' she announced in reply to some remark of Leake's, her penetrating but weirdly inanimate voice falling like a wooden plank across the silence.

Mrs ffrench-Sullivan looked as if a stranger had pinched her bottom during Holy Communion.

'The trouble is, unless she's careful, that's just what Cherry will become,' Clare murmured to Nigel.

The Admiral coughed. His gentle, lisping voice was heard to say, 'In for more snow, I think. Feel it in the air. Wind's dropped. Bad sign.'

'Oh, Papa, won't it be smashing? I'll make a snowman. And couldn't you get me a sledge? I've never done any sledging.'

'I expect so. But one thing at a time, darling. We've got a week more here.' Wragby's voice was resonant, with a trace of his Yorkshire origin in the vowels.

The Admiral leant over to their table. 'You might have longer, Lucy. The last time there was heavy snow, in 1947, this valley was blocked for a fortnight.'

The little girl's eyes danced at him. 'Wouldn't that be super, Elena? Papa couldn't get back to work, and we'd be all together for a long, long time.'

Mrs Wragby's low-voiced reply was not audible; but Nigel caught on her face a spasm of some profound grief or disquiet. Would she ever be able to forget that dreadful dash across the frontier and the bodies lying in the snow? It was a face of remarkable character and distinction, though ravaged: thin, with high cheekbones and pronounced hollows beneath them: the hair had turned white: the eyes looked deep as wells. But it was Elena Wragby's voice which had first impressed him—a low contralto, vibrant, with an undertone of melancholy.

On their first evening at the Guest House, Nigel had seen Clare's eye dwelling upon Mrs Wragby, and felt her sculptor's fingers itching.

'There's a subject for you,' he said later.

14

'Yes. Would she sit?'

'Why not ask her? Portrait bust?'

'No, I'd like to do a full figure. Niobe Weeping.'

Nigel found her perceptiveness uncanny. While on the job, he could disclose nothing to Clare: he had not told her about Elena's dead child.

By tea-time today the Admiral's prognostications appeared to have gone astray. A slight thaw had set in, and the snow in the winding village street was turning slushy.

On the heights above Eggarswell, five miles off, the snow still lay, an inch or two deep. Along the rough track that led up from the village, past Mr Thwaite's farm to Smugglers' Cottage, the boy they called Evan was walking with Paul Cunningham and Annie Stott. He looked younger than his nine years in physique, older in face: a pale, narrow face, almost wizened; the bullet head topped by bristly flaxen hair which had recently been allowed to grow.

Evan was a polite boy, if rather taciturn, and no trouble to his uncle and aunt. It was odd, being consigned to a pair of total strangers, after a long journey to an unknown country; but Evan's short life had already been abnormal enough—he was used to being treated like an unwanted parcel with a label attached—sent from pillar to post, as it were, and a different label each time. He had learnt from hard experience that it was best not to ask questions. At the moment he was thinking of a promise they had made him—a promise that opened up the most incredible vistas: his hand went to the front of his rough blue jersey, feeling for the secret thing there, his talisman, the thing that told him who he was.

A snowball hit him in the back of the neck. 'Come on, Evan, wake up, old son!' said Uncle Paul.

Evan stared at him, wiping the snow from his neck. 'But is it cultured to throw snowballs?' he asked, in a puzzled voice, his accent—for he had been well taught—almost perfect English.

'Cultured? Good God, yes. Not in the People's Democracies, maybe, but it's O.K. in this benighted imperialist country.'

Evan reached down, rather dubiously, made a snowball and flung it at Uncle Paul. They walked past the farm. Buxom Mrs Thwaite smiled from the window as she saw the two bombarding each other. Nice young fellow, that Mr Cunningham, she thought:

15

that sister of his, Dr Everley, is a proper dragon, though—stuck-up, I call her, not letting the poor little boy play with my nippers. Said he'd had a serious illness, got to go easy for a while. Yellow-faced cow. Can't abide kids to enjoy themselves. God help her patients.

'You'd better stop now, Paul,' shouted the yellow-faced cow. 'We don't want Evan to get overheated.'

They passed through the farmyard gates. Smugglers' Cottage lay beyond, a two-storied building with Gothic-shaped windows on the upper floor, standing quite alone overlooking a broad expanse of country: its site had been dug out of the slope, so that at the back the hill rose steep and close, shutting out any view. Inside, the cottage was snug enough, if somewhat austere in its fitments, as became the head of an Oxford college. A log fire blazed in the sitting-room. A row of ash-trees stood at the far end, protecting the cottage from the east wind.

'What would you like to do tomorrow?' said Annie, as Paul got the tea ready. 'It's your last day. You must make the most of the time.'

'What can I do?' asked the boy in his gruff little voice. Then, greatly daring, 'Could I go to the movies?'

'I'm afraid not, dear. You see, in the country they only run in the evenings, and your train goes at 6.10.'

'And then I go back to London, and see——'

'Yes, Evan. But you mustn't get over-excited about it.'

'No, Dr Everley,' Paul put in. 'At all costs he mustn't get over-excited.' There was a rasp of bitterness in his voice which made Annie Stott raise her eyebrows. There was always the chance that Paul would go soft, but she had not expected it to show up so early in the proceedings.

'Have another bun, Evan,' she said.

Tea at the Guest House was just over. Elena Wragby and her husband had gone upstairs to write letters. The rest of the party was assembled in the large panelled drawing-room, having jockeyed for positions near the log fire—a contest in which Mrs ffrench-Sullivan, Lance Atterson and Cherry had dead-heated.

'Other people like to be warm too, Mr Atterson,' the first-mentioned of these was remarking from her vantage point.

'Sure, lady. It's the universal yen of mankind. First gratified, the legends do say, by a sharp schemer called Prometheus.'

'I don't know what you're talking about,' the lady replied with hauteur. She turned away in a marked manner to Cherry. 'In my youth, young persons were always trained to give place to their elders.'

'Oh, I sympathise with you madly,' said Cherry in her flat drawl. 'Personally, I feel older than the rocks on which I sit.'

Justin Leake broke in, a nondescript-looking man, with the attentive but disabused expression of a journalist. 'Which can hardly be true, Mrs Atterson. You look charmingly youthful. I mean that as a compliment.'

'Like hell you do,' muttered Lance, his teeth flashing white above his black beard.

Mr Leake persisted. 'I'm sure I've seen your face somewhere before. Could it have been in a photograph, now? In the Press?'

'As the stranger said to the Egyptian, "The name escapes me, but the fez is familiar",' remarked Lance. There came a fizz of laughter from Lucy, who was lying on the carpet chalking a picture.

'My husband and I had a most delightful stay in Egypt, just before the war. He was stationed at Alexandria,' Mrs ffrench-Sullivan gave out.

'Did you see any belly-dancing?' inquired Cherry.

'No, dear. I don't think they had a ballet company there.'

Lance Atterson turned up his eyes to heaven. 'But you had lots of slaves?'

'Servants. Certainly. The fuzzy-wuzzies are a spineless lot—look at that man Nasser; but I always say they make excellent servants. So attentive and good-mannered.'

'Whereas in this country——?'

'Exactly, Mr Leake. The lower classes are utterly ruined. It's the Welfare State, of course. No one will go into service now. The Admiral and I had to move out of our beautiful house at Stoke Trenton simply because we could not find staff. I dare say it's easier in London, Mrs Strangeways.'

'Not really. And by the way, my name is Clare Massinger.'

'A name to conjure with,' said Mr Leake, covering Mrs ffrench-Sullivan's confusion. 'Miss Massinger is one of our leading sculptors. I greatly admired your last exhibition.'

'Kind of you.' Clare could not make out why this man gave her the creeps. It seemed cruel to snub so inoffensive a person. 'What did you like best?'

Mr Leake hesitated. 'Well now, I can't just remember the names of——'

'Describe just one of the exhibits,' put in Lance, smirking at him.

'Well, there was that figure of a woman, a nude,' Mr Leake began uneasily.

'I don't believe you ever went to the exhibition,' announced Cherry in her penetrating monotone.

The Admiral's wife turned to Clare. 'Do you make those modernistic things out of wire? I think they're perfectly ridiculous myself. Can't see any art about them.'

'No.'

'But I suppose they're fashionable—make a lot of money?'

'Clare knocks up whopping great nudes. Stone or marble. Makes pots of money out of them,' said Nigel.

'What? Like those awful Epstein things?' Mrs ffrench-Sullivan looked both avid and petulant.

'Not very,' said Clare.

'I liked that "Virgin and Child" of his in Cavendish Square,' lisped the Admiral. 'But I find Henry Moore's work more to my taste in general.'

'Good for you,' said Clare.

'Those awful things with holes in them,' murmured Lance.

At this point, Professor Wragby entered the room and sat quietly in a corner. The Admiral's wife changed the subject with a crash of gears.

'What's that badge you always wear, Mrs Atterson? A cycling club badge?'

'No. C.N.D.'

'C.N.D.?'

'The Campaign for Nuclear Disarmament.'

Mrs ffrench-Sullivan recoiled, as if Cherry had uttered some frightful indecency. '*Really!* D'you mean you sit about on wet pavements, and go for those dreadful marches? On Good Friday too! It's absolutely blasphemous.'

Cherry's voice took on an unwonted animation. 'Well, *I* think

18

it's absolutely blasphemous to make plans for killing millions of harmless people all over the world.'

'You don't want to defend your own country? *Well*, I *must* say!'

'The atom bomb is not built for defence. It's to attack other countries.'

'You don't believe in it as a deterrent?' asked the Admiral gently.

'You'd rather be Red than dead?' said Justin Leake, scrutinising the girl with his fixed, attentive eyes.

'Yes, of course. Who wouldn't? At least, I'd rather be Red than be responsible for killing millions of innocent people, white, red, or black.'

'Cherry's a fanatic,' said Atterson, smirking into his beard.

'And I don't believe it will deter—not for long,' the girl stubbornly went on.

'It does seem to have, so far, Cherry,' suggested the Admiral, his faded blue eyes blinking at her in a kindly, worried way. She felt a certain sympathy there, and exclaimed:

'I'm not trying to get at you, Admiral. Honestly I'm not. Soldiers and sailors—well, I mean they have a job to do, and——'

'Ours not to reason why, my dear?' he said, smiling at her.

'Actually, you're a pet. No, what makes me sick—it's the bloody scientists who never seem to reason why.'

'Hush, dumpling,' said Lance. 'Scientists present.'

Lucy looked up apprehensively at her father; but she knew the signs when he was going to explode, and it was all right. The Professor strolled towards the fire, a tall man, broad-shouldered but stooping a little, reddish-haired.

'Well, young woman, you'd better enlarge on that.'

'Sorry, I didn't know you were in the room.'

'Never mind about that. I won't bite you. Just carry on.'

The girl clasped her fingers tightly together. 'Well, then, I think you scientists just go blindly ahead with your theories and experiments and never stop to ask yourselves what the consequences will be—for mankind, I mean.'

'You're saying we should be, not only scientists, but prophets *and* moral censors of our own work.'

Cherry flushed, but bravely hung on. 'You don't need to be a prophet to know that, when you make an atom bomb, you're making an atom bomb and it'll destroy a great many people.'

'Nuclear fission was a neutral discovery. It could be used for destructive purposes *and* productive ones. Surely you can see that? Would you have suppressed the discovery of the internal combustion engine because motor cars can kill people?' The Professor spoke unaggressively, but with a trace of pedagogic arrogance in his tone.

Clare said, 'So the scientist has no moral concern whatsoever with the end-products of his activity?'

'The pure scientist, no. The technologist, of course, has.'

'As a pure scientist, you have no concern. All right. But you're also a human being.'

'As a man, I must be concerned, Miss Massinger. I agree. It can be a very real conflict.'

'But why should there be any conflict about it?' said Justin Leake. 'Isn't it a first principle of scientific morality that every new discovery should be published and made accessible to humanity as a whole?'

'In theory, yes. In practice, if you broadcast a discovery, you merely enlarge the area of moral conflict. I mean, the authorities of every other nation, as well as your own, will have to decide what use to make of it.'

'But some scientists have stuck to the principle,' said Leake. 'The ones the rest of us call traitors. Do you approve their conduct?'

'That would depend on the individual. I wouldn't approve if he handed over knowledge simply to further the ends of some other power-group against his own country's.'

'Not if, by doing so, he redressed the balance of power?' asked Nigel. 'Isn't the whole argument for a deterrent based on both sides having an approximately equal force of it?'

Alfred Wragby laughed, and threw up his hands. The Admiral's wife was asleep in her chair.

'This is a drag, all this yakking,' remarked Lance Atterson, yawning. 'Anyway, scientists aren't all making bombs. What's your line, Prof?'

'I'm a mathematical physicist.'

'Which explains everything,' muttered Lance sourly. Nigel thought the young man was disgruntled by Cherry's bold stand and his own failure to contribute anything.

'We are luckier in the Services,' said the Admiral. 'The horizon's narrowed down to one's duty, and that's generally plain enough. Find the enemy, engage him, and destroy him, eh? No moral conflicts.'

'Oh, you sailors are fearful escapists, aren't you?' said Cherry.

The Admiral chuckled at her. 'Ah, here's Mrs Wragby. Come on, postman.' He tapped Lucy with his foot.

She sprang up, put on the blue anorak and sou'wester which Elena had brought down, and took the sheaf of letters from her hand. Most days since they'd arrived, Lucy had gone down the lane to catch the evening collection: she was an independent little girl, and liked going by herself.

'Don't dawdle, love,' said the Professor. 'It's very cold outside.'

After a few seconds Nigel unobtrusively followed Lucy and her stepmother into the hall. He heard Mrs Wragby's footsteps as she ran rapidly upstairs, and the front door closing. It was sufficiently obvious to him that Lucy was the Professor's weak spot. He could not imagine enemy agents, if they knew anything about Wragby— as presumably they would—making a frontal attempt: they'd know it'd be altogether too chancy. On the other hand, Nigel could not stand about over Lucy all day and night: the Department itself had discouraged any obvious surveillance. It was a thousand to one against an attempt upon Lucy being made, yet Nigel, unknown to the others—or so he believed—had kept her in sight every evening she went down to the pillar box.

Tonight it was not so easy. The moon, in its last quarter, was obscured by heavy cloud. The snow played odd tricks with what little light there was. Nigel went farther down the hill than usual. At the bottom, a hundred yards from the Guest House, the lane joined the road at the western end of the village. At the T-junction stood a pillar box, very faintly illuminated from a window of the post office round the corner. Fifty yards away from it now, Nigel could see that the wedge of darkness opposite the pillar box was in fact a car with its lights switched off. He hastened his step: and the next instant a blow from a heavy spanner struck him on the back of the head, and the world disintegrated in a shower of vanishing sparks.

Paul Cunningham rolled the body into the ditch, and hurried silently down the lane, congratulating himself on his idea of

21

waiting in the shadows to choke off anyone who might follow Lucy from the Guest House. It was gratifying, too, to find that he had the nerve to clobber someone so efficiently.

Annie Stott, sitting in the car, saw Lucy approach and leant out of the window. 'Could you tell me which way I go for Longport?' she asked, switching on the headlights to dazzle anyone who might approach along the village street, and getting out of the car.

'You turn right here. But——' Lucy had no time to say more. The woman snatched the letters from her hand, threw a rug over her head and bundled her into the back seat. Paul arrived that moment, took the letters from Annie's outstretched hand and posted them, then jumped into the car, slammed the door and drove off along the Longport road.

The whole business had not taken ten seconds. Lucy thrashed about on the back seat like a fish in a net, but she was firmly held and the rug stifled her cries. It smelt of paraffin. Paul said, over his shoulder, 'Chap was following her. I bashed him.'

'Did you?' remarked Annie unimpressed. 'Stop as soon as you get amongst those trees.'

A quarter of a mile along the deserted road, Paul braked, the car slewing dangerously on the snowy surface. He took a filled hypodermic syringe from the glove-compartment, and got into the back seat.

'Torch,' said Annie.

He switched it on. She parted the rug, seized Lucy's arm, rolled up a sleeve of the anorak, and stuck in the needle, while Paul used his other hand to hold the child down.

'Stop it! That hurt!' screamed Lucy. 'What are you doing?'

'Taking you for a nice long ride,' Paul said, a maniac excitement filling him.

Annie Stott swathed Lucy in the rug again, Paul drove on, and soon the whimpering ceased.

CHAPTER 3

Smugglers' Cottage

DECEMBER 28

Professor Wragby put on his overcoat and went out. It was nearly ten minutes since Lucy had gone down to the pillar box: of course, she did dawdle sometimes, lost in one of those dreamy states which made her school teachers impatient; but a certain indefinable disquiet had seeped into the Professor's mind. Ten minutes, and on such a cold night. Lucy was generally back in three or four.

A groan came from the ditch to his right. He threw his torch beam in that direction. A dark, snow-splashed lump was lying there.

'Good God, Strangeways, have you hurt yourself?'

Nigel, with Wragby's help, crawled out of the ditch, and on hands and knees vomited in the snow. It was agony to raise his head, but presently he did so.

'Lucy,' he gasped, and was seized with a fit of retching. He tried again. 'Is she back yet?'

'No. What the devil is all this?'

'How long since she went out?'

'About ten minutes. But——'

'Telephone. Guest House. Afraid they've got her. Quick.' Nigel struggled to his feet. As Wragby supported him up the hill, Nigel's brain began to clear, and he told Lucy's father what he had seen before he was knocked out.

'Tell Chalmers. No one else. Ring the police on his private phone.'

'Look here, you've had a nasty experience. Are you sure? She could have dropped in to see Emma.'

'Somebody bashed me. That proves it.' Nigel fumbled in his pockets, took out his wallet. 'Not been robbed.' He extracted his credentials. 'Here. Read this before you telephone. And mention it to *nobody* except the police.'

The light outside the front door gleamed on the Professor's face. He looked more dazed than his companion.

A minute later, Clare's fingers were feeling the back of Nigel's head.

'I don't think it's broken,' she said, trying to keep her voice steady.

'Of course it isn't,' he replied irritably, 'or I wouldn't be talking to you. Just bathe it and put some antiseptic on. A nice bloody mess I've made of things. Where's Wragby?'

'He went to telephone.'

After she'd bathed his head and wrapped a bandage round it, Nigel asked urgently, 'Clare darling, when I went out, did anyone follow me?'

She took her time. 'Well, we were in the drawing-room. Mrs Wragby had gone out with Lucy.'

'Yes, she ran upstairs. And then?'

'Mr Leake left the room soon after you.'

'How soon?'

'Oh, almost at once. And Cherry and Lance Atterson about the same time. Sort of general exodus. Only the Admiral and his wife and I were left. And now, what *is* all this about?'

'Lucy's been kidnapped.'

'Oh, Nigel! No! How do you——?'

Professor Wragby strode into the room. 'The village bobby is coming up. And I rang the doctor too. How are you feeling?'

'Bloody awful. And what the hell use is a village constable? We want County Headquarters,' Nigel grumpily remarked.

'He's getting on to them straightaway.' The Professor was keeping a stern control on himself. 'Pity you didn't get a better look at the car.'

'Yes.'

'Not that I'm blaming you, Strangeways.'

'You'd have a right to.'

Wragby handed him the Department's credentials. 'Here's this piece of bumf. Why the devil couldn't they have let me know what was in their minds?'

'Have you told your wife yet?'

'No. Fact is, I'm funking it a bit. She's devoted to Lucy. And I don't want to alarm her until we know for certain—after all, Lucy *may* have dropped in at Emma's house or somewhere else in the village.'

'Would you mind if Clare broke it to her?'

'Well, no, I'd be grateful, Miss Massinger. She'll be worrying.'

At a nod from Nigel, Clare slipped out of the room. He knew how well he could rely on her powers of observation.

Wincing, he looked up at Alfred Wragby, who was gazing out of the window as if he might yet see a small figure in a blue anorak dancing back along the drive.

'I simply can't take it in yet. The dirty bastards!' His slow Yorkshireman's anger was beginning to flare. 'If your people suspected this might happen——'

'It seemed to them only the remotest possibility conceivable.'

'Still, they might have warned me of it.'

'Yes, perhaps they should. But even then, you couldn't have stood over her night and day.'

Wragby stared at him, unseeingly. After a silence, he asked, 'What do they want, these chaps who——'

'They want your last discovery.'

'Yes. I knew that really, of course.' He swallowed. 'Would they give her back if they got it?'

It was the question Nigel dreaded. He was saved from trying to answer it by the entrance of the village constable, whom the proprietor showed in. Nigel said to the latter, 'Mr Chalmers, will you please let us know at once if any of your guests attempt to leave the house.'

The man looked puzzled, but gave an acquiescent nod and went out.

'Sorry, Constable. I'll explain. This is Professor Wragby. My name's Strangeways. The Professor's little girl was taken away in a car, when she went to post the letters. She'd been down to post them about the same time every night since the Wragbys arrived here. The kidnappers could hardly have known this and made the plans they did, unless they had an accomplice in the Guest House to give them the information. Now, what are County Headquarters doing?'

The constable, fortunately, was not one of the notebook-ruffling, pencil-licking school. Catching the urgency of Wragby's voice on the telephone, he had jumped into action with commendable promptness. County Headquarters had been alerted first. In the fifteen minutes before the Superintendent could take action, the kidnapper's car would not have got more than twelve miles from Downcombe on these treacherous, winding roads. Blocks were set up on the roads leading out of the valley, at distances of twenty miles from Downcombe: an outer cordon was being formed too. Every car would be stopped at the road blocks and examined. Mobile police within a radius of fifty miles were alerted, railway stations informed; a description of Lucy was being telephoned to every police station in this part of England, and the regional B.B.C. service would broadcast it in the next news bulletin.

'Well, that sounds like a good job,' said Wragby.

'Oh, we're not so sleepy in these parts as some do say,' the young constable remarked. 'Tom Oakes at the Lion, he's organising a search party, just in case the little girl is wandering round hereabouts.'

'No chance of that, I'm afraid,' said Nigel.

'I thought not, sir. After the Professor told me who you were and what had happened to you. But for that, I'd have had a job convincing the Superintendent. He'll be here within the hour.'

'You've done very well indeed. I suggest you go down to the end of the lane now. Keep people off the spot where the car was standing. There'll be tyre-marks and footprints for the Super to examine. And take a look at the place where that bleeder hit me over the head. Maybe he left a visiting card there. The Professor will show you.' Anything to give Wragby something to do: his expression of stony despair underlined Nigel's own failure.

Meanwhile, Clare was with Elena Wragby. When she knocked on the Wragbys' door, Elena called out, 'Lucy! Where have you been all this time?'

Clare went in. By the light of the bedside lamp, Elena Wragby's face looked almost distraught. 'Oh, it's you. What's the matter? Is it Lucy?' Her voice was vibrant with emotion. Actresses, thought Clare, cannot help playing up a dramatic moment, even when it's no make-believe: she said,

'I'm sorry, my dear.'

Elena crossed the room to her in three magnificent strides. 'Is she—has there been an accident?'

Clare gripped her outstretched wrists. 'No. She has not come back. Try to be calm. She has been taken away. Kidnapped.'

'No! But that's impossible.' The great eyes blazed into Clare's.

'Little Lucy? Kidnapped? But why? We are not rich. I do not understand this.' Horror broke slowly through incomprehension on Elena's face. 'Yes, you do mean it. Tell me—but how do you know this?'

Clare told her what little she could. Elena had slumped down on the bed. In the shaded light, her face looked marmoreal now, petrified in grief. Niobe, thought Clare; Rachel weeping for her children, for they are not. Then the marble dissolved, the mouth began to tremble, the thin body was shaken by a storm of sobbing.

'I'll fetch your husband. He's talking with Nigel. You mustn't distress yourself too much. We'll get her back.'

Elena moved convulsively in her arms. 'No, not yet. Stay with me! I can't face him.'

'But, my dear——'

'If I hadn't sent her to post the letters, she'd never—I wanted her to be independent. An only child can so easily—— Oh, I don't know what I'm saying. I'm distracted. It hurts so. She was like my own child.' The tear-stained face looked up wildly. 'You never had one, did you?'

'No.'

'I did. One of my own. They killed it. And now they've taken Lucy too.'

That night, out of a windless sky, it snowed heavily, silently, obliterating tracks, overlaying and penetrating—it seemed—even men's sleep, so that when they awoke next morning they had a sense, before they looked out of the window, that some change had come about.

Lucy Wragby, under the influence of the drug, drowsed till ten o'clock. When she came half awake, her head felt queer—the way it had felt during a bad attack of 'flu, like a shell stuffed with cotton-wool, unnaturally light, but congested. Vaguely she knew there was something she did not want to remember, and tried to sleep again. This did not work for long. Climbing heavily out of bed, she drew the curtains. Not till then did she realise that she was not in her own room at the Guest House. The lower half of the window was barred, like a nursery's. It was light outside—dazzling light, for through the bars she could see nothing but a wall of white and the sky above it. With a rush, last night's happenings flooded

27

into her mind: the snowy lane, the pillar box, the car, the woman, the stab in her arm, the paraffin-smelling rug.

She looked down at her forearm, and saw that she was wearing pyjamas, not her usual nightdress.

'I am Lucy Wragby,' she heard herself saying. 'I am Lucy Wragby.' As though there were some doubt about it.

When in perplexity, she had a habit of putting one of her long, dark tresses in her mouth and chewing it. Automatically her hand went to the hair that should have been hanging down her back. There was no hair. Lucy felt at her head. It seemed to be covered with bristle.

'But I *am* Lucy Wragby.'

Her voice was frightened and tearful now. Looking wildly round the room, she saw a mirror on a dressing-table. She stumbled over to it. It was the worst moment in her life: far the worst. The face that looked at her out of the mirror was not her own. It was a boy's face, with short, blond hair and blond eyebrows. The face gazed at her in horror, opened its mouth, began to howl.

Lucy rushed back to the bed, drew the bedclothes over her head, and sobbed as if her heart would break . . .

Downstairs at Smugglers' Cottage, Annie Stott was preparing some food to take up to the child, who presumably had not awoken yet or she'd have started bawling. Everything had been carried out correctly so far. Last night they had got back without misadventure, and informed Comrade Petrov over the short-wave transmitter. The next move would be his. Annie had then shorn off Lucy's long tresses and dyed what hair was left, burning the rest in the incinerator. She went into the living-room, put some more wood on the fire. Outside, the snow covered everything. She noticed that it was nearly half-way up to Paul Cunningham's knees, as he walked away down the track with Evan to get milk at the farm. It might be awkward if further snowfalls took place; but the sky seemed clear enough just now. Annie gazed out resentfully at the panorama of rolling, white-clad hills. She disliked the countryside: she had been bored by Evan and irritated by Paul for nearly a week already.

At the farm, while his milk-pail was being filled and Evan stared in a lack-lustre manner at the hens that scrabbled in the yard, Paul Cunningham was conversing with Mr Thwaite.

'Going to be any more of this?'

'Shouldn't be surprised,' said the farmer. 'Have you got chains for your car? You may need them.'

'I'm afraid not.'

'I believe I've got a spare set kicking around somewhere.'

'That's very kind of you.'

'Staying on much longer?'

'Well, we ought to get back to London on Saturday. But—' Paul lowered his voice—'young Evan doesn't seem awfully fit. Hope he's not sickening for anything. He's a bit delicate, you know. I wouldn't like to risk his travelling if——'

'Lucky you've got a doctor in the house.'

'What? Oh yes, my sister's very capable. Gave up her practice when she got married, but——'

'Here's your milk, then.'

Paul collected Evan and walked back, angrily conscious of having babbled in an unconvincing way to cover up a blunder. Still, he'd established the main point—always supposing Thwaite's bucolic mind was capable of taking it in . . .

Lucy had the resilience of a child who has always been given love and security. Moreover, she possessed the enviable faculty of entering into the spirit of any dramatic event in which she was involved. Her father, whom she hero-worshipped, had once said to her, 'Never be afraid of the truth. Face facts. Take them to the light and look at them. If you learn to accept them—especially the nasty ones—for what they are, you've won half the battle.'

She could understand this better now than when he'd said it. She sat up in bed. The facts were that she'd been kidnapped, and was a prisoner in an unknown house. Or was she? Lucy leapt out of bed, turned the door handle: the door was locked. Nor could she squeeze through the top of the window above the bars. Her captors had cut and dyed her hair. Why? So that if a policeman came to the house, he would not recognise in her the little girl whose disappearance would no doubt be in the papers and the broadcast news. How absurd to have been frightened by that altered face in the mirror. Lucy fingered the mastoid-operation scar under her ear, and pulling up the pyjama top inspected the mole on the left of her belly-button: they proved she was Lucy Wragby.

Whoever her captors were, they could not be like the kidnappers one saw on the telly. She was not incarcerated in a mouldering attic, compelled to lie on a heap of filthy rags while unshaven, greasy men played cards in one corner, uttering oaths and fingering their revolvers. She was in a neat, bare room: bright-patterned curtains: floor well polished: plenty of warm bedclothes. A dado of ducks and geese along the wall suggested the room was once a nursery. There were some tattered children's books on a shelf, and a cupboard which proved, on investigation, to hold a few toys. The only peculiar thing was that the pages on which the owner's names had been written were torn out of every book.

Lucy became aware of hunger, and even more of thirst. And at the same time she was conscious of a creeping dread. She did not want to see that beastly woman who had dragged her into the car. Never again. She struggled with this fear for ten minutes. Face facts. The filthy old cow is a fact. All right, face her. Lucy could almost hear her father saying it. There were sounds of movement downstairs. Lucy rattled the door-knob and called out, first in a dry little croak, then louder. She jumped back into bed. Lay there, trembling. Perhaps it wouldn't be the same woman.

But it was. Horrid mustardy-yellow face, over a pink jumper which clashed with it like an unlovely discord: skirt bagging at the knees. The woman laid a tray on Lucy's bed—it held two boiled eggs, some bread and butter, and a mug of milk—then as silently moved towards the door. She must be a deaf mute, thought Lucy, drawing upon her knowledge of sensational fiction. No, of course she isn't, you nit—she asked you the way to Longport.

'Just a minute,' said the little girl timidly.

The woman hesitated. 'Yes?'

'Suppose I want to go to the lavatory?' It was not at all what Lucy had meant to say.

'There's a basin behind that curtain, and a pot under the bed.'

'But I—I can't do everything in the pot.'

'You can, and you must.'

The woman's pebbly eyes looked past Lucy's shoulder.

'What's your name?' asked Lucy.

'You can call me Annie. Aunt Annie.'

'But you're not my aunt.'

'And your name is Evan. Don't forget it.'

Lucy was convinced she had a lunatic to deal with. A fantasy

30

began to bubble up in her mind—about a woman who had lost a boy called Evan and gone potty and stolen a little girl to replace him.

'Well, don't you want your breakfast?' said the loopy woman. Lucy drank some of the milk and started on an egg.

'I suppose you've stolen me,' she said in a humouring tone.

'You can suppose what you like.'

'Where is this house?'

Aunt Annie became, for her, quite garrulous. 'It's my cottage in Buckinghamshire. About thirty miles from London. We brought you a long way last night. You slept all the way.'

'How long shall I be staying here?'

'That depends.'

'This is a very nice egg.' It annoyed Lucy that she could not catch the woman's eyes, but that—she supposed—is how a mad-woman behaves.

'When you've finished breakfast, put on these clothes. They should fit you.' The woman took out from the chest of drawers a boy's jersey, short trousers, stockings, pants and vest. They all looked a bit tatty, thought Lucy: belonged to the poor child she lost, I expect. The woman departed, locking the door behind her. Lucy opened the second egg, and while she ate it addressed her mind to radical changes in her new serial. Perhaps she should scrap the chapters already written and start again: she had a real adven-ture to write about now. She thought of the exercise book on her bedside table at the Guest House. Papa and Elena would be worrying about her. Poor darling Papa. Lucy found the spoonfuls of egg difficult to swallow now. A feeling of desolation crept over her . . .

'How is she?' asked Paul Cunningham downstairs.

'Awake. Eating her breakfast. She's a queer little girl, I must say.'

'How d'you mean, queer?'

'Takes it all very calmly,' Annie Stott replied.

'You'd prefer her to be in hysterics?'

Annie curled her thin mouth so that it resembled the rind of some bitter fruit. She glanced at her companion. There was something faun-like about his face and the shape of his head, giving him a faint likeness to a certain Russian dancer who had recently run out on his ballet company and gone over to the capitalists: it did not endear him any the more to Annie.

'Poor kid,' he said.

'If you're so sorry for her,' snapped Annie, 'you can go and be her nursemaid.'

'Certainly not,' he coldly replied. 'The arrangement was that she should set eyes on no one but you. If she sees me, she might meet me again and recognise me. Oh, I forgot, of course you're going to cut her throat when all this is over.'

'Don't be a fool. The child believes she is in Buckinghamshire. So long as she has nothing to give away about us afterwards——'

'About me, you mean. You'll be quite safe, sunning yourself in the salubrious Crimea.'

'—violence would be quite incorrect. When I've passed on the information and it has been checked, I'll give the child another shot in the arm and you can drive her away and dump her wherever you like. You've nothing to get in a panic about,' the woman added contemptuously.

'I wouldn't have, if I could believe a word you people say.'

'*Now* what's the matter?'

'You know perfectly well.' Paul's voice became a little shrill. 'I don't set myself up as a model of the virtues, but at least I don't pretend that whatever suits my book is the truth, like you and your bloody Party do.'

'There's no need to shout at me. Where's Evan?'

'Digging the snow away from the garage doors. Thwaite says he'll lend me some chains.'

'Well, you'd better go and put them on soon. My appointment is for midday.'

'Don't get caught, my dear sister. I'll need the car this evening to take Evan to the station. I say, aren't you nervous about putting your hand into the hornet's nest? Belcaster'll be swarming with police today.'

'Not if Wragby follows his instructions.'

'But if he doesn't?'

'So much the worse for him.'

'And for you.'

'Oh no. I shall be informed if he proposes to try any tricks.'

'Do you think he will?'

'Search me. He might, once. Not a second time. Not after we've turned on the heat.'

'You mean, you'll saw off one of Lucy's fingers and send it to him by post?' asked Paul flippantly. Then, as the woman made no answer, he added in an appalled voice, 'Good God, I believe you would.'

'You should bring your reading up to date,' said Annie. 'What d'you suppose we have that tape-recorder for?'

'I thought you were going to practise some dreary political speeches.'

Annie's rejoinder was stopped by a banging on the floor somewhere overhead. 'Are you sure Evan's outside? He mustn't know there's anyone but us in the house.'

'Don't panic, comrade.' Paul went to the window and looked out sideways. 'Yes, there he is. Shovelling madly away.'

When Annie came downstairs, Paul asked, 'What does she want?'

'Paper and pencil.'

'Going to write a letter home?'

'No. She wants to write a story. It'll keep her mind occupied. Where's the foolscap you're supposed to be writing your book on?'

Paul collected some sheets and a pencil off the desk in the corner. As Annie ran upstairs again, there was the sound of a tractor. Paul went out. Farmer Thwaite was standing on the machine's platform, one of his men driving. He held out a set of rusty chains. 'Can you fit these, or would you like Jim here to help?'

'That's tremendously kind of you. If you could spare him——'

'You're welcome. I'm beating down the snow along the lane as far as the village. Milk float won't be able to get up otherwise.'

Jim climbed down from the great tractor, which towered over Paul with its canopied top. The rubber tyres were as broad as the length of his forearm. At the rear was a winch. Jim patted it. 'Always tow you out with this if you get stuck, Mr Cunningham.'

Just as the farmer was about to move off, Annie Stott ran out of the house. 'Where's Evan? Oh, good morning, Mr Thwaite. Evan! Come here at once! You shouldn't be outside. I told you this morning——'

'But I'm very warm, thank you. And Uncle Paul said——'

'Never mind what he said. Paul, take him in.' She laid her hand against Evan's forehead, then gave him a push towards the door. Above the noise of the idling tractor, she spoke up to Mr Thwaite. 'I know, I'm a bit fussy. But he's my sister's only child, and it's dangerous for him to over-exert himself. I must go in and take his temperature again.'

The tractor turned and moved slowly away. Paul took Jim to the garage. Annie told the boy to sit near the living-room fire and play with his Meccano. She herself knitted, waiting for the telephone to ring in the next room with a message from the Guest House. Ten minutes later, it rang.

CHAPTER 4

General Post Office

DECEMBER 28

Professor Wragby too had awaited a telephone call. It came soon after breakfast. He took it in the proprietor's room, Nigel Strangeways listening over his shoulder.

'Is that Professor Alfred Wragby?' said the operator's voice. 'I have a call for you from London.'

There were some clicking sounds. Then a man's voice spoke, with intonations which Nigel soon pinpointed as Slav, and an accent learnt first from an American teacher but overlaid by some period of residence in England.

'I am speaking to Professor Wragby, F.R.S.?' inquired the voice.

'Yes. Wragby speaking. Who are you?'

'My name will not be known to you. I have news of your daughter.'

The professor's knuckles went white as he clenched the receiver, but his voice remained impassive.

'I take it you are the person who stole her.'

'Let us say "borrowed", Professor. She is in good order, and will be returned quite soon, if our transaction proves successful.'

34

'Where is she?'

'In London.'

'Let me speak to her.'

'I'm afraid that's not possible. I am in a public telephone box. Alone.'

'Well? What is this transaction you speak of?'

'You have something my friends need, Professor Wragby. In your head. We have something you need. I propose an exchange.'

'So I imagine. Your methods of business are contemptible, but I should not have expected anything else.'

'Hard words break no bones, my dear sir.' The voice was calm, almost jovial. 'For you, it's simply a question of how much value you set on your daughter.'

'Don't lecture to me. Get on with it.'

'Very well. If you decide to complete the transaction, you will be at the General Post Office in Belcaster at midday today. You will find, on your left as you go in, a long counter for writing telegrams. At its near end, attached to the wall above the counter, is a holder containing forms for Premium Savings Bonds. You will place a sheet of paper on which you have written your information at the back of these forms, and at once leave the Post Office.'

'And then I get Lucy back?'

'In due course. Naturally we should have to make sure it was the correct—er—formula you had given us. On these terms, Professor Wragby, are you willing to close the deal?'

'Well, it looks as if——' began Wragby after a silence. Nigel made a slowing-down movement with his right hand. The enemy must not be allowed to feel that Wragby was giving in too easily. 'It looks as if this is a stalemate. If I refuse, you're back where you started. If I agree, I've no guarantee of getting my daughter back.'

'You have our word for that.'

'*Your* word!' The contempt in Wragby's voice was withering.

'You refuse, then?'

Wragby did a passable imitation of a man cracking. 'Look here, how do I know Lucy isn't dead already? Suppose I find I've exchanged a vital secret for a dead child?'

'Nah, nah, we don't kill unnecessarily. I like children, myself. Of course, I can't answer for my friends who are looking after her in London. They are impatient folk. There are so many things you

35

can do to a child without actually killing her. She's a pretty little girl, they tell me.'

Wragby drew in a sobbing breath—he did not have to act this time. 'All right, all right! You promise not to hurt her?'

'I promise you that, my friend.' Curiously enough, Nigel believed this—for a while, at any rate.

'Then I'll do what you ask.'

'You are wise, Professor. It is the fortunes of war.' The genial voice grew hard. 'But don't play any monkey tricks. I could not stop you broadcasting the news of your daughter's disappearance. The police will be expecting you to hear from her abductors. You must on no account tell them about the substance of this conversation, or your agreement to our bargain. No doubt, your fertile brain can think up some story to put them off. They are not, after all, very clever: they could not even prevent us getting the child to London. When your Special Branch takes the thing over, it will be more difficult for us. That is why the move must be made at once. You will naturally enter the Belcaster Post Office unaccompanied. Any attempt to set a trap for our agent there would have disastrous consequences for you. Good-bye.'

Professor Wragby looked at Nigel, his face white under the reddish hair.

'What am I to do?' His voice was stiff with agony.

'We'll have to play for time. Do what he told you. But write down some data, symbols, what have you, that look plausible but are in fact misleading. Can you do that?'

'Yes, but——'

'I shall drop hints here that the kidnappers have an agent in the Guest House; he may or may not be the person who's going to collect your information. If we can establish who it is, we'll have one end of the thread in our hands. I'll get in touch with the Superintendent of the County C.I.D., ask him to have the Post Office watched unobtrusively from midday on: one of his men will be stationed behind the grille, to keep an eye out for anyone who comes to pick up your information. No, we shan't arrest that person at once. He'll be followed, and the trail may lead us to where Lucy is—that's to say, if the agent isn't one of the guests here.'

'But good God, man, Lucy is in London. Do you suppose——'

'I wonder.' Nigel's pale blue eyes were fixed on a repellent print, above Wragby's head, depicting a scene of eighteenth-century courtship. 'I wonder. Our friend on the telephone did his best to impress on us that London's where they've taken her. He wants the search to be concentrated there.'

'She might be much nearer?' The mere possibility enlivened Wragby's despairing face.

'They *could* have slipped through the two police cordons last night. But my guess is they're holed up within a radius of twenty miles from here.'

'In which case, we're bound to have news of her soon. There'll be descriptions of her in the papers and news bulletins. Somebody'd be certain to notice——'

'Don't run ahead of yourself. There are plenty of isolated houses in the country. She could be locked away in one of them for days, and nobody know.'

'I must run up to Elena. Don't like leaving her too long. She's dreadfully distressed. You'll do your best, I know.' The tall stooping figure hurried out.

And what a wretched best it's been, thought Nigel. The chance of getting Lucy back is a thousand to one. Her captors would be too afraid of the child recognising them later. Of course, until they possess and verify Wragby's information it will pay them to keep her alive—*or delude him into believing she is still alive*. An old kidnapper's trick.

The Superintendent last night had found footprints and tyre-marks in the snow opposite the pillar box. Wellington boots: those of Nigel's assailant much larger than those of the person who had emerged from the car. A woman, probably. While impressions were taken, one policeman had followed the tracks of the kidnappers westward along the unfrequented road. At one point it had stopped: then moved on till its traces were lost among many others where the minor road joined a main one. The car's direction appeared to be north-west now; but the driver might well have done this to shake off pursuit, and doubled back towards London presently. The district was a maze of small, twisting lanes, and heavy snow later in the night had covered all traces.

But the snow could work two ways. If only there were more falls, heavy enough to block the roads out of the valley, perhaps break down the telegraph wires, it would be physically impossible for the

Professor to keep any more rendezvous. The other side must recognise this. For Wragby—and, one hoped, Lucy—precious time would be gained.

After a telephone conversation with the County C.I.D. Nigel got up and went into the drawing-room. All the guests were there except the Wragbys.

'Good gracious!' exclaimed the Admiral's wife. 'What have you been doing to yourself?'

'Somebody bashed me last night. The doctor told me it must have been an amateurish blow. If the chap had done it properly I should be dead. The doctor seemed quite annoyed that I wasn't.'

'Not enough drama for him in these parts.' Lance Atterson yawned.

'A footpad, no doubt,' remarked Mrs ffrench-Sullivan sapiently.

Nigel turned to Mr Leake. 'Did you catch a sight of him, by any chance?'

'Sight of whom?' Justin Leake, looking puzzled.

'The—er—footpad.'

'No, indeed, my dear fellow. Where did it happen?'

'Half-way down the lane.'

'Last night? I never went out. Why do you ask *me*?'

'Because you left this room immediately after I did.'

'Look here, Mr Strangeways, I don't quite like this catechism.'

'Good practice for you, Mr Leake. When they can get round to it, the police will be asking you all just where you were when the assault was made.'

Justin Leake's attentive eyes were fastened on Nigel.

' "When they can get round to it"? Are they particularly overworked just now?'

'Surely you know why?'

'I haven't the faintest idea.'

'Strange. You've struck me as an unusually observant person.'

There was an edge in Nigel's tone which caused the others to sit forward and give him uneasy looks.

'You haven't noticed,' pursued Nigel, 'that Lucy Wragby is missing?'

'I haven't seen any of them yet this morning,' Justin Leake returned. 'Except the Professor for a moment in the hall. He

seemed worried.' A light dawned in the man's nondescript face.
' "Missing"? You don't mean——?'

Nigel's eyes swept the circle slowly as he said, 'Yes. She was kidnapped last night. Don't any of you listen to the B.B.C. news?'

'The set's out of order,' said Cherry.

This was no surprise to Nigel, since he had disabled it himself. He wanted to see the first reactions to the announcement.

'You'll read all about it when the papers arrive. The snowfall has held up delivery.'

Justin Leake appeared to have drawn in on himself, like a snail. Cherry looked incredulous, Lance suddenly ill at ease, the Admiral's wife outraged.

'There's no doubt about it?' asked the Admiral.

Nigel shook his head.

'What a shocking thing! Poor little Lucy. Who on earth would want to——?'

'Don't be absurd, my dear man,' rapped his spouse—Nigel could imagine her terrorising the wives of junior officers—'it's obviously a Red plot. Those devils are capable of anything.'

'But my dear lady,' said Justin Leake, 'why should they want to kidnap a little girl?'

Mrs ffrench-Sullivan's pug-face grew still more animated. 'Perfectly obvious. They wish to bring pressure upon Lucy's father.'

'Everything nasty that happens in this country is blamed on the Reds,' remarked Cherry, scowling.

'Rightly, my dear girl. And I'll tell you another thing—if you ask me, the Professor has made some scientific discovery they want to get hold of.'

'Is that a guess, madam, or have you some inside information?' Mr Leake's tone, though perfectly polite, was loaded.

'Of course I haven't. I merely use my head. Hope the police will too, Mr Strangeways. What are they doing about it?'

'One might also ask,' said Justin Leake silkily, 'why Mr Strangeways should have private information.'

Nigel ignored this. He gave the company a heavily censored account of the police activities. Then, always glad to set a cat among the pigeons provided he was present to watch the results, added:

'One thing seems possible—that the kidnappers have an

accomplice in this house. The police may concentrate on finding out which of us it is.'

'Obviously one of the staff,' said the Admiral's wife.

'They have all been here several years. I'm afraid it's very unlikely.'

'Oh poof,' said the lady. 'Domestics are notoriously unreliable these days.'

'Servant problem rears its ugly head again,' murmured Lance. Cherry giggled.

Nigel took a firm grip. 'We shall all have to answer very searching questions. I hope none of us, apart from the unknown accomplice, has anything to hide. Police investigations range far and wide, you know.'

His statement produced a quite extraordinary atmosphere of uneasiness in the room, though from how many of the guests it emanated he could not judge. Even the irrepressible Lance Atterson had an unusually thoughtful look on his face.

At this point Professor Wragby came into the room, and there was a general murmur of commiseration. When the Admiral inquired after Mrs Wragby, the Professor said she had got up and was just walking down to the village: she wanted to ask at the Post Office if anything had been seen or heard last night at the time Lucy disappeared—he knew the police had investigated this, but he thought it would be a good thing for his wife to feel she was taking some action herself.

There was an awkward silence. Then the Admiral's wife asked, in her forthright way, 'Have these ruffians been in touch with you yet?'

'Yes. I had a telephone call. They say Lucy is safe and well.'

'What do they want? Money?' asked Justin Leake.

Alfred Wragby glanced at Nigel, who almost imperceptibly nodded, before replying, 'No. Something they consider more valuable.'

'You're not going to *give* it to them?' Mrs ffrench-Sullivan's eyes opened wide.

'More valuable to you than Lucy?' Cherry's flat drawl made the remark all the more shocking.

A spasm came over Wragby's face, and he shaded it a moment

40

with his hand. 'I'm not giving anything away without a fight, Mrs ffrench-Sullivan,' he said at last.

'You mean, you're going to have a trap set for these jokers when they come to collect the—whatever they're supposed to be collecting?' Lance Atterson's teeth flashed over his black beard, giving him a foxy, anxious expression.

'But won't that—I mean, if you double-cross them sort of, won't they do something horrid to Lucy?' asked Cherry in faltering tones.

'Lucy is only valuable to them so long as she's alive. Otherwise she can't be used as a weapon against me.' Wragby's voice was chill and impersonal.

'Jesus! You can't be human!' exlaimed Cherry. 'Sorry, I didn't mean that, but——'

'Then keep your mouth shut, child,' said the Admiral's wife. 'You can't understand these things. Great issues are at stake.'

'Oh, balls to that!' Lance broke out. 'What's some piddling little secret compared with a child's life?'

'No doubt you have to think in an adolescent way, but you must learn not to talk in one, young man.' A touch of the quarter-deck came into the Admiral's lisping voice.

'Well, I expect we all have our little secrets,' said Justin Leake. If it was an attempt to pour oil on troubled waters, it only succeeded in creating a kind of turbulent silence.

Wragby, thought Nigel, had carried out their preconcocted plan well enough. The enemy agent in the Guest House, whoever he was, would now know that the Professor was not tamely acceding to their demands, and that some sort of trap was likely to be set at Belcaster. The agent would presumably get in touch at once with the person deputed to collect Wragby's information at the G.P.O., and warn him to keep away. If he avoided the telephone, as any competent agent now would, he must rendezvous at Belcaster with the collector and warn him by word of mouth, or by some expedient like chalking a symbol on a wall or pillar box. Of course there was a third possibility—that the Guest House agent and the collector were one and the same person. For various reasons, Nigel thought this unlikely: even if it were true, the agent would have to get in touch with his principals in London, sooner or later, to tell them about the failure of the first attempt and get further instructions:

if he did this by telephone, his identity would be revealed.

Meanwhile, there was the problem of Lucy. Nigel remembered the thin, vivacious little face framed in a sou'wester, the long dark hair, the blue anorak; and his heart grew sick with apprehension . . .

At Smugglers' Cottage, Lucy was playing solitaire on a board she had found in the toy cupboard. Last time, she had finished the game with only three marbles left on the board. If I get it down to one, she said to herself, everything will be all right: these people will let me go; or I'll wake up in my room at the Guest House.

Annie Stott came in, carrying a tape-recorder. She seemed to be in rather a temper. Perhaps she'd had bad news on the telephone—Lucy had heard the bell ringing five minutes ago. Annie locked the door, placed the machine on a table and opened it.

'Do you know what this is?'

'Yes. It's a tape-recorder. Are we going to play with it?'

The mustard-faced woman took a sheet of paper from her handbag and unfolded it. 'I suppose you can read?'

'Of course I can read. Don't be silly.'

'Very well. I want you to read this into the microphone. It's a message to your father—just to tell him you're being well looked after.'

'You're going to send him the tape?'

'We—I shall let him have it.'

'But why can't I talk to him? On the telephone?'

'Don't keep interrupting. You must read out just these words and nothing else. As if you were talking to him. Get the idea? And where there are three dots, you make a pause. It'll be rather fun. Like doing a broadcast play. Now, let's have a practice.'

Lucy had got quite used to humouring this loopy female. She started reading from the typewritten paper.

' "Hallo, Daddy. It's me"—No, that won't do.'

'What d'you mean, won't do?'

'I never call him "Daddy". Papa, or Father.'

'Well, alter it then.'

Lucy began again. ' "Hallo, Papa. It's me. Lucy . . . Yes, I'm very well, and the people are being very kind to me. I have plenty to eat, and a nice room with lots of toys and books . . . No, I'm not

42

allowed to say where I am. It's somewhere in London. Is Elena well——?" '

'No, child,' Miss Stott broke in. 'You're *reading* it, as if it was a story book. *Say* it. Put some life into it. Don't you ever act at school?'

'How can I? The way you've written it makes me sound like a kid of six,' said Lucy resentfully: Miss Stott reminded her of her least favourite school-mistress.

'Don't waste my time,' snapped the woman, flushing. 'Do it again. Pretend you're talking to him on the telephone. Use your imagination, you silly little boy.'

Lucy blinked away the tears that had risen at the thought of talking to her father on the telephone, and tried again. After several attempts, Miss Stott pronounced herself satisfied, put Lucy in front of the microphone, and started the tape-recorder for a level test.

Desperately, Lucy tried to think of some way of putting a secret message to Papa into the script. Or suppose, at the end of it, she just yelled for help. Fat lot of good that'd be. As it happened, though, this fantasy became real; for, as she neared the end of the recording, Lucy glanced up from the script and saw that Annie was holding a hypodermic syringe. Lucy began to scream . . .

A few minutes later, Miss Stott left the cottage, got out the car, and drove cautiously along the snow-covered road to Longport where she posted the small parcel to London, then turned the car in the direction of Belcaster. It was now 11.25 a.m. . . .

Alfred Wragby put his car in the municipal car park, and turned to Elena.

'You wait, darling. The Post Office is a couple of minutes from here. I'll come straight back. Hallo, isn't that Leake's car parked over there?'

His wife's tragic eyes held his for a moment. 'I wish you hadn't decided to do it this way,' she said.

'Look, we've had it out. Even if I gave them what they want, there's no guarantee we'd get Lucy back. *You* know what they're like.'

'Yes,' she replied, almost inaudibly. 'But——'

'The only hope—don't you see?—is for the person who collects

43

the information to be followed. He might lead us to wherever Lucy is. I've told you—Strangeways thinks she may be quite near.'

He left Elena staring stonily in front of her. The clock in the tower of the eighteenth-century town hall was striking twelve as he entered the General Post Office. He took a folded sheet from his wallet, inserted it at the back of the Premium Savings Bonds forms in the holder above the long counter, and walked straight out.

The plain-clothes man behind the grille on the opposite side of the Post Office alerted himself.

In a side turning, a police car waited. Along the main roads at the edge of town, other police cars cruised, their radio operators on the qui vive. A plain van, with radio and souped-up engine, stood thirty yards away in the main street. Its driver was apparently asleep, its other occupants invisible: all five were armed. This was the one that would do the following, when a description of the quarry had been received.

As midday struck, Nigel was turning over the pages of a book in a bookshop whose window gave a clear view of the Post Office across the street. A man was polishing the letter-boxes in the wall of the building. He could see through the window his colleague inside. When the latter made a sign, he would know that the information had been collected and the collector was on his way out.

A dumpy, yellow-faced woman entered the shop. She took up a book and began leafing through it, then moved closer to the window as if to get a better light to read by. Nigel was aware of her eyes momentarily upon him; but he paid her no special attention, for a few seconds afterwards he saw Justin Leake stroll into the Post Office, a figure so unobtrusive that he might almost be wearing a cloak of invisibility. In the dim, quiet little bookshop, Nigel felt an extraordinary tension: he noticed that the book in his hands was shaking, and put it down, his eyes fixed on the Post Office door. Justin Leake. It could be a coincidence; but, if he'd been asked to pick out the secret agent from among the visitors at the Guest House, it was Leake he would have chosen: the man smelt wrong to him.

A couple of minutes passed. Then Leake came out of the Post Office and walked in the direction of the car park. Nigel sauntered out of the bookshop. But the man cleaning the letter-boxes gave no sign.

It was a bitter moment of anti-climax. A word with the plain-clothes man behind the counter satisfied Nigel that Justin Leake had gone nowhere near the Premium Savings Bonds holder: he had innocently bought some stamps, then written a telegram and handed it in. Nigel asked the plain-clothes man to arrange at once that his Superintendent should see a copy of the telegram, and waited, keeping the Savings Bonds holder under his eye till the man returned.

People clumped into the G.P.O. kicking the snow off their Wellingtons. Cars, passing up and down the main street, were turning the snow into a demerara-sugar slush. A lorry cruised slowly down, with men shovelling grit from it on to the road. A child on a brand-new fairy-cycle skidded and fell bawling on the pavement: his mother picked him up and shook him angrily, as if he had committed some shaming nuisance. The market town seemed to be afflicted still with an after-Christmas lethargy. A north-west wind was blowing up, biting into the bones, numbing the mind, as Nigel walked up the street, past the statue of some forgotten civic worthy wearing a snow top-hat, and entered the Police Headquarters.

'Thought we had a bite just now,' he said to Superintendent Sparkes, 'but the fish never went near the bait. Chap called Leake, staying at the Guest House. Mystery man.'

'Plenty of time yet, Mr Strangeways. Have a cup of tea—you look clemmed.'

'Thanks, I will. I've a feeling their chap's going to keep his nose out.'

'Meaning he's been tipped off from the Guest House that Professor Wragby was not playing? I expect you're right. But there've been no telephone calls from the place this morning, not suspicious ones.'

'Leake could have come here to give the warning.'

'My chaps weren't told to keep a special eye on him,' said the Super with a touch of resentment.

'I'm not blaming you. You can't follow everyone around. What did he say in that telegram, by the way? Has it come through?'

The Super handed Nigel a sheet of paper.

Sir James Allenby. The Red House. Altringham, Surrey. Nothing to report yet, but am on possible trail. Leake.

45

'Who's this bird Allenby?' asked Nigel.

'Big industrialist, I believe. Seem to remember seeing something about him in the papers last year. Daughter went off the rails, wasn't it? I can't exactly remember.'

' "Possible trail"?' mused Nigel. 'Well, he looks rather like some kind of seedy private investigator. Anyway, I shouldn't think it's relevant.'

The Super flexed his powerful hands on the desk. 'I'd like to get my fingers on someone's throat. Any kids yourself, Mr Strangeways?'

'No. But I know what you mean. And Lucy's a real winner.' Nigel found himself muttering, ' "How soon my Lucy's race was run".'

'That's Wordsworth, isn't it? Learnt it at school. We mustn't lose heart, sir.'

'It's this waiting about.'

'Like war. Ninety-nine per cent of waiting to one of action.'

'Yes, we're in a war all right.'

The two men discussed arrangements. County police would inquire at every isolated farm and cottage, on the chance that Nigel was right in his hunch that Lucy had not been taken through the cordon to London. As to the Belcaster G.P.O., plain-clothes men would be on duty there all night and watch the staff leaving this evening in case the enemy agent might be one of them.

It was shutting the stable door before the horse had entered, thought Nigel. The anonymous telephone call would hardly have instructed Wragby to deposit this information sharp at midday unless it was to be collected soon afterwards. As the afternoon passed by, without any alarm given from the G.P.O., it looked more and more likely that the collector had been warned off. But how? Nigel read through the monitored telephone calls made from the Guest House this morning: they were few, and seemed innocent enough; but the Super set one aside for further investigation. And he must find out if any of the guests other than Justin Leake and the Wragbys had come in from Downcombe before midday.

Nigel left Belcaster and drove back to Downcombe with the blowing snow clotting his windscreen and the wipers squeaking. On the way back a yellow Cyclops's eye winked at him from the darkness fifty yards ahead. It was the light of a snow-plough, shovelling its way through a drift in an exposed section of the road. He drew in to the side and let it pass.

'How far you going?' shouted the driver.

'Downcombe.'

'That's all right. You wouldn't get much farther. Valley's blocked beyond.'

CHAPTER 5

The Blizzard

DECEMBER 28–29

Half an hour before Nigel met the snow-plough, Paul Cunningham had set out for Longport with the boy called Evan. He had wrapped the boy from head to foot in a rug and put him on the back seat: it was essential that his passenger should not be seen by anyone on the road to Longport junction. The boy accepted Paul's statement that he must wrap up like this against the cold, as he had accepted all the other queer happenings of the last few weeks, with the stolid fatalism his short life had taught him. Of course, he wasn't a bit cold: he had something in his heart which was enough to warm his whole body—and now the lovely, miraculous event was only a few hours away. He felt for the disc on his chest, under the layers of clothing.

Paul Cunningham peered through the snow that danced and eddied in his headlights. Thank God they were getting rid of this boy at last. Evan had little attraction for him, with his sandy hair and subdued manner: he might as well be a little, stocky auto-maton, answering questions politely, seldom asking them—asking for nothing, really, except to be kicked around. There seemed to be no vivacity about him, no give: it was like the dead feel of driving this car with chains on the rear wheels.

The farmhouse echoed back the clink of the chains as Paul

passed it. The tractor had beaten down the rough road pretty well. Half a mile farther and they hit the secondary road through the village. Here and there the snow had blown through a field gate and formed itself into a peninsula stretching out into the road: the car slowed as it bit its way through these patches. Paul congratulated himself on having left forty minutes to get to Longport, though it was less than four miles away.

It was rough, rolling country here, protected from the north-east by a high ridge a mile distant. Paul had a choice of routes now. He could continue on his present road, over the ridge, and drop down to Longport half-a-mile beyond in the next valley; or he could turn left on to a main road a few hundred yards away, continue along it for a mile, then strike off on a secondary road to the right, which made a detour round the end of the ridge and would bring him to Longport in another two miles. Paul had made a reconnaissance of the two routes several days ago. His instinct was to avoid main roads. It would be disastrous if anyone flagged him down and caught sight of the boy in the back seat. Following his instinct, Paul crossed the main road and started up the long winding incline to the top of the ridge.

Not till he had almost reached the top of it did he realise the violence of the blizzard. Up here, with no shelter from trees, he ran into what seemed at first a runaway fog. The north-easter was blowing the snow off the heights, so that in front of the car there was a white spume which the headlights could not penetrate. Paul slowed down to a walking pace and opened his window to see better. The blizzard rushed in, hitting the side of his face like a hammer swathed in ice-cold cotton-wool. The impact made him swerve. The car buried its wheels in a drift that was piling up on the left of the road.

He got out, walked a few paces forward, and found himself up to his knees in snow, with flying snow fuming in clouds across the road ahead and cutting short his vision. He examined the wheels: all four were embedded in snow, and the rear ones must have skidded into a shallow ditch, for the car stood listing to the left. He had a spade in the boot, but by the time he had dug the rear wheels clear, backed down the hill, got on to the main road and made the long detour round to Longport, they might miss the train; and it was the last London train tonight.

Paul got into the car again. On the back seat the boy crouched, immobile and silent. He was inert, like a dreadful load on Paul's conscience, which somehow or other he must throw off. Paul felt the clutch of a monster panic.

'We're stuck. We'll have to walk. It's only half a mile from here. Plenty of time. Take ten minutes at the most. Out you get, Evan.'

Docilely the boy got out, clutching his cheap canvas zip-bag in one hand. The other, after a moment's hesitation, took one of Paul's hands. The pair floundered through the drift up towards the top of the ridge. Here was a clearer patch of road to walk on, and in a brief lull of the blizzard they could see the lights of Longport in the valley below. Then the white hell enclosed them again. They struggled on for another fifty yards.

Paul soon saw that on this, the exposed face of the hill, the going was considerably worse. If he took the boy as far as the station approach, he would have to climb back again up this bloody hill, and at the rate the snow was piling up he might well fail to extricate the car. To spend the night in it would wreck their plan—he must not be known to have come in the Longport direction at all; there must be no connection made between a boy who got on to the train at Longport and the 'boy' who was now staying at Smugglers' Cottage.

Cowardice—the fear of being stopped on the main road—had pushed Paul into taking this calamitous short cut. Cowardice now impelled him to a worse betrayal: the lacerating wind, the eldritch whirling of the snow had destroyed what little nerve remained to him. He pulled his hand out of the boy's clasp. 'I've got to turn back now,' he babbled. 'Dig the car out. Can't delay. You'll be all right. Just follow the road. Only quarter of a mile.' He turned round and plunged back uphill, feeling only a blessed relief that the devilish wind no longer blew in his teeth.

'Good-bye,' said the boy uncertainly, but his companion had already disappeared into the whirling night. The boy shivered in his shoddy overcoat, then started forward again. He must not miss the train. There'd be plenty of time, Uncle Paul had said. His face ached less atrociously—it was going numb. The snow seemed to get deeper at every step: he floundered through a waist-high drift, with the ungainly movements of a bather walking out through the sea. He caught a glimpse of the lights again: they were nearer, but not near enough. Now the biggest drift of all lay in a hollow section of the road. The boy could not get through it. He summoned all his strength and determination, and clambered up the bank at the side of the road, intending to join the road again beyond the drift.

But now, dazed by the lashing wind, he lost his sense of direction and stumbled round the rough field in a circle, to fall off the bank presently into the drifted road at the very point where he had left it. He struggled a few yards farther, without even the strength now to call out for help. Then he fell, and lay where he fell. The snow did not feel cold any more. A feather bed. To sleep on.

The boy put his hand into his breast, clasping the medal-shaped thing hidden there. He sighed, and soon he was asleep. He had a beautiful dream about the person who was going to meet him in London. Not long after the dream was over, he died. The snow blew into the corners of his smiling mouth, then over his head, his body and the cheap canvas zip-bag still clutched in his other hand. . . .

'My God,' said Paul, with the air of one who has come heroically through great tribulations, 'there's an absolute blizzard raging. I only just managed to get the car out of a drift we ran into.' He chafed his hands before the log fire.

'Did he catch the train?' asked Annie Stott, unimpressed.

'Oh, bound to. I walked him to within a hundred yards of the station. Had to turn back then and dig the car out before it snowed right under.'

'You should have taken him all the way.'

'And frozen to death during the night?'

'Oh, stop dramatising yourself, Paul.'

'You just don't know what it's like on the hills. You don't seem to have done so brilliantly yourself,' he pettishly added.

'I told you—Wragby tried to double-cross us. It wouldn't have been very sensible to walk into a police trap in order to collect a faked piece of information, would it?'

'So what do we do next?'

'Petrov will apply pressure. Then we'll carry out Plan B.'

'Looks like it'll be a five-year plan at this rate. Haven't you grasped the simple fact that we'll soon be snowed up, and so will Wragby? It'll be a stalemate. Or is the master-mind Petrov going to turn up with a squadron of Soviet snow-ploughs?'

Annie Stott gave him a contemptuous look, and went out to cook some supper. Paul poured himself a second glass of whisky. He dwelt for a moment on the little girl locked in upstairs, then shook free of such uncomfortable thoughts. The repellent Annie had called him an escapist several times during the last fortnight: well, who wouldn't try to escape from the nightmare he lived in now.

After supper they listened to the radio. Presently the regional news came on. Annie's knitting needles stopped clicking, Paul sat up tensely.

'. . . Lucy Wragby, the girl of eight who disappeared from the Guest House at Downcombe last night, is still missing. It is now feared that she may have been kidnapped. Police are making inquires throughout the county, and will concentrate particularly on isolated houses within a radius of fifty miles from Downcombe. When last seen, Lucy was wearing a blue anorak and sou'wester, with a green and blue plaid dress underneath it. She has long, dark hair, a thin, pale face, grey eyes, and a surgical scar beneath her left ear. The authorities believe that attempts may have been made to alter her appearance, however. Anyone who has seen a child answering to this description or has knowledge of any new child seen in their neighbourhood whose presence cannot be accounted for, is urgently asked to communicate with the local police or with Police Headquarters at Belcaster: Belcaster 390. I will repeat that . . .'

Paul Cunningham stared at Annie, trying to conceal his anxiety behind a light tone. 'So the bluebottles will soon be buzzing round our ears. Did the infallible Petrov allow for this one?'

Annie knitted her sallow brow. 'I don't quite understand it. He must have failed to convince Wragby that the child was taken to London. Still, there's no great harm done. The Thwaites can't possibly find out that we've substituted her for Evan, so there's no child in this cottage unaccounted for.'

'But if a bobby comes to search it——'

'He'll find a boy ill in bed. A sandy-haired boy who has been here for a fortnight. The Thwaites will bear that out. They have been told that Evan was delicate. Tomorrow I'll tell them we could not send him to London after all, because he's been taken

51

ill again. You really mustn't lose your nerve at this stage.'

'And when the policeman finds a child in bed, with a surgical scar under the left ear, don't you suppose he'll be a bit suspicious?'

'He won't find a scar. The child will be doped, and I shall wrap a bandage round her neck.'

'You think of everything, don't you?' said Paul sulkily.

'Somebody has to.'

'Except the child's feelings. Have you for one moment stopped to think what she's feeling like? And don't give me that blah about personal feelings being unimportant compared with great political issues.'

'If you're so sensitive about it, why don't you go and comfort the child—read to her or something?'

'You know perfectly well——'

'Because you're only interested in saving your own skin, that's why. You daren't let her see you in case you met again somewhere and she recognised you.'

The telephone bell shrilled in the next room. Paul started. 'Who the hell's ringing at this time of night?'

When Annie Stott returned, her face was dark and her thin mouth compressed. 'That was Petrov. He's furious. Evan never arrived at Waterloo.'

'But he must have.'

'Don't quibble. Why didn't you see him on to the station?'

'I've told you——'

'You lost your nerve at a bit of snow. My God, what a bloody fool you are! Obviously the boy missed the train and found refuge in somebody's house. No doubt he's been telling them all about you and me and Smugglers' Cottage. You've wrecked everything,' she went on furiously. 'I warned Petrov he'd be in for trouble, taking on a lily-livered queer like you.'

'Don't you dare talk to me like that, you dung-faced bitch!' Paul's voice rose to falsetto.

The woman struck him violently across the cheek. He shook her roughly, then thrust her away and sent her sprawling into the arm-chair, from which she glared up at him.

'I thought the Party didn't countenance acts of individual violence,' he said with a sneer.

The woman stared at him, panting a little.

'Never been handled by a man before, I suppose? Makes you feel quite sexy, does it?'

'By a *what*?'

Without another word, Annie stumped out and went up to bed.

Next morning, Lucy was awoken at eight o'clock by the mad-woman.

'Put on your dressing gown and come with me.'

Annie led her to a bedroom at the far end of the passage on the other side of the house. It was the room Evan had occupied. She pointed to a bed drawn up close to the window, whose curtains were closed. 'Get in.'

Lucy got in, trembling a little. She could not forget what had happened the previous morning.

'The man is just coming up with the milk. When I tell you, I want you to open the curtain, put your face close to the window-pane, and call down to him. Wave to him, and say, "Hallo, Jim". Remember, your name is—what's your name?'

'Lucy Wragby.'

'Oh no. Try again.'

'Sorry. Evan.'

'That's better. Jim'll probably shout up at you "Hallo, Evan, how are you?" Something like that.'

'What do I say then?'

'Just smile at him and wave again. Then I'll close the curtain. Quite an easy game, isn't it?'

Annie wrapped a bandage round Lucy's throat. 'You mustn't say anything else. And of course no nonsense like calling for help.'

'I see,' said Lucy in a small voice.

'Otherwise I should have to use this again.' The woman took from her bag the hypodermic syringe. 'You know that I always mean what I say?'

'Yes.' The child cowered away from her. She was frightened, but it did not stop her from thinking fast. She must try to memorise what she could see from the window when the curtain was drawn, then bring it into the story she was writing about a kidnapped child: at the back of Lucy's mind there was a vague hope that somehow she might have this story conveyed to her father, and it would give him a clue as to where she was, and he would come to rescue her.

In a couple of minutes she heard voices outside. 'Aunt Annie' drew the curtain. A man with a milk pail—that must be Jim; and another man, of whom she could only see the top of his head: he must be the one she'd heard quarrelling with Aunt Annie last night—the first time she'd realised there was more than one person in the house. There was an enormous great view from the window: snow-covered hills, one of which stood out because it had a clump of trees on top; and away to the right, a farmyard. She could not take in any more, for the woman beside her said, 'Get on with it.'

Lucy tapped at the window. The man Jim looked up, grinned at her, called, 'Hallo, Evan! Sorry to hear you're poorly again.' Lucy smiled back and waved to him. Aunt Annie closed the curtain.

'You can go back to your own room now. I'll bring your breakfast soon.'

'Did I do all right?' Lucy had already decided that, since this potty female treated her as if she were six, she'd play up to it.

'Yes, Evan. I'm glad you're being sensible.'

While she ate her eggs and toast in bed, Lucy jotted down on a piece of paper everything she could remember seeing in the fifteen seconds or so while the curtain was open. It was like that game of objects on a tray: at first she could recollect little, but presently even things she didn't remember noticing at the time came into her head.

She dressed and got out the sheaf of foolscap paper. In Chapter I the heroine, Cinders (a nickname her father sometimes used) had been kidnapped and taken to a lonely house, inhabited exclusively by a mad woman with a mustard-coloured face. Lucy read through this opening chapter with nods of approval: it was super stuff. She took up the pencil.

CHAPTER II.   WHERE AM I?

Next morning the madwoman, who Cinders had to call Aunt Annie, took her into a room at the front of the house. She let Cinders, who she called Evan for some loopy reason, look out of the window. Down below was a man called Jim. He had brought some milk. There was another man, but Cinders could only see the top of his head standing in

the doorway. 'I expect he lives in the house and is Annie's keeper,'
thought Cinders. Jim waved to her, and she waved back. He had on
Wellingtons, and old Army great-coat, and a red woolly hat with a
bobbel on top. 'Don't you dare call for help,' hissed the madwoman, 'or
I'll stick this hipodurmic sirynge into you.' So Cinders didn't. She hates
pricks, ever since she was so ill when she was a kid.

The pannerama from the window was truly spectaculer. Snow-
covered hills lay like frozen waves of a bumpy sea. One hill, to the left of
the picture, attracted her attention: it was connical, with a clump of trees
four or five of them on its top. The cottage stood on the side of a hill, at
least the ground went down into a valley beneath it. Cinders's observant
eye noticed some farm buildings quite near on the right, I expect it was
where the milk came from. It was the only house in sight. The window
she looked out of had a sort of arched top and white wooden bars on it,
which cut up the view. Cinders could see no more now, because the
mainiak closed the curtain and with a fowl othe bade her begone to her
own appartment. Cinders bewent, but not before she had seen a
photograph of a bearded man in a cap and gown like her father wears
hanging on the wall.

Lucy started chewing her pencil. The door opened. The 'maniac'
padded in to fetch her tray. She glanced over Lucy's shoulder. It
was a ghastly moment: Lucy repressed an impulse to cover up the
paper—which would have betrayed her. The woman went out
again, locking the door. Lucy hid the sheet she'd written on under
the lining paper of a drawer. Then she had a better idea. She took it
out, made a copy of it on another sheet, and hid this in the drawer.
If Aunt Annie found the story and destroyed it, she would never
guess that there was a duplicate one.

But how could she ever send this to her father? And even if she
did manage somehow, how would he know where the place was?
The woman had told her it was in Buckinghamshire, about thirty
miles from London—a conversation faithfully reproduced by Cinders in Chapter I. There must be millions of cone-shaped hills with
trees on top all over England. Then a brilliant thought struck her:
the postmark on the letter would tell her father roughly where she
was. You steaming nit, she at once replied to herself, how can you
send a letter? You haven't an envelope or a stamp; and if you had,
they'd never let you post it—why, they won't even let you out of

this room. But they did before breakfast. And you saw Jim. He brings the milk. If you were alone in that room when he calls, just for an instant, perhaps you could drop the sheet of paper on his head—make a paper dart of it . . .

'What beats me is why they should go through all this rigmarole—me having to leave the information in a Post Office. I'd expect them to tell me to put it in an envelope and post it—some accommodation address in London—or just dictate it over the telephone.'

Professor Wragby's voice was gritty with sleeplessness. He and his wife were sitting with Nigel in the proprietor's office after breakfast, waiting for the telephone call which they had been expecting for many hours now.

'What do you think, Mrs Wragby? You know these people better than we do,' said Nigel.

She seemed taken aback. 'These people? But—Oh, you mean the Communists? Of course, they do not trust one another. They can't afford to. Perhaps that's it.' Elena's thrilling contralto voice made the most banal remark sound dramatic.

'What's in your mind?' her husband asked.

'Whoever it was that spoke to you from London yesterday—he would not be the principal. His superiors may suspect him of being a double agent, or an opportunist who would sell the information to the highest bidder.'

'So they couldn't risk it going straight into his hands?'

'Not so valuable a secret as Alfred's. They would depute someone absolutely reliable to collect it and pass it on to the principals. They see to it that each agent has the minimum of contacts within the network: it is a most important rule of espionage.'

Elena took several flowing, actress's paces across the room, then stood against the door with her palms holding her temples as if her head was bursting.

'Oh, God! I thought I'd be leaving these horrible things behind me when I escaped from my country,' she exclaimed bitterly.

'Now, love, you must try not to take it so hard. You're not to blame for what's happened to Lucy.'

Elena stared at her husband, as if he was a stranger. 'What's the use of telling me that?' she broke out passionately. 'We sit about here talking, and little Lucy——'

'Of course there's another possibility,' Nigel's equable voice silenced Elena. 'They might use Lucy as a bait to catch her father. You'd be even more useful to them than this particular bit of information.'

'Good lord, man, are you suggesting they'd try to capture me and smuggle me out of the country?'

'Induce you to leave it.'

'Alfred would never go over, never betray,' said Elena.

'I believe that. But we've got to be prepared for any new tactic they may try. Suppose they ring you and tell you to go, alone, to a certain place where you'll find Lucy, what'd you do?'

'Go,' said Wragby.

'Walk into the trap?'

'If there was the slightest chance of finding Lucy that way, getting her released, yes. I can look after myself.'

'Oh, Alfred, you don't know these people,' Elena cried.

'I'm beginning to,' said the Professor grimly. 'Don't forget, I did some roughish work during the war. I still have my cyanide capsule, if the worst came to the worst.'

The telephone bell rang. Nigel ran out to the instrument in the hall, and listened in.

'I have a call for Professor Wragby from London.'

'Wragby speaking.'

'Go ahead, London. Your call to Downcombe.'

'Is that Lucy's father?'

'Yes.'

'You failed to do what you were told yesterday. That was foolish of you. Not only did you inform the police, but you tried to double-cross us over the document. It must not happen again,' said the rumbling voice.

'But it will.'

'Then your daughter is going to suffer for your obstinacy. Suffer very painfully indeed.'

'I don't believe you. I'm quite certain that Lucy is already dead, you see.'

Nigel opened his eyes wide at this departure from the script. There was a brief silence. Then the voice said:

'You are wrong there, Professor. She is in the room with me now. Lucy, come and speak to your father.'

Another silence. Then a child's voice came over the wire.

'Hallo, Papa. It's me, Lucy.'

'God! Lucy, darling. Are you all right?'

'Yes, I'm very well, and the people are being very kind to me. I have plenty to eat and a nice room with lots of books and toys.'

'But where are you, love?'

'No, I'm not allowed to say where I am. It's somewhere in London. Is Elena well?'

Before Wragby could answer, the child's voice changed. She began to whimper. 'No, don't do it again! Please don't! Not that thing! Take it away! Oh!' She was screaming.

Lucy's voice died away into background whimpers. The man's voice returned.

'You see, Professor? Lucy is alive. But life can be very painful for her, and it will get worse the longer you remain stubborn. You will hold yourself in readiness for further instructions. Good-bye.'

The receiver clattered from Wragby's hand on to the table. Elena, who had been sitting by him with her ears close to it, was biting her knuckles when Nigel returned to the room.

'This is a bit more than I can take,' said the Professor at last, his face ashen. Elena stumbled out, weeping.

'It was Lucy?'

'Yes. Poor little pet. So she is in London after all,' said Wragby dully.

'I doubt it.'

'What d'you mean? The call came from London.'

'She wasn't talking naturally.'

'Who the hell would, under the circumstances?'

'She doesn't talk in that stilted way. It was more like repeating a lesson, or reading something aloud.'

'For God's sake, man, you're not telling me that bit at the end wasn't natural?'

'No, I'm afraid that was the real thing. But didn't you hear a faint whirring just before she started?'

'I wasn't in a state to——'

'Tape-recorder. The thing was faked. Quite clearly.'

'Anyway, she must be alive.'

When they forced her to make the recording, thought Nigel: that's all we know. He said, 'Yes. She's alive. Whoever's got her would have posted the tape to London. They're trying to break your nerve *and* fix in our minds that London's the place.'

The Professor's brain was beginning to work again. 'Are all the inward calls here monitored?'

'Yes.'

'You know, Strangeways, I can't imagine a man taking a tape-recorder machine into a public call-box. He'd have to hold it up to the mouthpiece and get it going. Damned awkward to manage; and he'd be calling a lot of attention to himself.'

Nigel rang the Superintendent at Belcaster, and asked him to find out where the call had come from. In a few minutes, the Superintendent rang back. It was a number on the Acorn exchange, and not a public box.

'That's Acton way,' said Nigel. 'Maybe we've got something at last. Will you get on to that division and ask their D.D.I. to find out the address of the subscriber and investigate the place. Pronto. We've just been rung from there. More threats.'

'I'll have the place taken to bits,' said the Superintendent.

CHAPTER 6

Ask Me Another

DECEMBER 29

Snow splattered across the windscreen of the police car as it brushed past the shrubs that, bent over by wind and weight of snow, leant out into the Guest House drive. Superintendent Sparkes emerged, followed by a sergeant. He moved with the deliberation of generations of ancestors who had farmed in the next county. After pausing for a few words with the group of newspapermen in the hall, he went on into the proprietor's office, where Nigel Strangeways was awaiting him.

'Hell of a job getting here,' he said, peeling off his overcoat. 'The snow-ploughs have only been able to keep the valley road open

single track. This is Sergeant Deacon. Mr Strangeways. Main road
to London is blocked. Looks like it's going to be worse than 1947.
When did those news hawks get here?'

'Yesterday evening. The London ones took the train to Longport and hired a car from there.'

'Where are they staying? No room here, is there?'

'Oh, they got beds in the village. Downcombe's pleased to find
itself in the news. They're mugging up on their background stories
just now.'

'Not much for them in the foreground. What about this latest
telephone call?'

Nigel gave him the gist. Sparkes clenched his fists at the final
part of it. 'The bastards! Using a kid like that to——'

'What does seem clear is, their collector was tipped off—not only
about the police trap but that Wragby was going to hand over
incorrect or incomplete information. The chap who rang said,
"Not only did you inform the police, but you tried to double-cross
us over the document".'

'Who would know here?'

'Wragby. His wife, I presume. And myself.'

'None of the other guests?'

'I don't see how. Wragby told them after breakfast he was going
to make a fight of it. That's all. Of course, it might have been just a
good guess.'

The Superientendent lit his pipe, gazing meditatively at Nigel.

'You wouldn't say the Professor is up to some funny game of his
own?'

'No. I'm as certain as I can be about that.'

'Which leaves his wife. A Hungarian by birth, you said.'

'Yes. She was thoroughly screened by Security when she came
over. They say she's absolutely in the clear.'

'Would she let her own daughter be kidnapped? It's a bit much.'

'Step-daughter. Still, I agree. But she did go down to the village
after breakfast yesterday. To the Post Office. There's a public
telephone outside it. I asked Miss Massinger to look into that.
Apparently Mrs Wragby asked the postmistress for some change to
make a call.'

'Which she'd hardly do so openly if—still, we'd better ask her.
Sergeant, will you find Mrs Wragby.'

'Have you any news of her?' asked Elena breathlessly as she came in.

'I'm afraid not, Mrs Wragby. But don't lose heart. I've got the best part of my Force looking for her today. And there's a possible lead from London too.'

'If only I could *do* something!' she cried.

Sparkes patted her on the shoulder and made her sit down. 'Perhaps you can, madam. I'm sorry to be asking you more questions again just now, but you might be able to help.'

'Oh, *yes*! Anything.'

Sparkes glanced towards the sergeant, who took out notebook and pencil. 'Now, madam, yesterday morning, before your husband came in to Belcaster, you discussed the blackmailer's demands with him?'

'Well, they hadn't rung up then—I mean, while we were talking about it. While we were having breakfast in our room.'

'He told you he was going to resist any demands they made?'

'Yes. I'm afraid we had a little quarrel about it. You see, I could think of nothing except getting Lucy back.'

'Very natural. Did the Professor say exactly how he intended to deal with the demands when they came?'

'Oh yes. He wanted to play for time. He would give them what seemed the information they wanted, but when they checked it, it would be meaningless.'

'And he said he was going to inform the police as soon as the kidnappers got in touch with him?'

'Yes. I thought it unwise; but Alfred is a stubborn man.'

'When the call came, he told you about it at once?'

'Yes.'

'That was soon after 10 a.m. Then you walked down to the village, by yourself?' The Superintendent's tone was positively sleepy; like drugged honey, thought Nigel. 'Your husband said you wanted to inquire at the Post Office if anyone had seen or heard anything at the time Lucy was kidnapped.'

'Yes. I just had to do something. Don't you understand?' Her small fists beat together.

'Of course. But you found out nothing new.'

'I'm sure your men had asked all the same questions.'

'And then,' said Sparkes, 'you telephoned?'

Elena's great, sad eyes dwelt upon him. 'Yes.'

'A private call, I take it?'

'Oh, I don't mind you knowing. I'd just remembered we'd been asked out to lunch by some friends in Lymouth—it had gone out of my head, I was in such distress—so I wanted to explain to them why we wouldn't be coming.'

'Just as a routine matter, may I have the name and telephone number of these friends?'

'Certainly. Mrs Ellaby. Lymouth 263.'

Sparkes gave his sergeant a slight nod, and the man went out to the telephone in the hall.

'You do not believe me?' exclaimed Elena, with a flash in her eyes that reminded Nigel she had been a heroine of the rising. 'You think I would take part in this filthy plot against——?'

'Calm yourself, ma'am. I have to find out who warned the kidnappers, and how, yesterday morning.'

Elena's face closed up. She began to chew a strand of her thick white hair; then, aware of Nigel's eyes upon her, said to him, 'I know. It's a childish habit. Lucy's caught it from me, too.'

Sergeant Deacon returned. 'All correct, sir.'

Sparkes gave Mrs Wragby his slow smile. 'That's over. Didn't hurt much, did it? Now then, you went into Belcaster with your husband. You waited in the car park. Did you see any of the other Guest House people there?'

'I saw Mr Leake's car. It was empty, though. And I noticed a young couple pass the far end of the street: they looked like Mr and Mrs Atterson, but I couldn't be sure at that distance. I'm afraid I was not noticing very much.'

'Naturally. And your husband returned——?'

'In four or five minutes. Then we drove back here.'

'And you saw nobody else you knew?'

'No, Superintendent.'

When she had left them, Nigel said, 'Well, that lets her out.'

The Superintendent relighted his pipe before replying, with what Nigel found a rather maddening deliberation. 'I wonder. She could have fixed with X to contact her in the car park.' Puff, puff, puff. 'Or she could have made a *second* telephone call while she was in the public box here.'

'Didn't her indignation convince you?'

'She was a professional actress, Mr Strangeways. They're paid to convince you. And she's the only person in this set-up known to have a Communist background. Let's see what these Attersons have to say. Deacon boy, go and chase up Mr Atterson for me.'

The bearded Lance tipped his hand at Nigel, and gave the Super a look in which bravado and uneasiness were blended. 'My first brush with the police,' he said, sitting on the arm of a big chair. Sparkes, riffling through some papers, appeared to ignore him for half a minute.

'Mr Atterson?' he then said. 'I am Superintendent Sparkes, the officer in charge of this case.'

'Well, I didn't suppose you were the Archbishop of Canterbury,' returned Lance, looking cockily around him as if he were entertaining a mob of teenagers.

'It's a very grave case, and I'd like to get on with it——'

'Surely, surely.'

'—with as few specimens of your humour as possible. I have here your first statement to the police. You are twenty-eight. You live in Chelsea. You married Mrs Atterson a week ago in a registrar's office. The Chelsea one?'

'No.'

'Which one?'

'What does that matter? I thought you wanted to get on with the case.'

'Which registrar's office?'

'Oh, get with it, man. Cherry and I have to pass as man and wife, or whatever corny phrase you——'

'Why?'

'Why? Because of all the squares in this joint.'

'Unmarried. You are a professional jazz singer?'

'You can say that again.'

'Successful?'

'Well, one has one's ups and downs.'

'Unsuccessful,' said Sparkes making a note.

'Hey, I never said——'

'Who arranged that you should stay here over Christmas?'

'Arranged? What are you getting at?' Lance grinned uneasily.

'Who made the booking?'

'Oh, I get you. Cherry did.'

'And she'll be paying the bill when you leave?'

'Look. I'm dead narked by this dialogue.'

'I'll ask *her*, then. Why did you go to Belcaster yesterday?'

'Cherry and I got a yen for the bright lights.'

'How did you get there?'

'The Leake character gave us a ride in his wheel.'

'Were you with him all the time? I want you to describe your movements very carefully.'

'Well, Leake stashed the wheel in the car park. Then we had some coffee with him. Then we rambled round the shops for five or ten minutes.'

'He was still with you?'

'Couldn't shake him off. He's a drag all right.'

'Carry on.'

'Finally, he said he had to send a telegram, and fixed to meet us in the car park in five minutes.'

'All the time he was with you, did Mr Leake talk to anyone else?'

'Only the chick who brought our coffee.'

'Could he have left a message there? On the bill, say? Or chalked a mark on a wall in the street? That sort of thing?'

'Not on the bill: Cherry paid it. Chalking?—that's spy stuff, isn't it? What a gas! He might have. I just didn't see him doing anything like that.'

'Thank you. That's all for the present. Deacon, will you ask the young lady to step this way. Mrs Atterson—Miss Cherry—what's her real name?'

'Smith,' said Lance Atterson, sliding out of the room in front of sergeant.

The Superintendent raised his eyes to heaven. 'That young man's going to run into trouble before long.'

'If they find Leake such a bore, why do those two hang around him so much?'

'Or him around them? Ask me another.'

'You could ask *her*.' Nigel gazed non-committally down his nose. 'I'm interested in that telegram Leake sent.'

'I'm expecting word from the Surrey police. They're visiting this Sir James Allenby today. Another blind alley, I expect.'

Cherry slipped into the room. Her head and most of her face were covered by a silk scarf, which she now took off and threw on to a table. Nigel rose.

'Ah, Miss Allenby, I don't think you have met Superintendent Sparkes. He's in charge of the case.'

Cherry stood rigid, staring at him. She licked her lips. 'Allenby? What *is* all this?' she said at last.

'Isn't that your name?'

'Of course it isn't. I'm Mrs Atterson.'

'Not according to Mr Atterson.'

'The rat! The bloody berk! I——'

'What's your unmarried name, then?' asked Sparkes.

'Smith.'

'We'll leave that for the moment. How long have you known Mr Leake?'

'Since we came to stay here.'

'What made you choose the Guest House for a holiday?'

'Oh, Lance saw the name in some mag or other,' she vaguely replied.

'You and your—Mr Atterson—seem to enjoy Mr Leake's company.'

'*Enjoy!* He clings to one like a parasite. It bugs me.'

'What does he want?'

Cherry's lethargic voice had an almost animated note. 'Oh, I should think he'd like to blackmail us.'

'Good lord! Over what?'

'Living in sin, of course.'

'*Has* he tried to blackmail you?'

'Well, not exactly. But he sort of makes with sinister hints. You know. And he's madly inquisitive. Trying to worm his way into one's confidence. Honestly, I don't dig him one little bit.'

Cherry's anomalous mixture of deb and beat had never been so evident.

'Has he ever tried to make you do anything for him? Pass a message yesterday morning, for instance? Any out-of-the-way suggestion he's ever made?'

'No, I can't remember anything.'

The Superintendent took her through the visit to Belcaster yesterday. Her account tallied with Lance Atterson's: she had seen nothing suspicious. 'But you know,' she added with one of her sallies of devastating honesty, 'I wouldn't notice a polar bear in the street unless you dangled it under my nose. I'm neurotic, you see—got an ingrowing ego.'

'Are you telling me the truth about all this, Miss—er—Smith?'

'Oh yes, I usually tell the truth. Only sometimes I get bored telling it, then I try making things up for a change.'

Superintendent Sparkes could seldom have had so unconventional an interview. Cherry's bursts of appalling frankness obviously disconcerted him. He fiddled with his papers, while she sat lumpishly, staring in front of her, like a subnormal child in class.

'Have you a record, Miss Smith?'

'Oh, dozens. Lance made the top ten a few years ago. But I really prefer the classical stuff.'

'A police record, I mean.'

'Well, I've not been in jail yet. I did get fined for sitting in Trafalgar Square. It was one of those Committee of a Hundred picnics.'

'I see. You believe in unilateral disarmament?'

'Every sensible person does.' Cherry took a deep breath, about to launch on a political speech, but Sparkes forestalled her.

'Would you say that betraying your country's secrets to an enemy advanced the cause of nuclear disarmament?'

The girl's pasty face flushed. 'That would depend. But if you mean, did I have anything to do with kidnapping Lucy, I didn't. I think it was absolutely foul.'

Sparkes asked a few more questions, but his edge was blunted by Cherry's curiously placid kind of non-resistance. As she draped the scarf round her head to go, Nigel said:

'No need to cover up your face. The reporters have gone down to the village.'

Cherry shot him a startled glance, then sidled from the room. Sparkes raised his eyebrows inquiringly at Nigel, who said, 'Didn't want to be recognised: therefore, she's been in the news. Maybe she's below the age of consent and her parents are trying to find her, break off her relationship with that preposterous Atterson character. They've engaged Leake to search for her. Leake's playing some double game of his own—"am on possible trail"—I'd guess she gets a big allowance, has prospects of a lot more when she comes of age, and Leake sees some nice pickings for himself.'

'You should be a book-writer, Mr Strangeways.' The Superintendent smiled. 'If Leake tries to blackmail that piece, I pity him. By the way, you noticed *she* said that Lance had chosen the Guest House to visit? Deacon boy, we'll try Mrs ffrench-Sullivan next.'

Sparkes handled the Admiral's wife with kid gloves at first. She treated him as though he were an upper servant, her somewhat raddled pug-face set in a look of command which Nigel found both ludicrous and pathetic.

'Well, Mr Sparkes, what are the police doing about this disgraceful outrage?'

'We're doing our best, ma'am.'

'I don't know what the country's coming to, with Red agents allowed to snatch little girls from under their parents' noses.'

'It's a shocking state of affairs indeed,' agreed the Superintendent. 'Whom do you suspect? The kidnappers must have a contact in this house, you know.'

'It's obviously that dreadful Atterson person.'

'What makes you think that?'

'He's a rotter. Do anything for money. We service wives get to know the type. Very rare, fortunately, in Her Majesty's Navy.'

'What about Mr Leake? Have you formed any opinion about him, ma'am?'

A wary look came over Mrs ffrench-Sullivan's face. 'Mr Leake? He seems a well-mannered person, though not quite a gentleman. Of course, I've had no dealings with him.'

'Dealings? What sort of dealings would you have?'

The woman looked flustered. 'I said I've *not* had any. I mean, beyond a little conversation. One must be civil. He's not quite our class, after all.'

'I see. So you've no reason to suspect him of anything but inferior social origins?' said Sparkes dryly.

'Well, there was just one thing.'

'Yes.'

'I greatly dislike anything that smacks of tale-bearing.'

'Any communication to the police, ma'am, is a privileged one,' said Sparkes, respectfully—and meaninglessly.

'Quite. Well, the morning after Lucy disappeared, as I was coming down to breakfast, just before nine, I passed Mr Leake's door. Do you know what I heard?' She made a dramatic pause. 'A *woman* was talking in there.'

'Indeed? Did you recognise the voice?'

'I'm afraid not.'

'Or hear anything she said?'

'No. Naturally, I passed straight on.'

'Naturally.'

'She sounded rather distressed. Or angry, perhaps.'

'Well, that may be a useful piece of information,' said Sparkes, giving Nigel a disillusioned glance. He sorted through the papers on the desk. 'Now, ma'am—just a formality, you understand?— you telephoned a wire to Belcaster yesterday morning. Let me see now—yes, here's the message: *Do not accept offer: am writing.* Could you——?'

'This is the most abominable interference with my affairs! How dare you intercept a private telegram I sent!' The woman's face had gone peony-red.

'You refuse to divulge any information about this message?'

'Most certainly I do. And I shall see that the chief constable hears of this.' The Admiral's wife stormed out of the room, Deacon following her.

Nigel grinned. 'Burnt your fingers there, mate. What's it all about anyway?'

The telegram, said Sparkes, had been sent to a Mrs Hollins, who kept a dress shop in Belcaster. Nothing was known against her, except that her business was a bit rocky: interviewed by the police, Mrs Hollins had said that she could not discuss the telegram without her client's permission.

'Unlike Miss Cherry What-have-you, Mrs ffrench-Sullivan has a record—or ought to.'

'Good lord, what for?' asked Nigel. 'Assaulting a Labour politician with an umbrella?'

'Shop-lifting. In the next county. During the war. The Admiral was in the Med—may never have heard about it. Her classy friends used influence, and the matter was hushed up. No conviction. But a friend of mine who handled the case told me there was little doubt about it. There was another woman involved, I seem to remember; but she gave a false name and address, and slipped out——'

'The real name being Hollins, perhaps?' Nigel gazed meditative-ly at a hunting print on the wall. 'You know, Mrs ffrench-Sullivan seems to bit too Blue to be true. She's a snob. But she's also greedy, and can't afford all the things she'd like. The shop-lifting bears that out. The sort of person the other side could easily put pressure on. Just do this little thing for us and you'll get £50: refuse, and we'll reveal your horrid slip-up in the past: what *would* the neighbours say?'

'Where the hell's that sergeant of mine got to? Could you round him up, and ask him to bring the Admiral along?'

Nigel found them in the drawing-room, with Deacon standing beside them rather at a loss: he had been instructed that no one who was still to be interviewed should communicate with anyone who had been; but the Admiral's air of authority, together with the unstaunchable flood of resentment his wife poured out, had in-hibited Deacon from the performance of his duty.

'Been getting my wife's back up, eh?' said the Admiral, when Sparkes had introduced himself.

'I can't understand why she should be so annoyed, sir. I only asked her to tell me a bit more about a telegram she wired from here yesterday morning. This is a copy of it.'

The Admiral put on reading glasses and took the paper. 'Mrs Hollins? Well, it could be the widow of my Jimmy the One. Poor fellow got killed in the Med. Muriel and she were quite thick during the war: shared a cottage in Devon. We lost sight of her after 1945. Didn't take to her very much myself. So she's living in Belcaster now?'

'If it's the same person, sir. Keeps a dress shop. Can you tell me any reason why Mrs ffrench-Sullivan should be so upset about this?'

'Can *you* tell *me* what it has to do with the case you're in charge of, Superintendent?'

'I'm concerned to check every outgoing call made yesterday morning. The kidnappers have a contact here. He tipped them off about our plans. It's a matter of eliminating the rest of you.' Sparkes trod as gingerly as if he were in a minefield.

'I see. "Do not accept offer." Yes, it could look quite sinis-ter.' The Admiral gave his gentle smile. 'I can assure you my wife is not an enemy agent, though. Dress shop, you say? Will you keep this quite confidential, if it is not relevant to the case?'

'Certainly, sir.'

'Of course it's only a guess; but it might be Muriel's mink.'

'Muriel's mink?' stammered Sparkes, utterly dumbfounded.

'Yes. Haven't seen it lately. Perhaps she asked your Mrs Hollins to dispose of it for her privately. Muriel wouldn't like to advertise, you see: she worries about keeping up social position—all that sort of thing. Fact is, I lost a lot of money—hers and mine—speculating in the fifties—and we've had to shorten sail pretty drastically. Comes hard on a woman, y'know. Different for me: never minded roughing it.'

Nigel had a wild impulse to embrace the old fellow: he had such gentleness, dignity, decency.

The Superintendent was asking him about their fellow guests. No, he had seen or heard nothing in the least suspicious. 'You've come to the wrong man, though, Superintendent,' he lisped. 'My head's rather in the clouds these days. Don't notice things like I did. Comes of reading the eastern mystics. Ever tried Buddhism, my dear fellow?'

'No, sir, I can't say I have.'

'Wait till you get old and useless like me. Perhaps I ought to take up that chap Leake's idea. Write a gossip column.'

Sparkes looked as if he had been struck by a torpedo. *'Gossip column?'*

'Yes. Well, not exactly write it. Send stuff in. Leake knows some journalist-johnny who runs a column. Gets stuff in from all over the place. They *pay* you for it—everything they use—quite a decent sum: five or ten pounds maybe.' The faded blue eyes beamed at them. 'This johnny apparently hasn't got anyone sending in from our part of the world. And I know the county folk and so forth. What d'you think, Strangeways?'

Nigel thought it was easy to imagine how this lovable innocent had lost all his money. The Admiral continued, not without relish:

'Bit of extra cash'd come in useful, y'know. Trouble is, they'd want the dirt. Saucy pars. Local scandals. Don't think I could manage that—not that I don't know plenty. Eh?'

'I'd stick to Lao-tze,' said Nigel. 'But don't decide yet. Keep Mr Leake on a string.'

'Might raise his offer? Ha. Very sound advice.'

'And don't tell him you've discussed it with us.'

'No? No, of course not.' The Admiral gave Nigel a crafty wink, and took his leave.

Nigel turned to Sergeant Deacon. 'When Mr Sparkes has recovered his power of speech, he'll probably want to interview Mr Justin Leake.'

Forehead in hand, Sparkes nodded, and the sergeant went out.

'What *is* it about the Navy?'

'Jane Austen was affected in the same way,' Nigel answered. 'Captain Wentworth is my favourite. Four-square chap, *and* intelligent. You remember that bit——'

The pair were launched on a discussion of *Persuasion* when Justin Leake entered. The Superintendent, who varied his tactics like a good fly-half, was evidently going to play this one close, and give the man no inkling of previous witnesses' curious evidence about him. Full name? Address? Occupation?

'I run an inquiry agency,' was the reply.

'What sort of inquiries, sir?'

'Things people don't want to put into the hands of the police. Search for a missing person, for instance. And of course a certain amount of divorce work. Snooping.' Justin Leake said it in his usual colourless way, with no trace of embarrassment or self-defensiveness.

'I take it your telegram to Sir James Allenby was on professional business?'

'Surely.'

'The nature of this business, Mr Leake?'

'That is a confidential matter between my client and myself.'

'You told him you were on a possible trail.'

'Yes.'

'Of a missing relative?'

'My clients would cease to have any confidence in me, Mr Sparkes, if I divulged their private affairs. It'd be as good as my job's worth to betray them.'

'I understand.' The Super dropped this line of questioning—to Leakes's not quite perfectly disguised relief—and began to take him through his movements in Belcaster on the crucial morning.

Nigel studied the witness. He was certainly a cool card. Almost inhumanly so. The head went straight up at the back, with no bulge. A bald spot on the top of it. Unobtrusive dark suit: shirt cuffs a little grubby: fingers tobacco-stained. A voice almost without inflections. And that attentive, oddly neutral gaze.

An inquiry agent, thought Nigel, would have unrivalled opportunities for blackmail. Blackmail today was a notorious weapon of persuasion in espionage work. If Leake himself were not the X they were looking for, he could be the one who had put pressure on this X, to organise the Guest House end of the kidnapping. But, if so, Leake would be unlikely to show up here in person: unless he was killing multiple birds with one stone. Who would the X be, then? Cherry? Lance? The Admiral's wife?

Leake's account of his visit to Belcaster tallied with the Attersons'. The Super suddenly abandoned his safety tactics. 'Do you suspect the Attersons of complicity in this kidnapping affair?'

'The Attersons? Not particularly. Why?'

'You go about with them a lot. You're in a better position than I am to pick up anything they let slip, and you're a trained observer. Are you sure they did not communicate with anyone in Belcaster?'

'As far as I can tell. I wasn't watching them all the time.'

'Nothing abnormal in their behaviour? Suppressed excitement? Nervousness?'

'Can't say there was.'

'Yesterday morning before breakfast—who was the woman you were talking to in your bedroom?'

For the first time, Justin Leake showed positive animation. 'Woman? I had no woman in my room. Where on earth did you get that idea?'

'Information received, sir.'

'Damned unreliable information. Wait a minute, though. I had a brief chat with the maid who brought my early-morning tea. At eight o'clock. Would that be it?'

'No. Just before nine.'

'That's absurd. Nobody in my room then.'

'Nothing that would account for this evidence? You weren't playing the radio, or a tape?'

'Oh lord, I'd quite forgotten. Yes, I have a transistor set. I believe I put that on while I was dressing.'

'Which programme? Home or Light?'

'Blest if I can remember. I wasn't really listening, anyway. Light, I should think.'

Should you indeed? thought Nigel. The Light always broadcasts a weather report at 8.55, which would not have sounded to Mrs ffrench-Sullivan like a woman's voice, 'rather distressed or angry perhaps'.

'But surely you can remember if the programme you listened to had a woman's voice in it?'

'Most of them do. Sorry, I wasn't paying attention. I'm a background listener.'

An appropriate designation, Nigel reflected, for this unobtrusive, shadowy fellow.

'Well, thank you for your help, Mr Leake. I'll be seeing you.'

'When shall we be allowed to leave this place, Superintendent?'

'How long had you planned to stay, sir?'

'Oh, another few days.'

'Your agency can look after itself?'

'I have a competent assistant, and a secretary.'

'Well, that's fine. Of course, nobody can leave till the main London road is unblocked. Good morning to you.'

Sparkes watched the man out of the door, then said: 'They ought to keep him on a table in an express restaurant car.'

'Oh?'

'The one thing that couldn't be rattled.'

'Who's telling the truth about that woman's voice in his bedroom?'

'We'll find out,' said Sparkes grimly. 'Get a *Radio Times*, Deacon boy, and see what the programmes were yesterday morning. And verify that he has a transistor . . . You know, Mr Strangeways, we're getting nowhere: and it's not as if we had time to play with.'

CHAPTER 7

Little Girl Lost

DECEMBER 29

At 10.30 that same morning, P.C. Hardman was plodding up the hill from Eggarswell towards Mr Thwaite's farm and Smugglers' Cottage. He walked in one of the grooves made through the snow by the great farm tractor, casting an eye now and then at the sky, which to his countryman's instinct threatened more snow. Small birds huddled in the snow-laden hedges, their plumage fluffed out, too cold and disconsolate to take alarm as the constable walked past. Above him lay the ridge, shaped like the body of a woman lying on her side beneath a white coverlet.

As he neared the farm P.C. Hardman heard two explosions, followed by a wild clapping of wings. It was Jim Stocks, in his red woollen hat, Wellingtons, and Army great-coat, shooting at the hordes of starving pigeons which marauded amongst his master's brussels sprouts.

The noise of the shot-gun alarmed Paul Cunningham. He and Annie Stott had taken turns during the daytime, since they had heard on the news that police would be searching all outlying houses in the country, on the lookout from a window upstairs. If the visit came at night, the plan was for Paul to keep the police in conversation downstairs while Annie made the necessary arrangements.

Paul now saw a constable entering the farm gates. He hurried to tell his companion. Thirty seconds later, Annie was in Lucy's room, holding out a glass of orange juice to the child. Lucy drank it eagerly. The knock-out drops in it took effect almost immediately. Annie stripped the unconscious child, put the pyjamas on her, carried her into the room that had been Evan's, tucked her into the bed, safety-pinned round her neck a cloth soaked in camphorated oil and laid a similar dressing on the child's chest under the pyjama jacket. Lucy was flushed now and breathing heavily.

Before closing the curtains, Annie took a quick glance round the room. Everything seemed in order. No, it was much too cold for a

74

sick-room. She should have kept the electric fire on permanently: her childhood poverty had trained her never to waste fuel—that was the trouble. She switched on both bars of the fire, inwardly blanching at the disastrous mistake she had so nearly made: they must not let the policeman in here till the room had warmed up.

Annie Stott was aware that, since Evan's disappearance, the whole position had altered. There'd been nothing about him on the radio or in the newspapers. Which could mean that the wretched boy had blown the gaff, and the police were here to inquire about him, not to search for Lucy. The anxiety set up by this dilemma impaired Annie's mental efficiency: she kept parting the curtains and peering right towards the farm buildings, forgetting that the bed in Lucy's room was not yet made.

P.C. Hardman entered the farm kitchen. 'Morning, Mr Thwaite. Another bad one. You been kidnapping any children lately?'

'Not bloody likely, Bert. Got enough of my own. Nasty business, though.'

'When's this weather going to break? My missus' chilblains are playing her up fair horrible.'

'We're in for a longish spell, if you ask me. Mother!'

Mrs Thwaite came bustling in. 'Thought I heard your voice, Mr Hardman. What's to do? Master been filling up his forms wrong again?'

'Give Bert a cup of tea, mother. He's chasing after this kid that's been stolen.'

'Well, he won't find her here, poor little thing. A downright shame, I call it. Three lumps, Mr Hardman?'

'Thank 'ee.' Hardman sucked the tea noisily through his shaggy moustache. 'Your kids not seen anyone about answering to the missing child's description?' he portentously inquired.

'You'd have heard from us if they had,' replied Mrs Thwaite a little sharply. 'You want to search the place?'

' 'Tis not what I want, missus. 'Tis what I'm ordered to do.'

'Don't take on, mother. Bert has his duty.'

'A process of elimination, like,' said Hardman, blowing out his moustache. 'Just a quick look round presently, see? What about the folk at Smugglers'?'

'They don't have much truck with us,' said Mrs Thwaite. 'That Dr Everley—a proper old pill she is. Thinks her nephew too good for my kids.'

'Now, now, mother. Evan's delicate. Ill in bed again today, Jim says.'

'They been here long?'

'A fortnight. Young Mr Cunningham—that's her brother—he came down first, a few days before Dr Everley and the boy. Quite a nice-spoken gentleman. Funny, him and that sour-faced creature hatching out of the same egg.'

'Twins, are they?' asked the literal-minded Bert.

'No. You know what I mean. He doesn't favour her at all.'

'Ah. Heredity. Queer do sometimes, Mrs Thwaite. Look at our Dudley and our Marlene—never think they were brother and sister, would you now?'

'Cuckoo in the nest, Bert?' said the farmer jovially. His wife looked shocked. Bert Hardman shook with silent laughter. 'Remember when I first joined the Force—Charlie Pearce—used to farm Knowhill—he married one of old squire's daughters. Flighty piece she was too. Well . . .' The anecdote wound itself to a laborious end. Bert Hardman reluctantly rose. 'Thank 'ee for the cup, missus. I'll just have a look round, then I'll walk along to Smugglers'.'

'You're wasting your time, Mr Hardman,' said Mrs Thwaite tartly. 'Sir Henry wouldn't let his cottage to a gang of kidnappers, would he now?'

'Never know. What you read in the papers nowadays, some of these Oxford and Cambridge bigwigs are no better than Bolsheviks.'

'Well, listen to him!' Mrs Thwaite chuckled maliciously. 'Maybe you'll get promotion at last, Bert.'

P.C. Hardman's intelligence quotient was not a high one. But he possessed a faculty which had served him well enough in his undistinguished career—a countryman's instinctive reaction to certain types of human beings and behaviour. He had not been with Paul and Annie above a minute or two before this instinct told him that the pair were frightened of something, and that, while Mr Cunningham was a gent, Dr Everley was not what he recognised as a lady. On the other hand, he knew by experience that even the

76

gentry—especially its younger members—could be nervous in the presence of the Law.

He faced them stolidly in the sitting-room, refused a drink, and took out his notebook.

'I am inquiring into the recent disappearance of a young girl, Lucy Wragby. You may have heard——'

'Oh yes, it was on the news.'

'Just a routine matter. May I have your names and addresses?'

Paul gave his own, Annie those of a woman doctor called Everley she had found in the Medical Directory.

'Is there anyone else residing here?'

'Yes,' said Paul. 'Our nephew. Evan. We brought him here for a holiday. He'd had a bad go of bronchitis.'

'I'm afraid he's ill again,' said Annie. 'I'm a bit worried it may turn to pleurisy. We meant to send him back to his parents in London yesterday, but I decided it was better not to move him yet.'

So that's what they're worried about, thought Hardman, not a visit from the police. Nevertheless, he ploughed on.

'I understand, sir, you rented this cottage from Sir Henry——'

'Yes. He's Warden of my old college at Oxford. I've got this letter somewhere, if——' Paul made a gesture towards the desk, kicking himself the next moment for having been so unnecessarily forthcoming.

'Well, sir, just to get everything in order.'

As Paul Cunningham searched a drawer, P.C. Hardman glanced at Dr Everley: she was sitting, balled up in her chair, immobile, in a way that reminded him of the clemmed birds he had seen in the hedges on his way. A sour-looking female, right enough. He read carefully through the letter which Paul handed him. Sir Henry had addressed him as 'Dear Paul', which made a favourable impression on the constable.

'Well now, sir and madam, do you have any objection to my searching the house?'

'None at all,' Paul answered. 'Go ahead.'

'I suppose it's all right,' said Annie grudgingly, 'though no one could conceal a child here without our knowledge.'

'Just a formality, Doctor.'

'And may I see your own identification first. Just as a formality?'

Sarcastic old cow. Mrs Thwaite was right, thought Hardman as he fumbled for his card. He decided that, after all, he would spend a very long time searching the house, just to annoy the woman.

Annie Stott leading him, and Paul Cunningham trailing behind, Hardman inspected the ground floor rooms, opening cupboards, stooping to peer under tables, Annie growing visibly more impatient every minute.

'What's in here?' he said, pointing to a door in the hall at the back of the stairs, then rattling its handle.

'I believe Sir Henry keeps his wine there.'

Paul was correct in this belief. He did not mention that the large cupboard accommodated Annie Stott's shortwave transmitter.

'Open it up, please.'

'Sorry, Officer, we don't have the key to it.'

'I don't want to have to break it down.'

'I fancy Sir Henry wouldn't want you to, either,' snapped the woman. 'My brother has told you, Sir Henry did not leave the key with us.'

Paul Cunningham felt a trickle of sweat run down his spine. He asked himself whether, as an honest householder—tenant—he ought not to be showing a bit of indignation; but before he could answer the question, the constable rattled the door-knob again, made a note in his notebook, and began clumping upstairs at Annie's heels.

In Annie's bedroom, then in Paul's, P.C. Hardman went through the same slow-motion rigmarole. His two companions were silent now, for the real test was coming any minute and they dared not betray themselves by the slightest flutter in their voices. Hardman postponed it intolerably, electing to investigate the bathroom and lavatory next.

'What about that room along there?' he asked, emerging at last.

'That's Evan's. He's ill in bed. Asleep,' said Annie firmly. 'You surely don't need to——'

'Duty is duty, Doctor. My instructions are to——'

'Oh, very well. If you must, you must. But you are on no account to wake him, or disturb him in any way. He's under mild sedation.'

P.C. Hardman tiptoed into the room. It was pretty warm now, and there was a smell of camphorated oil. Light seeping through the curtain fabric revealed a sandy-haired boy lying in the bed, breathing rather stertorously, a high flush on his cheeks, a cloth pinned round his neck. The constable looked down at this figure for a few moments, gently touched the damp hair on the forehead, whispered 'Poor little chap', and went out into the passage again.

'Hope he'll soon be mending, Doctor. Pretty little nipper.'

'He's very feverish just now, Got to keep him quiet.'

Irritable with the relief of it, Paul said, 'What *is* the point of all this? I thought you said it was a missing *girl* you were looking for.'

Annie cut in sharply. 'Don't you remember, Paul?—the news bulletin said that the kidnappers might have tried to alter the child's appearance.'

'So it did. But——'

'Don't you fret, sir. The child answers to the description Mr and Mrs Thwaite gave me of your nephew. What it is—I have to give my superior officers a report that I've examined every house in this vicinity.'

'You are acting quite correctly, Officer,' Annie reassured him.

' "Slow but solid, that's him",' quoted Paul *sotto voce*.

'Any rooms at the back?' asked Hardman.

'A lumber room and a spare bedroom.'

'Better just put my nose inside them.'

The lumber room was filled with junk. Hardman prodded about for a bit, then they went into the room in which Lucy was normally incarcerated.

'Sort of nursery, eh? Yes, I remember Sir Henry used to have grandchildren staying. Not much of a view.' The constable glanced out of the window, turned round. 'You didn't tell me there was another occupant in the house.'

'But there isn't. Just the three of us,' Annie protested.

'Somebody's been sleeping in that bed, sir.'

Annie Stott was staring at the unmade bed, the rumpled bed-clothes, incapable of speech. Paul suddenly felt in absolute command of the situation.

'Why, you forgot to make it, Annie.' He turned to the constable. 'Evan's being using this as a sort of playroom. We made him lie down for a rest every afternoon: till he got ill again yesterday.'

Hardman again felt his animal intuition that something was wrong, but he could not put a finger on anything suspicious. At a loss, he took up a sheaf of foolscap that lay on the table. 'Nipper writing a book, eh? The things they get up to! *"Chapter One. The Snatching of Cinders"*,' he read.

'Sorry. Thought I heard Evan calling.' Annie Stott ran from the room.

'Who's this Cinders now?' asked Hardman.

'Evan heard of the kidnapping on the news. Started to write a story about it. Don't know why he called the heroine "Cinders". Heartless little bastards these kids are,' said Paul coolly, fighting down a wild urge to tear the foolscap from the constable's hands. As it happened, this would have been unnecessary as well as unwise. Hardman put the manuscript down on the table again, without reading any further. 'Well, sir, I'm much obliged. Sorry to have troubled you. I must be on my way now. Let me know if there's anything I can do for the nipper. Good-day to you.'

'It was a near miss,' said Paul some minutes later, after describing the episode to Annie. He still felt a certain exultation at having kept his nerve when she had lost hers: it evened the score for his panicky desertion of Evan in the blizzard, and for the first time Annie was treating him with something like respect.

' 'You did well,' she said. 'What about this story she was writing?'

'Oh, I've burnt it. Made me feel rather a brute. How much longer shall we have the wretched child on our hands?'

'That depends on Petrov's next move.'

'*He*'s making the next move, is he?'

The woman did not answer. She had been in communication with Petrov over the short-wave transmitter last night—that was all her companion knew.

'If only we could be sure what's happened to Evan,' she said. 'Well, he can't have given anything away, or we'd be in jug by now.'

'You know what I think? Evan did get to London all right, and Petrov is pretending he didn't.'

Annie studied the faun's face of her companion. 'Why on earth should he do that?'

'Search me. To keep us on tenterhooks, maybe. He enjoys power and intrigue and deception—for their own sake, I mean.'

'Oh, rubbish,' retorted Annie, not with entire conviction though.

'Well, do *you* trust him?'

'Of course I do.'

'More fool you. If this scheme of his falls through, do you realise what he'll do? He'll duck out and leave us holding the baby.'

The woman's expression hardened. 'I see. You're suggesting *we* should duck out, before it happens?'

'*You* would, Annie, if you had any sense. I can't—he's got me by the short hairs, as well you know. Oh, of course you'll stick it out—Party discipline and all that cock. It must be nice to feel that nothing matters in life except the victory of the Cause.'

'Lots of other things matter, Paul. You talk as if we weren't human beings. It's just that we know what matters most. And act on the knowledge.'

There was something softer, almost appealing in her expression, more disturbing to Paul than her usual indifference or hostility. He found himself mentally shrinking from her, as if she were making a sexual advance towards him. 'The trouble with your lot is that your morality encourages you to tell lies, to us or to each other, whenever it's expedient.'

'Do you suppose capitalist politicians never tell lies?'

'That's not the point. Your creed that there's no truth except the truth of expediency means in effect you can trust nobody. And people who won't trust are condemning themselves to hell. All your dreary slogans—the solidarity of the masses, that sort of cant—they're just covering up the truth, that your solidarity is an abstraction, a paper façade, which prevents you making any real contact with others. You can't, not if you must always be suspicious of them, ready to distrust or destroy individual human beings in the interests of humanity. You're living in hell, though you don't know it. Hell is isolation. You worship a Purpose, historical necessity, like other people worship God: and you worship it so servilely that when your God tells you, go to hell for my sake, off you trot.'

'You should be a Quaker,' she said, not aggressively. 'You and your bourgeois romanticism, Paul.'

'There you go again. When you can't answer an argument, you dismiss it with some meaningless catch-phrase.'

'After what I've told you about my childhood, you can still talk as if I had no contact with—with reality? We know reality by acting upon it, not by sitting about contemplating it from a respectful distance, theorising about it.'

'But——'

'You belong to a working group yourself. You must know that, as a Party member, a shop steward, I have a close, active relationship with other people. We're in it together, working to make a better world for——'

'Oh good God! So that children shan't have to go to school cold and hungry like you did, and be given hell by bigger children, you feel justified in putting that kid upstairs through hell.'

'You're doing it too.'

'I was forced into it. You've done it of your own free will—if I may use that dirty word to a determinist.'

'You could have refused.'

'I *should* have refused. No need to remind me that I funked it, Annie. Why can women never resist an opportunity to use their claws?'

'You could assuage your conscience, my dear Paul,' she said with a return to her acid manner, 'by keeping the child company now and then. If you consider your presence would mitigate the hell you say she's living in.'

After a pause, Paul said, 'Very well,' as if he were issuing a threat, and flung out of the room. In a few moments, however, he was back. 'Asleep still. She's breathing awfully heavily. You didn't overdo that sleeping-draught, I hope.'

'Of course not . . .'

Lucy did not in fact wake up properly till 2.15 p.m. When she did, it was with an aching head and the memory of horrid dreams. She recollected the madwoman giving her a drink of orange juice: nothing after that but the things that had mocked and gibbered at her in the nightmares, stalked her as she ran down endless streets to find her father, who himself turned into one of them when she found him. The horror of this last betrayal was all too vivid still. Lucy buried her head in the pillow and began to cry. She knew she would never see her father again: the adventure-fantasies which had sustained her so far shredded to nothing and she was left alone, alone, all all alone.

After some time, a new voice said, "Hallo there, Lucy'. The electric light was switched on. She started up in bed, rubbing her eyes, not sure if this wasn't another of the dreadful dreams beginning.

'How are you now?'

'I'm so hot.'

'We'll turn off the fire then.'

Lucy saw she was in the room at the front of the house, not her own. A man was gazing at her: a man with rather long hair and a rather small buttony sort of mouth. The mouth opened and said, 'You've been crying, my dear. No need to cry.'

'I couldn't help it,' she replied miserably.

'There's shepherd's pie and tinned peaches for lunch. Can you force them down, you poor invalid chee-ild?'

Lucy gave a tentative smile. She liked this sort of talk.

'I expect so. Have I been asleep long?'

'Several hours.'

'But I *never* sleep after breakfast. And I've got a foul headache.'

'Bad luck. That'll go soon.'

'Will it . . . ? Who are you?'

'My name's Paul.'

'Are you that loopy woman's keeper?'

The man giggled in an agreeable way. Lucy noted that he had long eyelashes. When the eyes weren't dancing at you, they had a queer hangdog sort of look.

'Aunt Annie's keeper? Well, as you mention it, I am. But don't tell her. The cow stood up, the keeper stood up to keep the cow.'

Lucy began to laugh, though she could not tell why.

'You sound as mad as she is. Oh, what's this smelly thing around my neck? And there's another on my chest.'

'Aunt A. thought you were sickening for bronchitis or something. I think we can take them off now. If you promise not to open the window. Cold air really would be dangerous after being wadded up with wormogene and perforated oil——'

'Don't be silly. It's Thermogene and camphorated oil, you nit.'

'So it is. Promise?'

'I promise.'

Paul unpinned the dressings and threw them into a corner of the room. 'Here, put on this jersey. I'll get your lunch.'

The man sat watching her while she ate it. He seemed a nice man, thought Lucy; but he couldn't really be nice if he was helping to keep her prisoner, and besides there was something about the way he looked at her that made her vaguely uncomfortable.

Paul was thinking what a pretty boy she made, with that well-shaped head and shining grey eyes.

'Can't we have the curtains open?' she asked presently.

'Why not?'

Lucy gazed out over the great vista of snow. 'I wish we could go tobogganing,' she said wistfully.

'Perhaps we will one day.'

'Oh, when? Tomorrow? It may all melt before——' Lucy's voice quavered, and she could not go on, remembering how her father had promised to get her a toboggan.

'You're not going to start crying again?'

His tone, making her indignant, braced her against tears. 'That isn't fair. You can't expect me to feel happy here.'

'You're well looked after, aren't you?' said Paul, averting his eyes.

'But I want to go back to my father, and Elena. I don't know why you're keeping me here.'

'You will before long, I hope—go back to them.'

Lucy gazed steadily at him, trying to measure the truthfulness of what he'd said. 'Do you swear that? Cross your heart.'

Paul swallowed hard. 'Cross my heart.'

'I had some horrid dreams this morning. I dreamt I was looking everywhere for Papa and couldn't find him.'

'Come on, Lucy, cheer up. Shall we have a game of draughts?'

'I'd rather have a bath. I'm poofy.'

'All right.'

He took her into the bathroom, ran the water. When she had finished, he was waiting outside. He sniffed the air over her head theatrically. 'You smell nice now, Lucy.'

'Do I have to be shut up in that other room all day?' They were back in the room at the front of the house. 'It's so dull there, I can't see anything out of the window.'

'I'll have to ask Annie. I don't see why we shouldn't let you roam around the house a bit.' Now that Evan is no longer here. 'But—do you know what *parole* means?'

'It's what prisoners give.'

'Yes. Will you *promise* not to try and escape—you couldn't get far anyway, the roads are all deep in snow. Promise on your honour?'

It might possibly have worked with a boy. Lucy gave him a wide-eyed guileless look. 'Of course I'll promise. On my honour.' She was woman enough already to have no time for that sort of 'honour' and to be dimly aware that Paul was a weak spot in the prison walls, worth playing on.

'Well, I'll see what Annie says.'

'But I thought—you mean she isn't really mad at all?'

The man's little fat mouth pouted. 'Not all the time. One has to humour her, though.' He was thinking that, whether or not the blackmail attempt succeeded, they would have to make up their minds what to do about this child, and it would be just as well to have her on his side. He had closed his mind, as he did with all disagreeable things, to the idea that Petrov might have planned to stop her mouth for ever.

He stroked her stubbly hair. 'Don't worry. I'll look after you, Lucy.'

She automatically moved her head away—she didn't like being fondled by strangers—then, remembering she must play up to him, squeezed his hand. 'Can I stay in this room?' she asked.

'But all your books and things are in the other one.'

'Couldn't you fetch me something to play with? I was writing——' Lucy broke off.

'Oh, that story of yours. I'm terribly sorry, but Annie found it this morning and destroyed it.'

'Destroyed it? But *why*?' A whine came into her voice.

'She does funny things occasionally. Never mind. You can start another one.'

'But she has no right to——'

'And I'll see she doesn't lay her long, long claws on it.'

Lucy was not mollified. 'I suppose she tore it up because it was about a girl being kidnapped. I call that mean of her.'

'Don't nag at me, young woman. You females will go on and on so. Now, what shall I get you?'

'That Ransome book beside the bed, please.'

'O.K., chum. How's the headache now?'

'Gone, thanks, matey.'

So far, so good, thought Lucy. Paul had brought her the book and retired. A soppy sort of man, she decided, though he spoke to her much more pleasantly than the potty woman. Who apparently was not potty—all the time, anyway. Lucy verified that Paul had not locked the door: but she could hear their voices arguing downstairs, and decided against trying a dash from the house.

Tip-toeing out, along the passage, into the nursery room at the back, Lucy recovered the sheet of foolscap she had hidden under the lining paper of a drawer. Back in bed, she read it through again. *Chapter Two. Where am I?* Then she pushed the folded paper inside her jersey and settled down to think.

People must come to this house sometimes. The man who brought the milk, Jim. When someone comes, as long as they let me stay in this room, I'll see him. No use just talking to him through the window-pane—he'd not hear what I said. And if I yelled, the woman would hear it and rush up with that beastly hypodermic. Of course, if the window opens—

She stood up in bed and tried it. The lower half was absolutely stuck: she could pull down the upper, with a great effort, but only a couple of inches, and she couldn't get her mouth near enough to this opening to talk quietly through it and be heard by a person outside. If she just made faces and signs through the pane, the person would think she was ragging him, or potty. Nobody would be looking for Lucy Wragby in Buckinghamshire.

They won't even have heard of me here. So it'd be no use writing a message, 'Help! S.O.S. I am Lucy Wragby. I've been kidnapped. Get the police!' and throwing it out of the window. The person would think it's some sort of kid's game.

Lucy knew all too well the inability of grown-ups to understand when you were being serious and when you were larking. Then she had an idea. Suppose she wrote on the back of the foolscap sheet that the finder should post this at once to Professor Alfred Wragby, F.R.S., The Guest House, Downcombe. Reward of £5. It is a scientific experiment.

Exhilarated by the promise of this idea, she took her pencil and wrote those words, in large capitals, on the back of the sheet. With luck, she could shoot a paper dart through the gap at the top of the window. Lucy folded the sheet carefully into a dart. But where could she hide it, so that her captors didn't find it before someone turned up to throw it to?

After some thought, she pushed it gently behind the framed photograph of the man in cap and gown on the opposite wall.

So it was just a matter of waiting patiently for someone to turn up. Now that she had worked out a plan, time dragged worse than ever. Nothing to look at outside except the landscape of snow, which bored her now. Sounds of mooing came from the farmyard. She took up her book, but the exploits of Mr Ransome's desperately resourceful children could not hold her attention long: I bet they'd look pretty silly in real life, she thought, if they got into an adventure like mine. Fat lot of good being able to sail a boat and cook their own meals would do them.

She watched a tree shadow, bluish on the snow, willing it to lengthen visibly. Hurry on, time. No, because it'll grow dark soon and the person wouldn't be able to find my dart—white paper stuck in the white snow below the window—and I'd have to wait till tomorrow.

But what person? A dismal thought struck her. Supposing it was the man from the farm, or a stranger? How could she know if he'd be on her side? They might be accomplices of her captors. The farm man, Jim—if he wasn't in the know, why should Annie have made her wave to him through the window early this morning? Was it this morning? It seemed a week ago.

Wait a minute, though. Annie had put her into this bed, made her wave to Jim: he'd called up something about her being poorly. But of course she'd look like a boy to him, a sick boy. The mustard-faced hag would tell Jim that she—Evan—had some infectious disease, measles or leprosy, so she'd have an excuse for not letting him, or any of the farm people, come to visit her. Therefore Jim could not be in the plot.

Lucy was so ravished by this elegant train of reasoning that she almost did not hear the squinching of boots in deep snow growing louder, aprroaching from the direction of the farm.

She leapt out of bed, took the paper dart from behind the picture, pinched out a ridge that had been crumpled, stood on the bed close to the window.

It *was* Jim, carrying a basket with some big oranges in it. Lucy rapped on the window, afraid to rap too loud. Harder. Jim looked up, waved. She put her finger to her lips, saying a 'ssh' which he certainly could not hear. Before he could shout up at her and bring the other two out of the house, Lucy projected the dart through the opening at the top of the window. It sailed in a beautiful arc, falling right at his feet.

Then the triumph of it turned to disaster. Jim picked it up all right; but he threw it straight back at her. Having a game with the kid. Good sport, young Evan was.

The dart struck the window-pane and eddied down like a shot bird into the snow, a foot from the wall of the cottage.

Lucy made frantic signs through the window, jabbing her finger downward, then opening an imaginary paper dart and pretending to read it. Jim grinned up, looking bemused. And at that moment Lucy heard footsteps in the hall, going towards the front door. At all costs she must stop them going out and seeing the dart. She screamed out 'Help! Help!'

The footsteps changed direction and came pounding up the stairs. Bursting into the room, Annie Stott clapped a hand over Lucy's mouth and dragged her away from the window.

'How dare you make that disgusting noise? You're a very naughty child.'

'I'm sorry,' said Lucy, when she could speak. 'I had a horrid dream. I dreamt the house was on fire.'

Annie went to the door and called down. 'Paul! Come up at once, please.'

Jim started to knock on the front door.

'Paul, see this child keeps quiet. She says she had a nightmare. Did you open that window, child?'

'I felt so hot. Then I went to sleep and had a beastly dream.'

'Shut it, Paul, and stay here. Keep her away from the window.'

Annie Stott hurried downstairs, in a furious temper.

'What do you want?' she asked Jim. 'What's been going on? Have you been talking to Evan?'

Like most rural persons Jim, though slow-thinking, could be both obstinate and crafty. He didn't want to get the little fellow in trouble with this sour-faced aunt of his. Better say nothing about the paper-dart throwing.

'Nothing's been going on—not that I knows of. I waved up to young Evan. Then you come screeching out at me.'

'The boy's delirious. He must be kept quiet.'

'Sorry to hear that. Bert Hardman asked me to bring up these oranges for Evan.'

'Hardman?'

'Our village copper.'

'Oh, yes, the one who came up this morning. Very kind of him, I'm sure.'

Annie Stott gazed suspiciously around: but Jim was standing between her and the dart. When she had gone indoors with the basket, he bent down, picked up the dart, scrumpled it into his great-coat pocket—and forgot all about it.

Lucy had no means of knowing whether its message had been taken, or whether it still lay at the foot of the wall, for she was removed at once into the nursery room at the back of the cottage.

CHAPTER 8

The Bug

DECEMBER 30

Elastic, kept stretched too long, loses its tension. At the Guest House on Sunday morning there was an atmosphere, slack and sagging, of nervous exhaustion. Elena Wragby had sat at breakfast, stony-faced, eating little, eyes downcast as if to avoid looking at the chair occupied once by Lucy. Her husband was attentive to her, in an absent-minded way, but she could make little response and his ear kept waiting for the expected sound of the telephone. Why hadn't they rung him since yesterday? The morning dragged on, and still there was not a word. They'd said he'd be getting new instructions from them: but no instructions came—which preyed upon Wragby's nerve all the more because he had privately made up his mind what line to take when they did come.

The wind had dropped again in the night, and a very severe frost turned the road-surfaces, on which the snow had begun to melt a little yesterday, into stretches of ice. At 10.50 the Admiral and his wife went off to the village church, slipping and supporting each other like drunks.

In the sitting-room, Lance Atterson was strumming on his guitar, while Cherry's fat little body jerked to the rhythms, unconsciously, like the body of a dog twitching in its sleep. Justin Leake was reading a paper-back with a lurid cover: that is to say, he had the book open in his hand, but he never seemed to turn a page, and the book might just as well be reading him—as Nigel would have liked to, but the man was indecipherable. There could be little doubt what game he was playing here: but was he covertly playing another game at the same time?

Superintendent Sparkes had rung Nigel last night.

'The Surrey chums have come through at last,' he said. 'Sir James Allenby wasn't at home—called away suddenly to Stockholm, but they interviewed the housekeeper.' A note of wry amusement came into Sparkes's voice. 'Your Cherry—it seems she really *is* Miss Smith. Frobisher-Smith, to be precise. Sir James's ward. Aged sixteen years, ten months.'

'Well, that tidies up that one. You're going to let it ride for a bit?'

'I certainly am. If she lays information against our friend, or vice versa, I'll have to act. Not till then.'

'Conniving at malpractices, eh?'

'Just so.'

'Nothing about Lucy yet?'

'Nothing. We've combed nearly all the likely places hereabouts. It's getting me down.'

'What about that telephone call to Wragby from London?'

'Came from a flat whose tenant is abroad. Can't trace him yet. Maybe an undercover Party member. Wish you could break through to the contact at this end.'

'The informer? I think I know who that is.'

'You do, do you?'

'Yes.' Nigel told him a name. There was a long silence. 'Well, that'd be a turn-up for the book,' said Sparkes at last . . .

Nigel and Clare had talked till midnight. He had gone into her room, adjoining his, and sat down on the bed. 'You look more beautiful than ever, Clare love,' he said, admiring the magnolia-white skin of her face and shoulders, the gloss of the black hair that cascaded about them.

'Shall we make love?' She gazed up at him. 'No, you want me to do something else for you. Tell me.'

'This is what comes of living with a witch. Simply can't have a private thought of my own.'

'You know you couldn't live with anyone else, my darling,' she replied, not possessively, not anxiously—with the affectionate detachment that kept her so charming for him.

'You could say no. I wouldn't blame you. It's a fairly beastly job.'

'Well, go on.'

'Like being given a knife and asked to go and twist it in someone else's wound.'

'Yes?'

'And that person may not deserve it, may be quite innocent.'

Clare's eyes were fastened upon his worried face. In her high, light voice, she said, 'You mean Elena Wragby.'

'Clairvoyant again.'

'No. It's just that we know each other so well, bless you. Also, I've got some brains.'

'And the loveliest body. Put on your bed-jacket. I want to keep my mind on the problem.'

Nigel began to talk, her hand in his, her fingers stroking his. The problem was the identity of the kidnappers' accomplice. They had been tipped off about the trap at the G.P.O. How? Either by telephone from Downcombe or by making some sort of contact in Belcaster. The only suspicious call from the Guest House that morning was Mrs ffrench-Sullivan's. But she had telephoned a wire. You don't do that unless you are not sure whether the recipient will be at home: if the friend, Mrs Hollins, was in the kidnapping plot, she would certainly stay at home awaiting any message that might come from the Guest House.

'Neither the Admiral nor his wife left the Guest House that morning. Leake, Lance Atterson and Cherry went into Belcaster. Unless they're all in the plot together, which I don't believe, they clear one another fairly adequately for most of the time they spent there. Of course, one of them *could* have given a warning sign to the kidnappers, unnoticed by the other two. But our X must have thought it more than likely that the police would shadow any of us who went into Belcaster: I don't believe he'd have risked making any sort of contact there. And remember, he could have nothing more than Wragby's hints to go on: Wragby said he'd make a fight of it: he did not even hint that the information he was going to deposit in the G.P.O. would be bogus. But the kidnappers knew it was bogus without seeing it.'

'So you're left with Elena?'

'Elena rang some friends after breakfast, from the village call-box. Unfortunately we didn't have those calls monitored till a little later. There was nothing to prevent her putting through another, and there's no evidence that she didn't. But the main point is this—Wragby told her exactly what he and the police had planned. She was the only person here, apart from myself, who knew the details of it.'

'I see,' said Clare after a pause. 'I see, but I don't believe. She loves Lucy. That I'm sure of. Nothing could induce her to—why, it's utterly fantastic. And I thought she'd been thoroughly screened by the authorities.'

'So did they. I've been in touch with the department, and they're bringing out their fine-tooth combs to start all over again. But it'll take time. And time's what we haven't got. It may be too late already,' Nigel added bleakly.

'You must assume that Lucy's alive still.'

'Or pack it up. I know. I admire Elena. I like her. But we've no notion what pressures the other side may not be able to put on her . . . Tell me again what happened when you broke the news to her.'

Clare told him.

'Doesn't it strike you that she overplayed the scene? You knocked at her bedroom door and went in. Before you told her anything, she assumed that Lucy had met with some accident. She looked distraught. If she'd genuinely been so worried about the child's absence, wouldn't she have come downstairs, asked if Lucy had returned, gone out to look for her? Her behaviour was that of a woman who knew what had happened, was appalled by it, couldn't face it. She tried to explain her distraction by telling you she blamed herself bitterly for having sent Lucy down to post the letters. That was clever. It was also genuine. I've no doubt her conscience was torturing her about it. She's not a wicked woman.'

Clare's eyes opened at him, dark and lustrous as pansies. 'I see. It's an intelligent deduction all right. But you say she's not wicked. What on earth could compel a decent woman to sacrifice a child she loves for a Cause she hates?'

'That's for you to find out, my dear.'

'*Me?* But, good God——'

'If I'm wrong, I'm wrong. I'll eat dirt. If Elena's innocent, it'll be another turn of the screw for her. I hate the possibility. But Lucy is more important than her stepmother's feelings.'

After a long silence, Clare said, 'What do you want me to do . . . ?'

That afternoon Clare went up to the Wragbys' room with her sketching block and charcoal pencils. Elena had been persuaded by her husband to sit for Clare.

'It's very good of you to let me——'

'I'm honoured. Alfred said it would be—what is the word?— therapeutic,' Elena replied with a sad, bitter little quirk of the mouth. She sat down as Clare directed, on an upright chair by the window, falling fluently into an attitude of repose which belied the tautness of her face, the nervous tic that now and then twitched the skin at the side of her temples. Clare gazed for a minute or two at the proud, ravaged profile, feeling for the bone structure beneath, trying to clear her mind of everything but the forms it presented, before she took up her pencil. With the instinctive respect of one artist for another's work, Elena remained silent during this scrutiny. When the pencil made its first bold sweep on the paper, she asked, 'Do you generally start your portrait heads with sketches like this, my dear?'

'No. I prefer modelling straight off with the clay, but I haven't brought any. Raise your chin, just a fraction: that's it . . . You must have sat for many painters in your own country.'

'Ah, yes. In my young days. I was beautiful then. My husband— my first husband—painted me often.'

'Your face is the kind that will age into greater beauty. Tell me about him.'

'Oh, he was a wild one. But very talented. Very brave. As an artist he chafed under the regime.'

'Socialist realism?'

'Yes. He said such indiscreet things. I was always afraid they would come to the ears of the Party officials. Of course, he was very young—five years younger than me. Well, they killed him in the end. He died in my arms, in a barricaded house. He was angry to die, poor man. You know what he said, dying?—"Just when I was learning to paint. All those pictures—I shall never paint them now." I never thought I should live to envy him his death.'

Oh, God! thought Clare, I can't go on with this. Bloody Judas. Damn you, Nigel. She tore off the sheet, scrumpled it up, threw it on the floor, and started again.

'Do you miss the stage?' she asked presently.

Elena shrugged. 'That is all of the past.'

' "Drive your cart and your plough over the bones of the dead".'

'I do not know this.'

'William Blake. One of the Proverbs of Hell.'

'Proverbs of Hell? I should be familiar with *those*. I think I must be one of the people who have doom in them, like a disease. Carriers, you call them?'

'You mustn't feel like that. You've brought joy and understanding and love to many people too.'

'Thank you, my dear.' A tear rolled down Elena's cheek. Her next words seemed to spurt out of her, uncontrollably, like blood. 'But not to . . . my child. I'd have given it all up, gladly—the bouquets, the applause, you know?—for being a good mother. And now they say I cannot be a mother, ever again.'

'You're thinking of the baby you lost?' asked Clare gently.

Elena's head swung round. Her eyes looked as if a beautiful dream was dying out of them, visibly fading and dying. 'My baby? Oh yes. That was very sad. But it too is of the past. No, I am thinking of the poor little Lucy. Her too I have failed.'

The agony in the woman's face was so naked that Clare had to turn her own eyes away. 'To have to choose,' Elena muttered. 'Did I do wrong? I could not help myself. It's like a cancer eating at me . . . I am sorry. I don't know what I'm saying. You never had a child, Clare?'

'No.'

'You are a creative artist. You make things. I only passed them on, interpreted them. The work of your hands is your children, and *they* can't be taken from you.'

Clare was silent. She felt that she and Elena had been on the brink of some revelation, only to step away from it.

'It is strange,' Elena resumed, 'that the children of our bodies should have such power over us. Your works—the children of your mind and hands—you have suffered as much to make them, done much more to make them, and yet when you have made one, you don't mind what happens to it—is it not so?—you are detached from it as if it were a stranger's child?'

'Well, in a way it is.'

'It cannot be taken from you because it never belonged to you.'

'That's also true, in a sense.'

Elena's eyes stared intensely into Clare's. 'But if you saw a man with a hammer raised to beat one of your works into fragments, what would you do? Beseech him to spare its life?'

'I'd hit him first, with my mallet.'

Elena sighed heavily. There was silence for some minutes while Clare worked on, wretchedly postponing the moment when she must do what Nigel had asked her, more and more conscious that her recalcitrance about doing it had impaired her skill as an artist. Finally, it was Elena herself who took the initiative out of Clare's hands.

'Oh, damn it to hell!' Clare tore the sheet off the block. Before she could throw it away, Elena said, 'May I see it?'

'It's no good. Yes, if you like.'

Elena studied the drawing. 'No,' she said at last, 'it is interesting, clever; but you are not perhaps in form today? Your mind is not on it, perhaps. Why is this?'

Now the crisis had come, Clare found she could not be Machiavellian or equivocal. She must declare herself. 'Elena, I must tell you. I'm here under false pretences a bit. Nigel believes you were a party to Lucy's kidnapping.'

Elena stared at her, then she shook her head incredulously, then she rose and stood over Clare in formidable indignation.

'*No!* This is beyond everything! Have you gone mad?'

'I hope Nigel is wrong. I honestly believe he must be,' said Clare truthfully.

95

'He has sent you to spy on me?' Elena's eyes looked hard as agates.

'It's not a question of spying. I'm being quite open with you. Someone here informed the kidnappers about your husband's plan to outwit them and trap them at the Post Office. Only you and Nigel and the police knew about this plan,' said Clare bleakly.

'Why does not your Mr Strangeways come and make these accusations to my face?' Elena exclaimed.

'He thought you might be able to speak more freely to me than to people in an official position like himself or the Superintendent.'

'Speak more freely? Speak what?'

Clare gazed out of the window at the snow-blossomed trees. 'Well, for instance, did anyone here put pressure on you to tell him your husband's scheme for dealing with kidnappers?'

'Certainly not. If anyone had tried, I would have gone straight to the police myself.' Elena's eyes were distracted. 'But this is madness. Why, why, why should I help the people who took poor little Lucy away? I loved her. Could you not *see* that?'

'Yes, Elena.'

'And even if I didn't, I love Alfred—how could I bring this sorrow on him?'

Clare turned from the window to face the most difficult moment of all. 'I'm sure there's some explanation. But Nigel is worried about—he thinks you must have known Lucy was being kidnapped. When I came up here just after it, before I actually told you, you were overwrought; yet she'd not been missing long, and you hadn't even come downstairs to ask about her. So, you see——'

'Yes, yes, yes. I do not need every "t" to be crossed. This is typical policeman's logic. Don't they understand that a woman, a mother, may have premonitions about a child? Good God, you are a woman, can you not imagine such a state of mind? I *felt* something dreadful had happened: but my reason told me not to be a fool, not to go chasing after Lucy, like some possessive mother, just because she was a little late.'

Elena was superb in her indignation and grief. It was not, Clare felt convinced, an act: no actress in the world could simulate the inner violence of the conflict which was tearing Elena apart. Never again, she swore, will I do Nigel's dirty work for him.

There was a silence in the room, where exhausted emotions stirred like bits of rag flapping on a barbed-wire fence. Clare was about to retreat when sounds of altercation came up from the lawn outside. She moved to the window again, brushing past Elena who sat huddled in the chair . . .

Downstairs, Nigel, hearing the sounds, hurried out and went round the house, to see Lance Atterson thrusting a snowball down Justin Leake's neck. 'Stuff it, you crappy old bastard!' he was yelling. 'You bug me. Why don't you go away some place and drop dead. Can't you get it into your lousy head that Cherry isn't playing?'

'Dead right, I'm not,' said the girl, emerging from behind a bush on the drive's edge. 'Let's pelt the stinker.'

She and Atterson began hurling snowballs at close range at the unfortunate Justin, who at first, seeing Nigel watching him, tried to pretend it was just a romp and flung snowballs back, but soon began to swear at his tormentors. He tried to run past them into the house, but Lance tripped him up and put the boot in. Yelping, Justin Leake wrenched at Lance's foot, dragged him to the ground and jabbed a thumb into his eye. Cherry hurled herself on Leake as he struggled to his feet, tore at his hair and ran her nails down his cheek.

'Why don't you stop them, Mr Strangeways?' called the Admiral's wife through a drawing-room window. 'This is the most disgraceful exhibition I've ever——'

'Don't worry,' Nigel called back, 'they're amateurs, they can't do each other much harm.' He was already running for the house, a certain phrase of Lance's stinging him on like a gadfly. Without knocking, he rushed into the Wragbys' room. The two women stared at him in speechless amazement as he loped round the room, subjecting to a close scrutiny the electric light fixtures fastened to the head of the double bed, the ceiling light, the wainscot plugs for the electric fire.

'What on earth are you doing, Nigel?' said Clare.

Elena's voice was shaky, between anger and stark incredulity. 'I believe the man really is mad.'

'Sorry. Hope you don't mind,' muttered Nigel, tearing open the wardrobe door, pushing Elena's clothes aside and examining the back of it. Then, to Clare's increasing consternation, he crawled on hands and knees under the dressing-table and looked upwards, seized the bed, lifted it on end, stared at its underside, let it down again. Finally he pulled a chest of drawers away from the wall, went down on his knees again, uttered a sound of satisfaction.

'Let this be a lesson to me, Mrs Wragby. I owe you a very humble apology.'

'I think you certainly do, breaking into my room in this extraordinary way. Will you please explain——'

'You've been bugged.'

'Bugged? What *are* you talking about?'

'Look. Hole bored through the wainscot here. See? And a few fragments of sawdust. Untidy operator, should have swept them up. The microphone was out of sight behind the chest of drawers: the wire ran through this hole into—whose is the room next door?'

'Mr Leake's,' said Elena.

'The naughty man. So the voice Mrs ffrench-Sullivan heard in his bedroom that morning was yours.'

'*Mine?* But I've never—what morning?'

'Friday last. Your husband was telling you how he intended to deal with the kidnappers' demand when they got in touch with him. You were upset, protesting. Leake in his room was listening in. He must have tipped off the kidnappers somehow in Belcaster, three hours later. After that, he didn't dare leave the bug in position any longer.'

Elena Wragby's fine eyes were alight with relief and excitement. 'Thank God we know this. You will arrest him now?'

'No. Not yet. We can't afford to.'

'But he must know where Lucy is.'

'I doubt it. And if he does, he's not going to tell us.'

'But the police could extract it from him.'

'They're not allowed to torture prisoners. If Sparkes finds the apparatus in Leake's room, it would help: but he's enough sense to have got rid of it. No, we mustn't say a word yet to anyone about this discovery. If Leake knows we know about the bug, he'll not attempt to contact the kidnappers again. We want him to do just that—he's our only lead to them. From now on, he'll be watched more closely than ever.'

'I've just thought of something, Nigel,' said Clare. 'All telephone calls from the Guest House and Downcombe are being monitored—right?'

'Right.'

'And none of us can leave the village without being followed?'

'Right.'

'But suppose one of those newspapermen is bogus—I'm trying to think how Mr Leake could get a message out to the kidnappers—'

'It's a good idea; but Sparkes has had all their credentials very carefully checked, and confirmed them with their offices. I must ring him now.' At the door Nigel turned. 'Mrs Wragby, I have your promise not to breathe a word about this discovery?'

'But surely I can tell my husband?'

'I'd rather you didn't.'

'Very well.'

'And if you're talking to Justin Leake, behave quite naturally. Don't let him suspect——'

'I understand. You can rely on me.' Elena smiled charmingly. 'I was trained as an actress to wear a mask.'

'What they call "a false face" in Scotland,' put in Clare. 'I believe I could make a better go of your real face now, Elena. Could you bear to sit again?'

Nigel had a telephone conversation with the Superintendent, the result of which was that Sparkes transmitted orders for the plain-clothes man established in the Guest House to search Justin Leake's room. It must be done at dinner tonight, when the detective would be sure he would not be interrupted.

When Nigel entered the drawing-room, he found three of the guests there.

'Finished snowballing?' he asked Cherry, who sat hunched up by the fire thawing her hands. 'How's the victim?'

'Oh, all right, I expect. He and Lance did each other up a bit. They're having a lie-down upstairs.'

'Perfectly disgusting—grown-up people brawling like that—on a Sunday too,' said the Admiral's wife.

'Well, there doesn't seem anything else to do here on Sundays.'

The Admiral looked up from his book of oriental philosophy. 'You don't carry the doctrine of non-violence to extremes, Cherry?'

'Well, I wouldn't actually murder Leake. Not actually.'

'Would you kill a scorpion if you found it on your pillow?' asked Nigel.

'Oof, no! I'd run away.'

'But you don't run away from Mr Leake,' said the Admiral's wife. 'You three seem as thick as thieves.'

'A curious expression,' remarked her husband dreamily. 'I've always understood that members of the criminal classes don't trust one another an inch.'

'Hey, I'm not one of the criminal class!'

'No, no, my dear, of course not. You misunderstand me. I was going to say, if you hold all life sacred, like these fellows'—he gestured at his book, and Cherry interrupted him.

'Sacred? Why should it be? I think life is a bloody drag. I hate it. What's it for, anyway?' Her voice rose. 'You're born, you go through the motions of being alive, then you die. You eat, you shit. What a gas! It's all wasted.'

' "Thy lot esteem I the highest who wast not ever begot. Thine next, being born, who diest and straightway again art not",' quoted Nigel. 'You'd apply that to Lucy?'

'What d'you mean?'

'You'd say she'd be best off if the kidnappers killed her?'

'You know I don't mean that. She's an angel child.'

'That's the point, Cherry,' said the Admiral. 'One may not see any arguments for being alive oneself, but one feels—*knows*, without an instant of doubt—the value of Lucy being alive.'

'Yes. But does *she* feel it? Is she feeling it now, about herself?' Cherry's voice quavered. Mrs ffrench-Sullivan struck in, with the acidity of one who must destroy a mood into which she cannot enter.

'The trouble with you, my girl, is that you don't take enough exercise. Makes you morbid.'

Cherry glanced at her. 'I was always taught not to make personal remarks.'

'Mrs ffrench-Sullivan is right,' said Nigel. 'And you're coming for a walk with me now.'

Three minutes later they were going down the drive. At the gate Nigel turned right, up the hill. 'You'd prefer this way,' he announced.

'Would I? Why? I don't care a damn which way we go.'

'You might meet one of those newspapermen in the village and be recognised.'

Cherry stopped dead, and began scuffling in the snow with a knee-length black boot. Her eyes glanced at him, swivelled away.

'I don't——'

'Yes, you do. Don't be absurd. And for God's sake keep walking or we'll freeze to death. You don't want it to get to your guardian's ear that you've actually run off with Atterson, or where you're staying.'

Cherry plodded on at his side, silent.

'Sir James got wind about your affair with Atterson. He knows the chap's after your money—I presume you come into the capital when you're twenty-one, and at present you get an allowance through your guardian. He could apply sanctions. But what he's really worried about is whether you marry Atterson. Right so far?'

'O.K.,' she sulkily replied.

'He doesn't want a public scandal, so he hires someone to find you and detach you from the egregious Atterson. That's what I'm interested in. Oh, look!—there's a hare. See it?'

Nigel pointed towards a pair of long ears lolloping away over the snow-covered breast of a hillock to their left. They stood a moment, watching. Cherry's fur-gloved hand stole into his. 'I've never seen a hare before, except hanging up at the butcher's. It's lovely. Well, what are you going to do about us?'

'If you really want to tie yourself up with a heel like Atterson, that's your affair. The person I'm interested is Justin Leake. What's he up to?'

'You could ask him.'

'I'm asking you. And if you don't come clean about him, I'll get in touch with your guardian this evening. Leake's been trying to blackmail you, hasn't he?'

Cherry looked up at him, a sly smile on her dead-white face. 'No comment.'

Seizing the puppy-fat shoulders, he shook her till she felt her teeth were starting from their sockets. 'Don't give me that,' he said, releasing her at last. 'Leake is blackmailing you. Go on from there.'

'I rather liked that.' She grinned at him shamelessly. 'Yes. The idea being that I should make him monthly payments until I come into my money, and then give him a slab of that. I was to write a statement about me and Lance, which he'd show to my guardian if I double-crossed him about the payments.'

'But you refused?'

'Bloody true I refused.'

'You didn't care if Leake spilt the beans to your guardian?'

'Why should I? James can't *do* anything to me.'

'Only break it up between you and Lance.'

'Oh, I don't mind that.' Cherry's voice was at its flattest and most childish. 'You see, I've just about had Lance. Mind you, I was dead chuffed when he first took me on. But I don't dig him any more. He's all right in the sack, I admit: but I get narked with that show-off act of his. He's phoney to the gills.'

Nigel looked down at the girl trotting by his side like a fat, woolly dog. 'It must have been a disillusioning moment for our Mr Leake when he found you impervious to his fiendish suggestions.'

Cherry giggled. 'The really funny thing was him being shocked—I swear he was—at my just not caring what he told my guardian. Fancy a blackmailer being shocked! But he's such an old square, he simply isn't with it. You should have seen his face when I said to him. "But all my generation is promiscuous"—it's not strictly true, I was sending him up a bit—"you're thinking in terms of damaged goods, a lady's reputation being ruined for life by a breath of scandal, all that antediluvian stuff. You ought to have stayed in the Ark, my poor Leake," I said, "your mind's as jokey as your clothes." Well, I *ask* you!'

Nigel cut into the girl's merry prattle. 'When did he declare himself? He started off by insinuating things, didn't he?'

'Oh yes. Trying to soften us up, scare us, I suppose. He put on the screws—tried to, I mean—the morning Lucy was snatched.'

'Will you tell me the truth about this? Did he, at that point, try to put pressure on you to do anything except sign a document and start handing over money to him?'

'Oh, no.'

'Hinted at nothing else you might do for him? "We might forget about the money if you helped me to"—that sort of thing?'

'No. Truthfully.'

Nigel frowned in thought. How far could one rely on this

extraordinary girl's evidence? 'We'd better turn back,' he said brusquely.

'All right. Don't you believe me?'

'I'd like not to. It complicates things.'

Cherry took off her glove, slipped a naked hand into Nigel's overcoat pocket, and twined her fingers with his.

'Are you going to seduce *me* now?' he inquired.

'I'd like to.'

'Well, you can't. Tell me, Cherry, if you find Leake such a bore, and you're so hopelessly unblackmailable, why do you still go about with him so much—you and Atterson?'

The girl's fingers stiffened round his, then tried to withdraw: he held them firm.

'That's not my secret,' she said at last, head bowed.

'Shall I ask Atterson, then?'

'Oh, no! . . . Well, I suppose I might as well tell you. When Leake found he couldn't get change out of me, he started putting the bite on Lance. He'd evidence that Lance peddled tea—for reefers, you know. And snow too. I didn't know about the heroin, honestly.'

'Leake's idea was that, if you wouldn't cough up to preserve your own reputation, you would to protect Atterson? Pertinacious fellow, Leake.'

'Yes.'

'But that angle failed too? Because you've gone off Atterson?'

Cherry looked uncomfortable: her fat little body wriggled. 'Well, it's not as simple as that. We've been stringing him along, I know, but—oh, you'd never understand.'

'You've come to realise Atterson is a hollow man, but you still don't want to see him prosecuted for this drug racket?'

Silently Cherry nodded agreement.

'Sort of perverted sense of loyalty? You'd pay up for him because it'd make your conscience easier about giving him the pay-off?'

'I suppose so. I know he's a shit. But he's sort of pathetic, underneath.'

'Oh, God,' muttered Nigel to himself, 'when will they ever learn?'—and startled Cherry by bursting into the plangent song with that refrain as they approached the drive gate.

CHAPTER 9

The Beleaguered Café

DECEMBER 31–JANUARY 1

On Monday morning Professor Alfred Wragby woke up soon after seven. The room was dark: his eyes went automatically in the direction of Lucy's bedroom door, as if she had called out to him from a nightmare. He was wryly conscious that for the last two nights, in spite of everything, he had had almost his full usual quota of sleep. He ran over a mathematical problem in his mind, as a pianist might play scales to limber up his fingers: then he addressed himself to the graver problem.

Why had he not received the instructions which the kidnappers had told him two mornings ago he would be getting? Perhaps they were afraid of telephoning again.

But it seemed more likely that they had dropped their attempt to secure his knowledge; and they would not do that unless they had lost their bargaining counter—unless Lucy was dead.

Wragby's heart began to ache, with the torturing, throbbing persistence of an abscessed tooth. Suppose they had carried out their threats to hurt Lucy, and gone too far and killed her? He remembered giving her a rather pompous lecture once on facing the facts: he'd better instruct himself on that subject now. He was grievously aware how the intellectual demands and discipline of his work had too often taken him away from Lucy, prevented him from giving the child the fatherly attention which was her due. It was the kind of vain regret one feels for one's failures towards a loved person now dead.

It was little consolation to know that his work must be the most important thing in his life: that is no excuse for neglecting the living. Face the facts.

Elena stirred at his side. He must do more to support her through this terrible ordeal: she had suffered far worse things in the past than had ever befallen him, and she had no work to distract her mind now. In sleep, her hand came out and grasped his. He recalled the first time he had seen Elena, and how her likeness to his first wife had made his heart miss a beat. What could he do for her? She had seemed more cheerful yesterday evening, but later she relapsed into the dumb misery which he could find no way of breaking through. Such contact as they had now was a physical one only.

Wragby's feelings of helplessness was increased by their present situation, snowed up in the Guest House with little to do except eat, talk to their fellow guests—a pretty odd lot anyway—and tramp along the deep lanes. They were living in a limbo on the very edge of hell . . .

At seven o'clock this morning, Jim's wife put a packet of sandwiches into the pocket of his great-coat. As she did so, her hand encountered a crumpled ball of paper, which she extracted.

'What's this, Jim? Someone written ee a love-letter?'

'Dunno. Oh, kid up at Smugglers' threw it to me. Out of window. Paper dart, see?'

'It's got writing on it. "Chapter Two, Where am I?".'

'Evan bin writing a story, looks like.'

'Paper dart! Paper dart! Give it I!' yelled their little boy, Ernie.

Jim folded the paper into the lines marked on its surface, and threw it at Ernie, who hurled it back. The dart struck his elder sister, Sue, who was just coming into the kitchen.

'Give over now, do,' said Jim's wife. 'Time your dad was up to the farm. Give him a kiss, you two.'

The dart lay on the floor, where it had fallen, while the two children ate their porridge. Through the window they could see snow falling again in the little village street of Eggarswell as their father tramped off to work in his Army great-coat and red knitted hat . . .

Justin Leake turned in bed, wincing at the bruises Lance Atterson had inflicted, looked at his watch, switched on the transistor set to hear the regional weather news. It was unpromising. No break in the weather. The section of the London road between Belcaster and Longport had been cleared by snow-ploughs, but was still blocked farther west by a ten-foot drift. Whether or not, in view of recent developments, it was worth staying on here, apart from police surveillance, it would be physically impossible to get out of the valley at all yet. Justin Leake, a townsman born and bred, cursed at the uncouthness, the unco-operativeness of nature—and of that bloody little whore, Cherry. Then his mind, like a spider darting over a web, moved to another part of his design . . .

Nigel Strangeways sat up in bed, thinking. No suspicious evidence had been found in Leake's room last night. Well, he'd hardly have left it lying about for the police to find. Nigel meditated for a little on the visit he had paid last night to the shed at the back where the proprietor of the Guest House kept a carpenter's bench and tools. Then his mind turned to Lance Atterson: perhaps he should have paid more attention to this preposterous and unlikeable individual: a person who trafficked in drugs would be easy meat for the other side. Atterson could have given them the tip-off in Belcaster that morning; but how could he have obtained the information? A wire laid from the Wragbys' room into Leake's could have been protracted out of the door, under the passage carpet, into Atterson's room; but surely Leake would have seen it. And whose was the voice the Admiral's wife had heard in Leake's room that morning, if it wasn't Elena's over the bug? And if, as Leake claimed, he'd had the transistor set on, and if the wire led into Atterson's room, Cherry must have known there was a speaker operating there, and concealed the knowledge to protect her lover . . .

At nine o'clock in the nursery room at the back of Smugglers' Cottage, Lucy was trying to eat her breakfast. She could not be sure what day it was, but she thought it was Monday. Uncle Paul had spent some time with her yesterday; talking and playing draughts—a game at which he lost his temper rather easily for a grown-up. The rest of the day she had been alone. There didn't seem much point in going on with the story of Cinders, for the dreariness of her own existence blanketed her imagination from any more fictitious adventures in which Cinders might be involved. Lucy had little hope that the paper dart she had thrown yesterday—two days, two weeks ago?—could reach its destination.

If she was not to be rescued, she must escape. She had given much thought to this yesterday. Being a sensible child, she knew she must find some boots and her anorak, or some sort of overcoat, to wear over her boy's clothes, or she would freeze to death in the snow. The farm was only a hundred yards away; but its occupants might be on the side of her captors—she would not risk going there for help: which meant she must creep out of the cottage and hurry past the farm in the dark. And, if she succeeded, the nearest village might be miles away.

After supper last night, however, Lucy's problem was solved for her. When Uncle Paul took away her tray, she did not hear the key turning in the lock outside. She crept to the door and opened it, stood listening at the head of the stairs. Now would be an opportunity to reconnoitre the ground floor and find the quickest way of slipping out, when she was properly equipped to escape: she might even find her anorak and Wellingtons down there. But, before she could move, Lucy heard the woman Annie's voice saying, 'He's coming himself,' and Uncle Paul's voice in reply, 'How the hell does he think he's going to get here? Fly?'

Lucy slid back into her room. It was the most wonderful moment. Her papa was coming—she had not the least doubt who the 'he' was—to rescue her. Perhaps they'd make him pay a ransom. Lucy hoped he'd be able to afford it. But he was coming at last. She undressed, got into bed, and was soon asleep, a smile on her face.

Now, this morning, she could hardly eat her breakfast for the excitement of it. The snow outside was thick as ever. Papa would fetch her, and she'd have hours, days of tobogganing after all . . .

Half a mile away, Jim's wife left the cottage in Eggarswell to do some shopping, with strict instructions to her children not to go near the oil stove. Presently Ernie picked up the paper dart, and asked his sister to read him what was written on it. Smoothing out the paper, she did this, then happening to turn it over saw that there was writing on the back too.

'Hey, Ern, it says to post this to Professor Wragby, F.R.S.'
'What's F.R.S.?'
'Dunno. Gives his address and all. Over to Downcombe.'
'So what? 'Taint nothing to do with we.'
'Says it's a scientific experiment.'
'Jees! Dropped from space like?'
'Says there'll be a reward. Five pounds.'
'Get on!'

'Shall us then?'

'It's an April Fool, Sue.'

'April Fool yourself. We're in December.'

'Mum says we're not to go out.'

'Five quid, Ern. Think of it. You could buy that tommy-gun we saw in Longport.'

'And billions of bubble-gum packets. Go on then, pinch one of Mum's stamps. I dare you.'

Sue opened a drawer, took an envelope and copied out the address on it. Then she folded the paper dart and sealed it up in the envelope.

'Cor! Mum won't half wallop you, pinching one of her stamps,' said Ernie in awed tones.

'I don't care. I'll just slip round and post it. Shan't be a mo . . .'

The postman did not reach the Guest House till 10.50 this Monday morning. Wragby had conceived it possible that X, knowing the police would intercept communications, might try to contact him by post, using some name on the envelope which he would cotton on to himself, but which would arouse no suspicion in the police. Now, as he passed the hall table, he saw an envelope addressed to one of his former colleagues in the Establishment, now dead. Assuring himself he was alone, Wragby opened the letter. It told him to go this evening to the Bellevue Café on the Belcaster-Longport road, and await instructions. A map reference was given—not that he needed it, for he knew the place, a pull-up for lorry-drivers a few hundred yards from where one of the roads out of the valley climbed steeply to join the main London highway. The letter told him it was his last chance—and Lucy's.

Entering the drawing-room, he threw the crumpled flimsy on the fire, aware of Mrs ffrench-Sullivan's eyes fixed inquisitively upon him. A gust of wind blew the sweet smell of wood-smoke into the room. Outside, it was snowing, not heavily but steadily, the flakes dancing and dithering against the screen of trees beyond the lawn.

'No news, I suppose?' asked the Admiral's wife in a sick-room voice.

'Afraid not,' he answered curtly. The woman meant to be

sympathetic, no doubt, but he could not stand being treated as an invalid.

'You mustn't lose hope,' she persisted.

'I'll endeavour not to, ma'am.'

'How is Mrs Wragby today?'

'She had a bad attack of migraine in the night. I'm keeping her in bed.'

'I have some Veganin, if——'

'No. I shall go into Belcaster and get a special prescription she has, in case the migraine recurs.'

Alfred Wragby left the room, Mrs ffrench-Sullivan gazing after him in an affronted way. 'He may be a great scientist, and I'm sure we're all very sorry for him; but the man's a boor,' she remarked to the company at large.

Going into the little writing-room, Wragby set down in his clear, decisive hand certain facts which he desired, if things went wrong, to be known, addressed the envelope to the Chief of his Establishment, and enclosed it in an envelope to his solicitors with a covering note that the document should be forwarded in the event of his death or disappearance.

He sat on a little longer. Now that there was a prospect of action before him, his mind was working again with its usual speed and clarity: he felt almost exhilarated.

The Bellevue Café was barely two miles from Downcombe. He would do best to go there on foot, for he must throw off the police and there was always a danger that his car would be recognised. The Admiral's wife would no doubt tell others of his expressed intention to go into Belcaster and get the special drug for his wife. It would gain time, when he was missed, if the police searched in that direction first. But Wragby did not know to what extent he himself was under surveillance. Would he be allowed to leave Downcombe, by car or on foot, unaccompanied?

'I'm fed up sitting about here,' he said when he'd found Nigel. 'Any reason why I shouldn't drive into Belcaster? I want to get a prescription for Elena.'

'Telephone it to Sparkes. He'll bring it out when he comes this afternoon. Sorry.'

So that was that. Wragby didn't argue the toss. The authorities couldn't afford to lose him too: here he was protected, but on the road to Belcaster anything might happen to a solitary driver.

Wragby became aware of his companion's pale blue eyes gazing fixedly at him.

'Funny you've not heard from them. I'd have thought, if they've given up telephoning, they'd write to you.'

'Perhaps they're going to call on me in person.'

'You've had no letter from them?'

'No,' the Professor dourly replied. 'And if I had, the police would have read it first.'

He went to the bedroom. Not made up, with her white hair and ravaged face, Elena looked like an old woman.

'No news?' she asked.

'Nothing.'

She walked listlessly into Lucy's room, took up the doll from the dressing-table, set it down again. Wragby went in, put his arms round her.

'What is it?' he said. 'What is it, love? There's something come between us.'

'Are you surprised?' she said harshly, disengaging herself.

'Now, love, you aren't still blaming yourself for Lucy?'

'*You* do, Alfred—in your heart of hearts.'

'That's simply not true. You're overwrought still. You——'

'I'm a hideous, vile creature, and I hate myself,' she burst out. 'Lucy, your work, your first wife—they mean far more to you than I do. I'm jealous of them.'

'That's wild talk, my darling. Haven't I shown you how much I——'

'I'm sorry.' She smiled palely. 'We mustn't shout at each other in Lucy's room. D'you remember how she hated it when we quarrelled?'

'Don't talk as if she's dead.'

'But you believe it. Don't you, my poor Alfred?'

'I shall soon know—one way or the other,' he found himself grimly saying.

Elena stood away, her tragic eyes searching his face. 'I see,' she said at last. 'Have they? . . . You will be careful?' She came into his arms now, her long fingers stroking his temples.

'Would you despise me, Elena, if I gave them what they wanted?'

'I would never despise you, my dear.' She gazed at him enigmatically. 'We must all do what we must—for what we love most . . .'

Professor Wragby was not missed till dinner-time. He had stolen out after dusk, two hours before, not using the drive but through a back door and the paddock behind the house. The snow soon filled in his footprints. He had no weapons, except for a heavy spanner in his overcoat pocket—and the lethal capsule tucked away where he had used to keep it during the most dangerous of his Special Operations during the war. What awaited him at the Bellevue Café, he had no idea: he would have to play it by ear, as his younger colleagues at the Establishment put it. Steadily uphill he plodded, snow falling fitfully now, the snowy lane unwinding ahead of him in the darkness like a bandage. For the first time since Lucy had been taken, he felt in command of things: it all depended upon him now, and he had made his decision—there were no complications left.

In less than an hour he had reached the crest of the hill, where the lane met the main road. A strong wind was blowing here, driving a thick mist of snow across the road, through which he presently discovered lights. A number of long-distance lorries were drawn up in the bay outside the café, and several private cars, their number plates caked with snow. A blast of heat and juke-box music came out at him as he opened the door.

'Another orphan of the storm,' someone called out cheerfully. The tables were occupied by groups of lorry-drivers. In a corner two children sucked Coca-Cola through straws while their harassed-looking parents talked to each other in undertones. Wragby went over to the counter and ordered coffee and sandwiches. Through the din of the juke-box the proprietor shouted, 'Nearly run out of grub, sir. Road's blocked again too—half a mile to the west. You from London?'

Wragby nodded, started looking around him as he sipped his coffee. The café was thick with smoke. He could feel the atmosphere, compounded of resignation, exhilaration and unwonted matiness, with which the British—the working-class in particular—greet any communal crisis. At a table by the door he noticed three toughs sitting, unshaven and glum, a sinister little enclave amongst the smoke and noise. One of them now rose to put a coin in the juke-box; a second went unobtrusively outside, to return after a minute and nod at a large, bear-like man in cloth cap and long overcoat who sat alone at a table not far from the counter. This man, catching Wragby's eye, beckoned to him. Wragby went over to the table, sat down.

'Good evening, Professor—' It was the voice Wragby had heard over the telephone—'I was expecting you. Come by car?'

'On foot.'

'Splendid! Wise fellow. I take it you've informed nobody of this little expedition?'

'Nobody. What's your name?'

'You can call me Petrov. I should make it quite clear to you at the start, Professor, that if you have attempted to lay another trap for us, we shall shoot you, then shoot our way out and be on our way to liquidate your pretty little daughter.'

'You wouldn't get far. The road west is blocked again.'

'So? But that will be temporary. The snow-ploughs—' Petrov broke off, his eyes hooding over. 'That is of no interest to me. So long as the London road is open—' whatever else he said was obliterated by a fortissimo blast from the juke-box. Wragby inwardly exulted: Petrov's slip indicated that Lucy, as Nigel had guessed, was not in London but somewhere to the west, perhaps not far away.

'Of course,' he said, 'snowing like it is, the London road too will be blocked again before long. Nature seems to be fighting against you, Petrov. It's an ironic situation, when you come to think of it—kidnappers and police all sitting around, immobilised. A stalemate.'

'You are a strange man, Professor, to be discussing such literary ideas at a time like this.'

Wragby shrugged. He scrutinised the man at his side. Immensely powerful body, sloping shoulders carrying a roundish head, the eyes small, the wrists thick and hairy. A formidable opponent, leaving aside the thugs he had brought with him. Wragby itched to drive his fingers into the fat neck, kick this ape into a jelly. But that would have to wait. He said, 'Why don't you take your overcoat off? It's hot as hell in here.'

'My dear sir,' the rumbling voice replied, 'I have a revolver in the pocket, that's why.'

The family party brushed past their table, one of the children whining. 'Have to go back towards London—see if we can get a bed in the next town,' the paterfamilias explained to all and sundry.

'Good luck, mate!' a lorry-driver called. 'We'll come and dig you out—just send us a message by carrier pigeon.'

'What the hell's he doing, taking kids around in weather like this?'

'Come to sunny Torquay!'

A cold draught shuddered the smoke as the door opened and shut.

'Well, to business,' said Petrov. 'Here's paper and pencil. Write it down, Professor.'

Wragby made no move. Petrov's eyes narrowed.

'What's this? Changed your mind? Come on, you've wasted enough of our time. I don't want to be here all night. Are you going to give me the information or not?'

'Yes,' said Wragby, 'but not yet.'

'You're giving it to me now, or your dear little daughter will die a most unpleasant death.'

Wragby's head was in his hands, his voice broken. 'You've killed her already. I know it.'

My baby's just the bestest baby rock, rock, rock, olly, olly, hoo, hi! bawled the voice from the juke-box.

'That is not true.'

Wragby's head came up and he stared bleakly into Petrov's eyes. 'Prove it.'

'Prove it? But, my dear sir——'

'It's quite simple. Take me to where you are keeping her, let the child go free, and I will then give you the information.'

'That is out of the question. It is not for you to make conditions—not now, my friend.'

'I have made my conditions. You can accept them or reject them.'

'And if I reject?'

'You fail to get what you're after—and your people don't forgive failures.'

'So now *you* are threatening *me*?' Petrov gave a jovial laugh. 'So, I get no information. And I hand little Lucy over to my friends there.' He jerked his head towards the group by the door. 'They are very rough men. Uncultured. The older one, with the white face—he was in prison for sawing the nipples off his girl-friend, with a fret-saw. Another time, for violating a child of five. The other two will do anything for money, you know, but *he* will do it for—er—love. You get me?'

'Oh, pack up this bogy-man line of talk. If Lucy were alive, it might serve a purpose, but——'

'But I tell you, she is alive. You heard her voice on the telephone.'

'That was two days ago. And anyway, it was off a tape-recorder.'

Petrov pursed his mouth, frowning. Wragby, pursuing an advantage, went on. 'That was just a trick to make us think you were holding her in London. Not a very subtle one, either. The inference is that she's somewhere not far from here, alive or dead. As the police have searched every house in a radius of twenty-five miles or so, the presumption is that she's dead, and buried. It's up to you to prove the reverse.' The café proprietor came to their table and gave it a perfunctory swabbing with a cloth.

'Two more cups of coffee, please.'

'Right you are, sir. Funny, you two gentlemen meeting in an out-of-the-way place like this. Coincidence, you might say.'

'You might.'

'Two friends from London meeting by chance at the back of beyond,' the proprietor amplified with relish. 'Well, it's a small world.'

The man padded off, to return with two slopping cups, then retire again.

'How did *you* get here, by the way?' Wragby asked.

'My friends drove the truck. I followed them in my automobile.'

There was a silence between the two. Presently the café door opened again to let in a flurry of snow and the family party: the whining child was now bawling, 'I want to go home!'

'Don't we all?' cried a joker at a nearby table. 'Roll on, summer!'

The paterfamilias announced that a drift had formed across the road to London, only a hundred yards from the café, and his car had been unable to get through it.

Wragby leant towards his companion. 'What did I tell you? Stalemate. You can't get out, the police can't get in. May last for

114

days. I'm told that death by starvation is extremely disagreeable. You realise that this place will shortly run out of food?'

'God, what a filthy country!' growled Petrov. 'Haven't they got a telephone?'

'You can't send food over a telephone. Which reminds me.' Wragby got up and moved smartly through a door at the side of the counter. Petrov was after him, light on his feet as a great tomcat. In the passage beyond, he caught him up. 'If you touch that telephone, I'll shoot you.'

'I'm looking for the lavatory, not the telephone. Don't be so excitable.' The massive Petrov glared at him suspiciously. 'And if you suppose I'm going to climb through the window and run away, you're even less intelligent than I'd thought you,' Wragby went on. 'I'm relying on you to take me to Lucy.'

A fantastic euphoria had invaded Alfred Wragby. The love of action, the boyish streak which years of arduous intellectual labour had not eradicated, the knowledge that he had got his vile and formidable opponent guessing—all combined to create a mood of buoyancy.

'You'll agree to my conditions?' he asked, when they were seated at the little table again.

Petrov's eyes were clear as ice. 'I will take you to your daughter, when we get out of this rotten dump.'

'And release her?'

'When you have given me the information.'

'Before I give it.'

'Now, now, Professor, that would never do. I let her go, and you then refuse your side of the bargain.'

'Don't be ridiculous. How could I refuse, once those filthy-looking friends of yours got to work on me?'

'My dear sir, if we'd thought that physical persuasion would work with you, we'd have kidnapped you, not your daughter.'

'Where is she?'

Petrov laughed genially. 'I am not a child to be duped. I shall take you to her.' He paused. 'You may not be able to recognise her at first . . .'

Gradually the conversation in the café petered out. The juke-box was silent at last. On benches, chairs or floor men tried to sleep. One electric bulb was left burning over the counter, revealing the nude pin-ups on the partition behind it. Snoring, grunting, restless shifting: the air growing fouler. Wragby, awake on his hard chair, felt the dark hours pass, slow as a glacier's movement. Petrov's last sentence kept recurring to his mind, and every time it was as if the blood ran out of him, leaving him faint and cold. If Lucy had been disfigured, he was responsible for it through his first refusal to co-operate with the kidnappers: he tortured himself, imagining tortures the child had suffered. Petrov was asleep beside him. Wragby could draw the revolver from the big man's pocket and shoot him—shoot his way past the thugs at the door; but it would be self-indulgence, for Petrov was the only road that could lead him to Lucy . . .

As light began to strengthen through the uncurtained windows, there was a stir in the café. Presently a few drivers went out to warm up their engines. The white-faced psychopath put a coin in the juke-box, baring his teeth and jerking his limbs at the music that issued. The proprietor was boiling kettles for those who wished to wash. There was a smell of bodies and stale coffee. Petrov's other two thugs began to demand food from the proprietor, refusing to believe he had not got some hoarded away: it could have turned ugly, but Petrov moved to the proprietor's side and, without any sign of recognising the men, made them retreat.

After a quarter of an hour the drivers stamped in again, blowing on their hands. The road was still blocked to the east, but a snow-plough was at work on the drift half a mile to the west. At this news, one of Petrov's men went out to run the engine of his truck: the rest of those in the café, who had looked like a bunch of refugees, dirty and dispirited, took on an air of activity.

'We'll be able to get off soon,' said Wragby. 'Hadn't you better start your engine running?'

'Patience, my dear sir.' Petrov gave him a comradely slap on the back.

Wragby could think of nothing but seeing Lucy again, comforting her.

And then, everything went wrong. It must have been half an hour later, though to Wragby it felt like half a lifetime, when voices were heard outside, the door was flung open, and a file of soldiers trooped in, some with spades, some carrying cartons of food. At their heels entered a policeman.

Wragby, in the bustle of welcome, dived under the flap of the counter and locked himself in the lavatory. He knew that the police would have been notified of his disappearance, and every police-man have a description of him. If he was found now, he would lose the chance of getting to Lucy: there would be long-drawn-out explanations, in the course of which Petrov would either be arrested or escape, and if he were arrested he would certainly not talk.

Petrov, for his part, believed that a trap had been sprung on him. Soldiers, police, and the Professor darting away, his job done, before Petrov could silence him. He jerked his head towards the three thugs by the door, who looked at a loss, standing in a tight little group, like sheep with a sheepdog prowling round them. They did not know what Petrov had hired them to do: but it was unlikely to be a legal activity, and their instinct was to withdraw from the vicinity of any copper. They pushed sharply out of the door, colliding with the corporal in charge of the military detach-ment, who began cursing at them.

This was enough for the white-faced thug. Whipping out a razor, he slashed the corporal from temple to jaw. Several of his men, hearing the altercation, rushed out. They saw their corporal writhing on the ground, his blood turning the snow scarlet, and three men running away. The soldiers dashed after them, dragged them away from the truck they were climbing into, and finding themselves attacked with a razor, a cosh and a bicycle chain, fought back with spades, fists and boots. Other soldiers streamed out to help them. The policeman carried the wounded corporal into the café and gave him first-aid. Under cover of all this, Petrov had slipped into the back part of the café, searching for Wragby.

Since the Professor could not be carried off, he must be silenced here and now. It would be unwise to use a revolver—the man must be strangled, as silently as possible. Petrov, moving lightly, peered into the sleazy kitchen and scullery: they were empty. He looked out from the back door: no footsteps led away from it. Petrov turned back, smiling, and rattled the knob of the lavatory door. 'It's me, Petrov, we can get away now. Hurry.'

Wragby emerged, to find his throat gripped by two tremendous-ly powerful hands.

Violence, as so often, had a farcical air about it. Two big men heaving, bumping and straining in a narrow passage, hopelessly at cross-purposes, the one convinced that his enemy had led him into a trap from which he could escape only by murder, the other knowing that everything depended upon not killing his enemy and thus keeping the road to Lucy open.

Wragby had been taken utterly by surprise and he had under-estimated his opponent's strength. If he could get those fingers off his throat, he'd have breath, maybe, to explain. He clasped his hands above his head and smashed them down hard on the hairy wrists. It had no effect. He brought up his knee, but Petrov had turned a little sideways to him. With a last convulsive effort, he threw himself backwards, sending Petrov in a somersault over his head. The fingers were loosened now and Wragby could whoop for breath. But before he could speak, Petrov was at him again in the narrow passage, moving smooth and irresistible like a piston in its cylinder.

And now Wragby forgot his intention, forgot the spanner in his pocket, even forgot Lucy, flooded by pure hatred for this man. He uppercut him, jolting the round head back: he slammed a right into Petrov's fat belly, low down—it was like hitting the bag of an octopus. The man reeled away, knocking open the unlatched back door behind him.

Now they were in the open, no longer constricted by the passage walls, Wragby knew himself at less of a disadvantage. But, with that, his brain grew cooler and the blood lust ceased to possess him completely. It caused an instant's hesitation, which was fatal. He opened his mouth to explain; but Petrov was up from the snowy yard, and the fingers clamped on Wragby's throat again.

When the body was limp at last, Petrov dragged it into the lavatory, and was about to assure himself that his victim was dead when he heard distant footsteps approaching from the bar. He slipped out of the lavatory, walked through the back door, and in full view of a soldier—to whom he genially waved—got into his car and drove off.

As he carefully negotiated the icy one-track way which the snow-plough had cut, Petrov worked out the report he should give to his superiors. They had approved, indeed enforced upon him, the plan of contacting the Professor personally. He had carried it out with skill and daring. It was no fault of his that the Professor should have been so stubbornly foolish as to have a second trap laid on. No fault, but of course a failure; and his superiors did not tolerate failure.

And only at this point did Petrov, who had himself been sufficiently battered during the struggle, find his brain working properly again. Was it a trap, after all? If it had been, surely the soldiers would not have allowed anyone just to walk out of the café and drive away? The soldiers, he now realised, had been armed with nothing more militant than shovels and cartons of food.

Petrov would certainly have to edit his report drastically. He would still put it that he had escaped from a trap, and in the course of his escape found it necessary to remove the Professor from his path: too bad that the stubborn fellow should later have died of it. The hired gangsters would not be in a position to contradict his version of the events, and in any case they did not know his identity.

To discover the late Professor's secret, they would now have to start again. A pity, but in this kind of work setbacks were bound to occur. If Petrov was to remain useful to his superiors, though, he must cover his traces—a process which would clearly demand, among other expedients, the liquidation of the child, Lucy . . .

At this moment, the proprietor of the Bellevue Café, entering the lavatory, found the body of one of the London gentlemen there. He called for help. The policeman had already left, but two soldiers assisted in carrying out the body. Professor Alfred Wragby—they got his name from his driving licence—was unconscious but not, it turned out, dead. If he had underestimated Petrov's strength, Petrov had underestimated Wragby's grip on life. They did what they could for him, while the proprietor telephoned for an ambulance. Half an hour later, having a slow brain, he realised that the unconscious man had been in the news lately, and rang the Belcaster police.

CHAPTER 10

Little Boy Found

DECEMBER 31

While her father was plodding up the lane towards the Bellevue Café, Lucy waited for the moment to escape. This afternoon her lovely hope had been smashed to pieces. When Annie Stott came in with the tea-tray, Lucy, bubbling with excitement, had said: 'Will he come today?'

'Will who come?'

'My papa, of course.'

'*He*'s not coming.'

Lucy's mouth began to quiver. 'But I heard you say "He's coming himself".'

'Oh. That's a friend of ours.' The woman gazed at her bleakly. '*How* did you hear this?'

'I—well, I was at the top of the stairs, and——'

'You're very naughty. You're not allowed to leave this room, you know that perfectly well. If you do it again, you'll be beaten.'

It was a double blow. Her father was not coming, and now they'd make sure to keep the door locked. For a while Lucy cried, heart-broken. Then exhausted with crying, she began to think of escape again.

The heroines of adventure stories often managed to soften the heart of one of their captors. No use trying loopy Annie—she was as hard as the batch of rock-cakes Lucy had cooked once, and nearly broken a tooth on. Uncle Paul? He was different, much nicer to her; but instinct told the child she could not trust him. There was something slimy about him, she thought—you couldn't get a grip on him: one moment he'd be smiling and joking, and the next he'd withdraw himself, his eyes went cold and uninterested, and he reminded Lucy of the princess with a splinter of ice in her heart.

In adventure stories the prisoner filed through the bars on his wimdow, or dug a tunnel through the floor. Such activities were not in her power. Her only way out was the door, and the door was

120

locked. Why didn't they teach you something useful at school, like how to pick a lock? She grinned to herself, thinking of the consternation there'd be if her captors found the room empty when they'd carefully locked her in it. Stinking Annie would get in a fearful bate. But——

But, why not? Another time-honoured device of escape fiction shot into her head. Why on earth didn't you try it before, you steaming nit? she reproached herself; and remembering the snow outside, deep and crisp and even, started undressing, put on her pyjamas, then the underclothes, then the boy's shorts and jersey on top of them. There'd be no time to find a pair of Wellingtons— she'd have to make do with the walking shoes they'd given her, though they were at least a size too big. But she'd better string them round her neck, and go down the stairs in stockinged feet. *If* the idea worked at all. She waited, sweltering.

When Paul came up half an hour later with cocoa and biscuits, he found the room in darkness. He had been drinking a lot recently, to dispel the shadows that were closing in on him, and his reactions had slowed. He put the tray down on the bed, felt a small body beneath the clothes (the child must have gone to sleep), and fumbled for the light switch: in the course of which proceedings Lucy slipped out from behind the door where she'd hidden, quietly locked it, and made for the satirs.

Before she could reach the front door, there was a frantic yelling and banging from above. Lucy slipped into the nearest refuge—a lavatory—as Annie rushed out of the sitting-room. Hearing Annie's footsteps pounding upstairs, Lucy slid out into the hall and through the front door, turned right and raced away as fast as she could through the snow. No time to put on the shoes yet. She had only got thirty yards away when she heard the sounds of pursuit.

Silly fool, she said to herself, why didn't you take the bedroom-door key away when you locked it? Then you'd only have had one of them after you.

The track glimmered ahead of her, the way to freedom. Panting and whimpering, Lucy floundered on. It was a game no longer, and there seemed nowhere to hide; she had left the protective bulk of the garage behind her. The only hope now was the farm. If they were enemies there too, she'd be finished. A stockinged foot slipped on an ice-hard rut made by a tractor, and Lucy fell to the side of the track. As she lay there winded, a figure hurried past her in the darkness. It was Annie, and she was calling in a low, urgent voice, 'Evan! Where are you? Come here at once!'

When Annie had disappeared, the child got to her feet, and gave a gasp of pain: she had turned her ankle. Behind her, she heard Paul searching around the garage and out-buildings of the cottage. Setting her teeth, Lucy limped towards the light of a farmhouse window, got to the door. No bell. She began hammering on the knocker. Mr Thwaite opened the door.

'Why, Evan, what're you doing out here, son?'

Sobbing, Lucy ducked under his arm into the house, found herself in a kitchen, dazzling bright after the darkness outside.

'I'm not Evan! Help me! I——'

'There, there, my little chap,' crooned the farmer's wife. 'Sit ee down a while. You're not well.'

'They've kidnapped me! Oh, you must believe——'

At that moment there came a thunderous knocking. Annie Stott, who had heard the child banging the knocker, had turned back. Lucy was paralysed, like a rabbit before a stoat: her voice wouldn't work any more. She threw herself into Mrs Thwaite's arms, hiding her head.

'Oh there he is,' said Annie's voice. 'Evan, you're really very naughty. Never mind, we'll forget it.' She lowered her voice. 'The child's delirious again, Mrs Thwaite.'

'He said something about being kidnapped. My gracious, he is hot, though, isn't he?'

It was not surprising, with the weight of clothes Lucy wore, and the running away.

'I must take him back to bed at once. I'm so sorry he's given you this trouble.'

'And the poor lamb's feet, soaking wet,' exclaimed Mrs Thwaite.

'Ah, here you are, Paul. Will you carry Evan back?'

Lucy began to kick and faintly scream; but Paul whisked her out while Annie explained that the child in high fever has this delusion of being kidnapped as a result of hearing the broadcast news about Professor Wragby's daughter. Mr and Mrs Thwaite, though disturbed by the occurrence, had no suspicion—the substituting of one child for another had completely deceived them.

Back in the nursery-bedroom prison, Lucy wept her heart out. She hardly heard Annie say, 'I've lost patience with you, you wretched child. You're very wicked. I shall give you the slipper,' or Paul say, wresting the slipper from Annie's hand, 'You'll do nothing of the sort. The child's had enough. Anyway, I disapprove of corporal punishment . . .'

At dusk, while Lucy was planning her escape, a snow-plough, its yellow Cyclops-eye winking, thrust its way over the crest of a hill above Longport. The driver congratulated himself on having only half a mile more to cover, then he could call it a day and stop off at the Kings Arms before going home to supper.

It was bitterly cold in the exposed cabin of the snow-plough. He envied his mates following him in the sheltered truck, with nothing to do but tumble out from time to time and keep warm by digging bays where cars could pass one another in the channel he had cut.

A continuous bow-wave of snow pushed whiskering and cascading out from the diagonal share. Lights sparkled up from Longport in the valley below. Suddenly there came a frenzied hooting from the truck. The snow-plough driver stopped, jumped out and ran back. The men in the truck had got out too. They were standing around a dark object embedded in the wall of snow which the plough had excavated from the drift and flung to one side of the road. . . .

Superintendent Sparkes had turned up at the Guest House about tea-time, delivered the prescription to Mrs Wragby and was now closeted with Nigel. His men had searched the house and grounds for the bug and speaker, but fruitlessly: if Justin Leake had buried them somewhere, the signs of interment were covered over by the fresh falls of snow. So, for all the county police could discover, were the traces of Lucy. It was inconceivable that a child should have been kept alive all these days, with no hint of it reaching the neighbours and every house searched now by the police.

'I'm afraid it looks as if we have to write her off,' said Sparkes, a slow flush of anger coming to his cheeks. 'I tell you, Mr Strangeways, I've had some failures in the Force but I've never felt so badly as I do about this one. It's a bastard.'

'Yes. I'm afraid you may be right. And that's why the other side have not tried to get in touch with Wragby again.'

'I wonder. Kidnappers have often kept the heat on after—look at the Lindbergh case——'

'If only we knew where to turn the heat on, ourselves,' said Nigel. 'That deplorable type, Leake, for instance——'

'I had another go at him. He's not giving an inch. He knows we know he's a blackmailer. We're searching his office and house in London—not got enough on him yet to make a charge, in spite of Miss Cherry's disclosures—can't see her evidence standing up in court. Anyway, proving blackmail is one thing, proving conspiracy with foreign agents is another.'

'Yes, and a successful blackmailer in his own right wouldn't be awfully likely to get mixed up with them.'

'Unless they'd rumbled him and threatened exposure.'

'That's true. Well, where do we go from here?'

'I'd like to clear up some loose ends. Your notion about Lance Atterson. And the Admiral's wife.'

After a brief consultation, Cherry and Lance were summoned together. Sparkes had them sitting on hard chairs, well separated, on the other side of the table.

'Now then, Atterson,' he said, 'I've wasted enough time on you already. You're in an awkward situation. It's known that you peddle drugs——'

'That's a lie! Who told you?'

'Information received.'

'You'll get me stroppy if you start bullying, you bloody flatfoot.'

'No lip from you, my bearded wonder, or I'll take you to pieces.'

'Big deal!' jeered Lance, but he went pale.

'I'm not interested at the moment in your filthy drug-racket—that'll come later. You enjoy ruining adolescents. Right. Do you enjoy kidnapping children too? How low can you get?'

'I simply don't know what you're talking about,' stammered Lance.

'It's escaped your notice that a child has been kidnapped? Are you a moron, or don't you care?'

'It's nothing to do with me,' Lance sullenly replied.

'Suppose I tell you that you listened in to a conversation between Professor Wragby and his wife on the morning of Friday last, and conveyed the gist of their conversation to the kidnappers?'

'Well, suppose you *do* tell me?'

Sparkes's huge fist crashed on the table. 'You admit it?'

Lance wet his lips. 'No.'

'You fixed up a bug in the Wragbys' room and a wire leading into yours.'

'Balls to that.'

'You were listening in just before 9 a.m.'

'I wasn't. I don't dig this. You were with me, Cherry. Did you see me with my ear glued to some gadget——?'

'No. But I couldn't have anyway. I wasn't in our room,' said Cherry with her flattest intonation. 'I was in Justin's.'

'You bloody little bitch!'

'Shut UP!' roared the Superintendent. 'Now, Miss Cherry. I'm talking about the period between, say, eight forty-five and nine last Friday morning. You were not in the bedroom then?'

'No, I started going down to breakfast, about ten to nine.'

' "Started"?'

'Yes. On the way I met Justin Leake and he asked me to come into his room. He wanted to talk about—well, you know what.'

'Another attempt at blackmailing you and Mr Atterson?'

'Yes. He was in a hurry for me to sign something.'

'And how long were you there?'

'Ten minutes maybe.'

'So you were out of your own bedroom at the operative time. Atterson could have been listening in, unknown to you,' said Sparkes triumphantly.

The girl took her time about it. 'I don't think so. I don't know about these concealed microphone things, but I suppose you'd need quite a bit of equipment. Well, we only brought one suitcase, and I unpacked it, and I didn't see any bugs or wires or stuff.'

So that was that. Sparkes couldn't shake her, and the staff confirmed later that she and Lance had arrived with only one piece of luggage and a guitar. Of course, Lance could have fixed up the equipment—from an agent in Belcaster maybe—after they had arrived. But it was pretty well a blind alley, since Cherry swore that Lance had made no attempt to hustle her out of the bedroom at

8.45—and besides, how could he know that the Wragbys would be discussing plans just then.

'You're very quiet,' said Sparkes when the pair had been dismissed.

'I'm feeling sick. At my own thoughts. Comes of looking through a hole and seeing hell beneath.' Nigel stopped abruptly, then muttered to himself. 'Why? Why? Why?'

Sparkes glanced at him sharply. 'A hole?'

'A small hole.'

'Ah . . . Well, we'd best tidy up the remains.'

'I suggest interviewing the Admiral and his wife together. Do you mind if I do the talking?'

'It's all yours. You'll be more tactful, I'm sure,' said Sparkes, a humorous gleam in his eye.

Tact, however, was not needed, though patience was. Mrs ffrench-Sullivan appeared at her most voluble. She made it clear, if not quite in those words, how gratifying she and the Admiral found it to have a gentleman in charge of the investigation (here Sparkes winked covertly at Nigel). She proceeded to express at some length her indignation at the state of the country, when Red agents were allowed to run riot. It was all the result of the late Labour Government and that dreadful Canon Collins. Nigel was unable to stem the flow. Finally, the Admiral interposed gently, 'I think they want to ask us some questions, Muriel dear.' Nigel leapt into the momentary pause.

'Yes. I would like you to tell us a little more about Mr Justin Leake.'

'Odious man.'

'About his attempt to blackmail you.'

'I sent him away with a flea in his ear, believe me.'

'May I have some more details? If you'd prefer to talk quite in private——' Nigel glanced at the Admiral.

'Oh no. My husband knows all about it now.' A flush came into her over-powdered cheeks, turning them an unpleasant shade of mauve. But her eyes were bright—almost girlish for a moment.

'Yes,' said the Admiral. 'The shop-lifting business. All my fault, really. Away in the Med. Mind rather occupied—convoys, y'know—didn't think about rising prices at home, should have increased my wife's allowance.'

'Well,' said Nigel after an appreciative pause, 'that's all over and done with. Justin Leake threatened to tell your husband about it?'

'Yes. He really became quite offensive, and——'

'Unless?' Nigel broke in firmly.

' "Unless"?'

'What did he demand in return for keeping silent?'

'Oh, I see. Well, it was perfectly absurd, you'd hardly credit it. He wanted me to persuade my husband to dig up *scandal* for him. As if Tom would lend himself to that sort of thing!'

The Admiral coughed, gazing poker-faced at Nigel, a mischievous glint in his eye. 'Hrrmph. Sort of gossip column. Y'know? Muck-raking amongst the landed gentry and so forth.'

'Extraordinary,' remarked Nigel, as if he hadn't heard it all before. 'Impudent fellow, asking you to be a blackmail scout. You were wise, ma'am, to inform your husband.'

'And courageous,' said the latter, smiling at his wife. 'Took a bit of doing, y'know.'

'There's just one more thing, Mrs ffrench-Sullivan. Did Leake put pressure on you to do anything else—not openly perhaps, but hinting?'

'I don't quite——'

'Did he ever insinuate that he'd like any information you could pick up about the Wragbys—or any of the other guests?'

'Oh, no, there was nothing like that, I assure you.'

'We've been a little worried about that telegram you sent to your friends in Belcaster.'

'It *was* about the mink,' put in the Admiral.

'Why did you send a telegram, instead of phoning her direct?'

Mrs ffrench-Sullivan bridled a little. 'That's surely my affair, Mr Strangeways, But I don't mind telling *you*. Susie Hollins was away for two days—I didn't know the address—and I didn't want to discuss the matter over the telephone with her assistant, the girl's a dreadful gossip.'

Sparkes's lips silently formed the words, 'never thought of that one, did you?' . . .

The interview with Justin Leake that followed was little more satisfactory than Sparkes's previous attempts to break him down. The Superintendent could neither intimidate nor wheedle him into any further admissions, except that he had talked a little with

Cherry in his room before breakfast on Friday.

'You were making another effort to tighten the screws?'

'Was I?'

'Don't box clever with me!' roared the Superintendent, smashing his fist down on the table. 'You were hired by her guardian to find her and prevent her marrying Atterson. You found her, then you started to worm out what pickings there'd be for yourself. You tried to get her to sign a document—pay you for not giving her away to your employer, with a promise of more money when she came of age.'

'That's your interpretation,' replied Leake equably. 'The actual fact is that I was trying to persuade her to leave Atterson. I told her that, if she did so, I would keep quiet about this escapade.'

'Without any money changing hands? Do you take me for an imbecile, Leake?'

'Do I have to answer that question?'

Sparkes controlled himself with difficulty. 'Your story is very different from hers. Why should she lie about the business?'

'I presume because she dislikes me, dislikes my having found her out, and wants to do me all the dirt she can,' replied the colourless man. 'You realise, of course, that she's a pathological liar. I don't see her evidence standing up in court.'

The impudence of it took Sparkes's breath away. Nigel came to his rescue. 'You're telling us, Mr Leake, that your attempts to ingratiate yourself with Cherry were motivated by an unselfish desire to rescue the young woman from a fortune-hunter?'

Leake looked at him cautiously. 'You could put it that way.'

'I do. You were prepared to break your agreement with her guardian?'

'If necessary. I——'

'And of course return the fee he's paying you?'

'Oh, no. I shall have earned the fee by stopping the marriage.'

'I see. Thank you, Mr Leake. You are', continued Nigel in the same unimpassioned tone, 'one of the nastiest and most contemptible persons I've ever had the ill luck to meet. But you have made one useful contribution to the case Mr Sparkes is working on, so I suppose we should be grateful to you. Good-morning.'

'You'd better put on your bullet-proof vest,' said Sparkes when the man had gone out. 'See that look he gave you?'

'Well, we know now who tipped off the kidnappers. The question is, what do we do about it?'

Nigel and Sparkes discussed this at some length. They were prepared to take action without waiting for absolute proof; but in so delicate a situation, a false move could wreck any plan of action. The one they finally worked out depended upon a preliminary talk with Professor Wragby.

But Professor Wragby was not to be found.

Sparkes and his sergeant hurled themselves into activity. The Guest House was searched, every room and outbuilding of it. No car had been taken out of the garage: if there were footprints they had been covered up by the falling snow. It was inconceivable that Wragby had been kidnapped from under their noses, nor were there any signs of a struggle. He must have voluntarily walked out and disappeared.

The last people to have seen him were his wife—after tea, when he told her he was going to write some letters—and the plain-clothes man on duty, who had noticed him going through the hall towards the writing-room. He had chatted for a minute with Mrs Wragby after her husband retired.

The Professor could have gone out by the other door of the writing-room into the back quarters of the Guest House, while Nigel and Sparkes were interviewing the guests, though neither the proprietor nor any of the staff had seen him do so.

One thing, after all these investigations, became clear. Since by 9 p.m. the Professor had not returned or sent any word back, he must somehow have received a communication from the kidnappers and gone out to meet them on foot. Whether he had walked to be picked up by a car, or to some house in the neighbourhood, the rendezvous could not have been very far away. Sparkes had alerted the whole county force, and road blocks were set up on the few roads that were not already blocked by snow.

'Do you think he's knuckled under to them at last?' said Sparkes wearily, looking up from the large-scale ordnance maps on which he had marked the clear roads.

'I can't believe it,' replied Nigel. 'He's not a quitter. We've failed to find Lucy, so he decided he must try himself. His only hope was to meet the other side's agent, and make some sort of bargain.'

'He's got nothing to bargain with except the information they've been demanding. So he *is* going to quit.'

'He'll try to trick them again. I'll give you what you want when you've shown me Lucy alive, and let her go. Then he'll hold them off as long as he can, and after that he'll kill himself. That's how I read it, anyway.'

'It's more or less what his wife told me, too.'

'Is it indeed?' Do you think she knew he was going to bolt?'

'Can't tell. I'd have doubted it, from her manner. But she's an actress. And she did hold my chap in conversation for a little—never talked to him before, he said—just at the time Wragby went into the writing-room.'

'That child found dead in the drift——'

'Nothing to do with the case. A boy. I told you.'

'Murdered?'

'No visible signs of injury. They'll ring me again if the autopsy finds anything.' Sparkes's voice was rough with exhaustion. 'Listen to the late night news bulletin and hear all about it. Now I must go and throw some meat to the vultures.'

'You'll have to fight them off Elena Wragby, when you tell them the Prof has disappeared.'

'She's in her room, with one of my chaps at the door,' said Sparkes. 'No one's going to get in. Or out,' he added grimly.

But Elena Wragby did. A little before the regional news was due, Nigel, who had arranged it with the man on guard, sent Clare to fetch Elena down. He knew the guests would all be in the drawing-room, waiting for the news bulletin, and he wished to observe reactions—one person's in particular. A theory had formed in his mind which could only be tested thus: a theory which had nothing to commend it except its cold logic, from which he shrank.

The other guests, who had been talking in a desultory way, fell silent when the two women came in. They knew the Professor had disappeared: they did not know how to take it. Had he been kidnapped? Had he gone over to the other side? Had he just, after the fearful strain of the last few days, lost his wits and wandered out into the snowy night?

The Admiral took Elena's hand and led her gently to an arm-chair by the fire, opposite his wife's. She moved, as always, with dignity, but her limbs seemed stiff, as though she had just come through some physical ordeal, and there was a far-away look in her deep eyes.

The others kept eyeing her covertly, with embarrassment or a shameful intentness, as one might eye the still-living body of a martyr. Only Mrs ffrench-Sullivan, after one glance, averted her eyes and began poking at the fire: her lips were set in a faintly complacent expression which might have been interpreted to convey a silent 'I told you so. No foreigners are ever reliable. You can take it from me—she's mixed up in all this somehow.'

Justin Leake had been playing patience, at a table apart from the others. Presently he resumed the game, his cards slurring one over another, but his whole mien suggesting a wary attentiveness to something quite different. Lance Atterson, looking half-dead with boredom, tickled the Guest House cat behind the ears. It was Cherry who broke the intolerable silence, moving over to sit on the floor by Elena's feet and saying:

'I'm awfully sorry. I'm sure he'll be all right. Try not to worry, Mrs Wragby.'

'Thank you, my dear.'

The Admiral glanced at his watch, turned up the volume of the muttering radio set, went back to his chair. Nigel, standing beside the set, saw Clare's fingers curl into fists: his own tension had communicated itself to her. The others moved a little closer, or leant foward, as if the announcer's voice were that of the Delphic oracle.

'Professor Alfred Wragby, F.R.S., whose daughter disappeared last Thursday and is believed to have been kidnapped, is now missing. He was last seen—' the well modulated voice began. A description of the Professor was given; an appeal was made for anyone who had seen him to come forward: the police believed he might have lost his memory . . . It was as cagey as an announcement could be. Only the handful of people in Britain who knew the nature of Wragby's work would realise that his disappearance could mean a major defeat for their country.

The announcer gave a gentlemanly cough, and apologised. There was a rustle of paper. He began speaking again.

'A snow-plough, clearing a road in the vicinity of Longport this evening, turned up the body of a child.'

Elena Wragby gasped, as if she had been kicked in the heart.

'The body, that of a boy of about eight, had been lying buried in a drift for several days. There were no signs of violence upon it. It is believed that the boy may have died in a blizzard, while making his way towards Longport station: a zip-bag containing articles of clothing was found near the body, and the boy had a return ticket to London in his pocket. His identity is at present a mystery, for no boy had been reported to the police as missing in this part of the country.'

Elena, who had relaxed in her chair when the sex of the dead child was mentioned, grew tense again.

'A curious feature of the affair is that there were no name-tapes or other distinguishing marks on the boy's clothing. The only clue is a thin silver medallion, about the size of an identity disc, worn on a chain under the boy's clothing. On one side of the disc is embossed a phoenix rising from the ashes. On the reverse, an engraved inscription——'

The announcer's voice was blotted out by the most terrible sound Nigel had ever heard. Elena's face had gone ashy; her eyes stared at the radio set as if the voice of her damnation spoke from it. A shuddering cry broke like blood from her bloodless lips—a cry all the more appalling because it was not loud and yet it filled the room and seemed to beat back off the walls in waves of agony after Elena had started to her feet, then fallen on the floor fainting. 'Ivan!'

CHAPTER 11

Confession

DECEMBER 31

Nigel carried Elena Wragby upstairs and laid her on the bed, where Clare attended to her. The plain-clothes man was on guard again outside the door.

Elena had made one last attempt, on recovering consciousness. 'I'm sorry to have been so stupid, giving you all this trouble,' she whispered, looking up at Nigel. 'The relief of knowing it was not Lucy——'

'No, Elena,' he answered gently. 'It's too late for that. Ivan was your child, wasn't he?'

'Yes,' she muttered at last, and broke down into dry sobbing, which seemed as if it would never end, and shook her whole body in spasms like an electric current. Clare held the woman's hands, giving her what little comfort the human contact could give: she herself was quietly crying.

It had to be Elena, Nigel was thinking. The way she had received the news of Lucy's disappearance; the fact that other sources of information to the kidnappers had been virtually eliminated. But above all, there was the hole in the wainscot by which she deceived him for a little. When she realised how grave was the suspicion that had fallen on her, Elena borrowed the auger from the proprietor's workshop and made that hole. She was a resourceful woman, who kept her nerve under the most acute strain: she had resisted the temptation to 'find' the hole herself and show it to Nigel. The notion of a bug was allowed to enter his mind, with no forcing from her. But, once it was established that it had been Cherry's voice, not Elena's, which Mrs ffrench-Sullivan had heard from Leake's room, the device of the imaginary bug had recoiled upon her: nobody else could have had a conceivable motive for boring that hole. In any case, it could only be a desperate and temporary expedient. She needed to delay her unmasking, to gain a little time for her employers.

Here, sobbing on the bed, was a woman who had helped in the

133

kidnapping of her own step-daughter, and very possibly wrecked her husband's life; yet Nigel could feel no disgust, no hatred, no contempt for her. Elena, like some heroine of Greek tragedy, had been caught in a dilemma of fate, the victim of impersonal forces which had exploited her deepest instincts to further their own ends, and ruined her in the process. There was no doubt in Nigel's mind that Ivan had somehow been used to put an intolerable pressure on Elena, as Lucy was being used to coerce her father.

Presently the sobbing ceased. Elena sat up, encircled by Clare's arm, and sipped the glass of brandy Nigel had sent for.

'You must despise me,' were her first words.

Nigel gazed at the once beautiful face, haggard now and racked almost out of recognition. 'No, Elena, I do not despise you. I can guess what happened. You must tell us all about it. But first, do you know where they took Lucy?'

'Oh, if only I knew, I would tell you! Do you believe me?'

'Yes. You can't even guess?—whether it was to London, or somewhere near by?'

'No. I'm sorry. Oh, my God, why did I trust them!' Elena wildly exclaimed.

'Because you had to. For the chance of being reunited with Ivan.'

'Yes,' she said eagerly. 'You are understanding. Perhaps if I could have had another child. I tried to love Lucy. I did love her. But she was not my own. My life is quite finished now. If I could get Lucy back for Alfred—but I'm afraid she is dead too. And I'm responsible.'

There was a distant jangle. The church bells were being rung up to herald the New Year in. It only needed this, thought Nigel bitterly.

'Tell me how it started,' he asked

'They got in touch with me, last September. I thought I'd left all that behind me when I escaped to this country. I should have known better.'

'They told you Ivan was alive, after all?' asked Clare.

'Yes.'

'And you believed them?'

'Not at first, oh no. I did not trust them; I am not a stupid woman, and I'd had experience of their methods. Too much

134

experience. Even when they told me about the medallion: it's a family heirloom of my first husband's—he was called Ivan too—and about a birthmark the child had on his body: even then I did not quite believe them. But I wanted to. I wanted so badly. Can you understand?'

'Yes, my dear,' said Clare.

'I thought, they would have found these things out after they'd shot the man who was carrying him to the frontier. It was snow then. I tried to run back to my baby, but my friends stopped me. They told me he too was dead. That was to make me feel better for not going back to him. He was quite silent, in the snow in no-man's-land. I expect he'd been stunned by the fall. My little Ivan! And now he is dead. In a snowdrift.'

Elena choked on the words, glaring sightlessly at the atrocious picture in her mind.

'But they convinced you at last?' Nigel prompted.

'Yes. The frontier guards who had shot at us picked up the baby and found it was alive. One of them took him to a farm, where he was warmed and fed. Now it happened the farmer was a secret sympathiser with us: we had hidden in the farm the day before we made our dash across the frontier. He and his wife kept Ivan for nearly a year, but they had no way of communicating with me. After that year, the regime decided Ivan must go to a State Orphanage. The man who contacted me last autumn, when he saw I did not believe him that Ivan was alive, arranged for me to get in touch with this good farmer. He also arranged that the farmer and his wife should visit Ivan in the orphanage, and assure themselves—by the birthmark—that he was the baby they had taken in. So at last I believed.'

There was a long silence in the room, while gusts of wind tossed the sound of pealing bells against the window-pane.

'And now we come to the difficult part,' said Clare, chafing Elena's cold hands. Touched by her sympathy, the woman gave a wan smile.

'Yes. Please remember, I am not trying to excuse, only to explain. I had never forgiven myself for abandoning Ivan; but when I learnt he was alive—learnt I had left him to have his childhood in that orphanage, and be indoctrinated, turned into a little automaton—then I suffered worse than ever. You see, when my husband died in my arms, during the rising, his last words were committing little Ivan to my care. It was a sacred trust . . . Oh, why do those bells keep ringing?'

'They'll stop soon. They're ringing in the New Year.'

'New Year! It can only be worse than the old one. They should toll for death, not ring for life—in this accursed world.' Even in her extreme anguish, Elena showed unconscious touches of the histrionic.

'You must see, please. I was fond of Alfred, and the poor little Lucy. They helped to heal my spirit. But Ivan was my first husband and the greatest love in my life. It only comes once. Perhaps never it comes. But if it does, nothing afterwards can compare with it—not for a woman at any rate. When I heard the little Ivan was alive, nothing else mattered except to save him—try to give him back the years he had lost, and keep my faith with his father.'

'Yes,' Nigel sighed. 'So they said they'd let you have him if you did what they asked. And because they had told you the truth about Ivan's being alive, you felt you could trust them about this too?'

Elena shaded her eyes with one hand. "I *had* to trust them. I could not let slip even the slightest chance of getting Ivan back. Alfred's formulas—what did they matter to me compared with my own flesh and blood? These scientists and their great inventions!— why should I care which side overreaches the other? Let them fight amongst themselves for their filthy secrets—how to destroy humanity most efficiently! I am a mother.'

'Yes,' said Nigel, 'but there was Lucy.'

'You have a right to reproach me. I am not hard in my heart about the little Lucy. Since I helped them to take her away, I have lived in such a hell no preacher, no religious picture could express. But they promised me she should come to no harm. And again I believed them. I was foolish, wicked, yes. But it was Lucy against Ivan. There was no choice for me.'

'When they had your husband's secret, Lucy would be returned to him, and you and Ivan would——?'

'I was to meet Ivan in London. They would smuggle us back to Hungary. I could think of nothing but to have him in my arms again.' Elena's face seemed to splinter with agony. '*Why* did they

136

bring him down here? Why? If they meant to double-cross me, why bring him out of Hungary at all?'

'The answer's easy, I'm afraid. To stand in for Lucy.'

'Stand in? I don't know what you are saying.'

'Ivan and Lucy were rather alike?'

'I don't know. I haven't seen him all these years, or a photograph of him even.'

'But he took after you, didn't he?'

'Why yes, as a baby people thought he was just like me.'

'And you happened to remind people of Alfred's first wife?'

'Yes. But——'

'And Lucy takes after her.'

Elena's great haunted eyes lit up with intelligence. 'Ah! I see. That is why I had to hide away the photograph of Alfred's first wife. So that it would not give your agents a clue—put into their minds the idea of a likeness, and a substitution. You mean Ivan was brought down here so that Lucy could be substituted for him?'

'It's the only possible inference. I imagine the kidnappers must have taken a house in the neighbourhood—somewhere near Long-port, probably. They'd bring Ivan, so the neighbours knew there was a child in the house. What colour hair had he?'

'Sandy. Like mine before it went white.'

'When Lucy was kidnapped, they'd dye her hair, put boy's clothes on her, let the neighbours see her but not talk to her. If police inquiries were made, there'd be perfectly good evidence that the child in the house was the same one who'd been there before the kidnapping. No suspicion could attach to the house.'

'And, when they'd used Ivan, those devils killed him and left him in the snowdrift?'

'But he hadn't been injured,' Clare put in.

'They have ways of killing that do not show.'

'He had the return half of a ticket to London in his pocket,' said Nigel. 'If they'd intended to kill him, they wouldn't have bought a return. No, my guess is that they meant to put him on the London train, and something went wrong on the way to Longport. They'd move him by night of course, so that neighbours wouldn't notice his departure. Perhaps they found the road blocked at some point and had to walk the rest of the way, and the poor little chap couldn't make it.'

'Then they did murder him. As surely as if——' Elena broke off, her face hardening into the stony look of an avenging goddess. 'They left him to die there.'

'It's a gentle death,' murmured Clare; but Elena made no response, sunk in her own thoughts.

The sound of bells clamoured round the house, like ghosts crying to be let in.

Nigel waited for a little, then began a series of questions about the agents who had first contacted Elena. She answered without reluctance, but such information as she could give was limited to a few facts—the initial telephone calls, two rendezvous with a large, bear-like man in a London tea-shop, and the method by which she was enabled to communicate with the farmer who had taken in the baby Ivan. It soon became evident that Elena's memory for these transactions was weak: no doubt she had wanted to forget their detail, and the horror of the last week had wiped many things from her mind. Unfortunately, it had obliterated, amongst them, the most crucial fact of all.

'You had to tell them how your husband was reacting to their demand for information. You put through a second call from the telephone booth here last Friday morning, to tell them he intended to leave false information at the G.P.O., and the police were laying a trap for the collector—right?'

'Yes,' she replied, almost inaudibly.

'What number did you have to ring?'

Elena looked up at him with an expression of despair. 'I'm afraid it has gone from my head. No, please, you must believe me. I have been trying, trying to remember, since I heard what they did to Ivan. They told me I must memorise it: but I have a bad memory, so I disobeyed them and wrote it on a piece of paper, which I destroyed after making the call.'

'But you can remember if it was a local one, surely?'

'Oh yes. It was the Longport exchange, and there were three figures in the number. A four and a nine, I think—479 was it? 497? No, it's hopeless.'

'Never mind. It may come back. Who answered you?'

'It was a woman. I had to say "Millie here". And if the person answered, "Hallo, how is Ingham?"—that's my husband's birthplace—I would give the message. Only a few words. If all was clear for them, I would say, "Much better, thank you". If my husband was not consenting, I'd say, "About the same". If a trap was being laid, "Not so well, I'm afraid". Oh, if only I could remember that number!' Elena beat her fists against her temples, frantic with the frustration of it.

'Please try not to worry,' said Clare consolingly. 'They surely wouldn't have taken Lucy to the same house whose number you were to ring. I mean, they'd not trust you not to change your mind after Lucy was gone, and tell the police the number.'

'Well, we've got a little nearer, anyway,' said Nigel. 'Clare darling, would you fetch my ordnance map and the railway timetable.'

When she returned, Nigel spread the map on the table. 'Here's Longport. Their exchange serves this whole group of villages—' he pencilled a rough circle on the map. 'Your contact was in one of them, or in Longport itself. Now this is where Ivan's body was found, on the hill going down to Longport'—he made a cross. 'I'm sorry if I'm being rather brutal about this, Elena.'

'My feelings do not matter any more. Nothing matters except to find Lucy.' Elena stared at the map, as if a vision of Lucy might spring from some spot amongst its colours and contours.

'Lucy was taken to a house somewhere here, and substituted for Ivan. A house whose nearest main line railway station is Longport. The last train to London leaves Longport at, let's see—six twelve. So, unless the kidnappers have two cars, they could not have taken Ivan to the station till the following evening, Friday. Of course, there may have been a whole gang of them with a fleet of cars; but the arrival of so many in a country house would set the neighbours talking. I'd guess there were only two or three of them—two perhaps, masquerading as Ivan's parents.'

Clare broke in. 'Surely we can narrow it down a bit more? Look, you said they'd not smuggle Ivan out till after dark. They'd want to make sure of his catching that train, and they knew some of the roads might be blocked. Now they got Ivan to within half a mile of the station. Even if they were able to drive all that way more or less straight, starting after dark and aiming to reach the station in good time, six o'clock say, they'd not have much over an hour's driving time. How many miles an hour could one average over hilly, snow-covered roads? Twenty-five? Thirty at the very most. So the house is within a radius of thirty miles from Longport. Doesn't seem to help much. But think of the conditions that night. They may have had to get out and walk some way to the place where Ivan was found. That narrows the distance they travelled.'

'Yes,' said Nigel, 'it's a fair inference. And I think we can take it further. We can find out tomorrow which roads were blocked on Friday night. But the point is, they had to make sure of getting Ivan to the train—otherwise there'd be two children in the house instead of one. They could not know how many roads were being blocked by the blizzard that evening. They'd have to allow for a number of detours. Under those conditions, they couldn't risk the chance of doing a thirty-mile journey in the hour they had at their disposal: but they could be reasonably certain of accomplishing a journey of say, ten miles as the crow flies.' Nigel drew a small circle on the map. 'I believe Lucy is somewhere inside that circle.' He did not add, 'If she is alive.'

'May I say something?' asked Elena. 'You are assuming that Ivan would not be removed till after dark. But he could be hidden at the back of the car, in a rug perhaps. They might have started earlier.'

'It's possible of course. But look, there are two other main-line stations, at which that train stops, in thirty miles. But it was Longport they aimed at. Longport must be the nearest one to the hide-out. That roughly checks the ten-mile radius.'

'But, Nigel, didn't the police search every house in that area?' said Clare.

'They were looking for a girl, not a boy. We warned them that Lucy's appearance might be altered. We didn't at that time allow for the substitution of a kidnapped child for a bona fide one. I wouldn't be surprised if some village bobby set eyes on Lucy during the search—she'd be drugged maybe, they'd say she was ill and mustn't be woken—and padded off quite satisfied that she was the little boy who'd been seen about the place for a week.'

'I wonder,' said Elena. 'Perhaps Alfred's there now.'

'They picked him up in a car, you think?' Nigel's pale blue eyes regarded the woman steadily. 'You knew he was going to meet them?'

'He did not tell me much. I believe he did not quite trust me any more. Why should he?' Elena added remorsefully. 'He just said one thing: we were talking about Lucy—whether she was alive or dead—and he said he'd know soon, one way or the other. Oh, yes, and then he asked would I despise him if he gave them what they wanted.'

'In exchange for Lucy? Would he do that?'

'I just don't know. He is a good man, and a strong man. He is a little inhuman sometimes—it's the nature of his work, perhaps. But he loves Lucy very dearly. No, I don't think he would give them anything till he could assure himself Lucy was alive, and saw them let her go. After that——' Elena shrugged.

'So the chances are he's now in the same house where Lucy is, or soon will be, if the road to it is not blocked.'

'Well, then, why do we sit here doing nothing, talking?' she exclaimed. She started pacing the room, with those long dipping strides, like an animal in a cage. 'The police must start searching that area again, at once. Or do you have to get permission from some bureaucrat in London first? Oh, you are so slow in this country.'

Nigel smiled wryly at such imperiousness from a woman who had lost all right to command. Yet it was impressive: her figure, as it must often have done in the theatre, seemed to add a cubit to its stature.

'Elena,' he said patiently, 'I can't just press a button and start the whole operation. It's dark. There are drifts everywhere. I'll see that Sparkes moves his men in as soon as it's light. If Lucy *is* still alive, they'll certainly not do anything to her now that your husband is with them; and he'll be playing for time. Maybe he'll be able to get a message to us.'

'But he's in deadly danger! Please! I've done him so much harm already, I can't bear——'

'He'd be in still deadlier danger, and so would Lucy, if we went off at half cock,' Nigel broke in firmly. 'If their captors knew we were so close on their heels, they'd shoot them both and make a bolt for it. The road blocks are out again: they'd not get far if they tried to take Lucy and her father out of the county.'

Elena was silent for a little. Then she said decisively: 'Very well. I will try to sleep now. In the morning you will take me to the Superintendent and I will make a statement. Ah, the bells have stopped.'

'It is 1963,' said Clare. 'Good luck to it.'

Elena turned to her. 'Good luck to Alfred and to Lucy. My dear, you have been very kind to me. Will you do one thing more—sit up a little longer with me. I cannot bear my own company.'

It was said with a pathos that brought tears to Clare's eyes: but it was also like a royal command.

Nigel left them, told the plain-clothes man outside the door that he must treat Elena as under arrest, and rang Sparkes's home number. He gave him a rapid résumé of Elena's confession.

'So what we have to look for,' he went on, 'is a house, probably within a ten-mile radius of Longport, where a boy answering to the description of the boy found in the snowdrift, was staying for some days before the kidnapping—a boy who was a stranger in the neighbourhood, with two or three grown-ups looking after him. They'd probably be strangers too: rented a cottage, perhaps, for the holidays—an isolated place, or quiet digs in Longport itself. Main thing is, if you find the place, don't alarm the customers.'

'I'll wake up every bloody member of the Force now.'

'Happy New Year, and good hunting.'

Sparkes spent the next two hours dragging his men out of bed to the telephone. He rang Longport first, then worked outward from village to village. And it was all quite fruitless. For it so happened that Bert Hardman, the village constable at Eggarswell, had been carried off to Belcaster hospital that morning with an acute attack of pleurisy.

CHAPTER 12

Dart Home

JANUARY 1

In spite of his long bout of telephoning, Superintendent Sparkes was at his desk by 8.30 on New Year's Day. And it was just as well, for this morning the log-jam of the last week began to break up. Sparkes had hardly started work when a telephone call came through from the owner of the Bellevue Café. A man answering to the description of Professor Wragby had been attacked in his café: an ambulance was conveying him to the General Hospital at Belcaster. There seemed to be no witnesses of this affray, but a large man from London, who had greeted the Professor when he arrived and talked with him for some time, had disappeared shortly before Wragby's half-lifeless body was discovered.

Sparkes obtained a description of this man, who was presumably the agent sent to contact Wragby, and had it disseminated throughout the country. The only theory he could form was that the Professor had been attacked and left for dead by this agent, after giving him the information: why should the man attempt to kill him before he had given it?

But Sparkes had no time to develop theories just now. The café owner told him about the brawl between three thugs who had spent the night there and the detachment of soldiers. These three would shortly be arriving at the Belcaster Police Station under a military escort.

'See what you can get out of them,' he said to his detective-inspector. 'And keep your kid gloves in your pocket. The bloke at the café has an idea they were in cahoots with the big chap we're looking for. You can get me at the hospital if anything breaks.'

By the time he reached it, the ambulance had just arrived and Wragby was being examined. Sparkes brushed aside the usual hospital delaying-tactics and made his way into the private room where the Professor lay, with two doctors and a sister at his bedside. The sister gave Sparkes an outraged look and tried to hustle him out, but she might as well have tried to shift one of the stone men off Easter Island. The senior doctor said:

'Hallo, Sparkes, you're up early. Interested in my patient? Who is he?'

Sparkes told him. The doctor gave a low whistle.

'How's he doing?'

'I think we'll keep him. Sound constitution. And he needs it. Looks as if he'd been fighting a gorilla. We've treated him for shock and given him a tracheotomy.'

'When can he talk, Doctor?'

'Not yet. Just take a look at him.'

On Wragby's dead-white face, freckles stood out like disease-spots. His breath was like the noise of sandpaper.

'We'll let you know when——'

'Sorry, I'm waiting here.'

'Now look, I'm in charge. My job is to save this man's life.'

Sparkes drew the doctor out of the room, and had a whispered conversation with him. 'Wragby may have given away a vital secret to enemy agents. Or he may not. And he may know where his kidnapped daughter is. I've got to find out. Every minute counts.'

But many minutes passed, slow as hours, while Sparkes leant against the wall, staring at the unconscious man as if willing him to give up his secrets.

At last Wragby's eyelids fluttered open. Sparkes moved forward. The doctor laid a hand on his sleeve. 'He is not to talk. You may ask a few questions, and let him nod or shake his head. But wait till I tell you.'

The two doctors busied themselves around the bed, while Sparkes stood fuming with impatience.

'Don't try to talk, old man,' said the house physician. It was an unnecessary order, for Wragby, desperately attempting speech, could hardly utter an articulate word.

Presently, at a sign from the doctor, Sparkes stood over the patient. 'Professor Wragby, you recognise me—Superintendent Sparkes? No, don't talk. Just nod or shake your head. I must ask you a few questions. You understand what I'm saying?'

Nod.

Sparkes described the big man who had disappeared from the café. 'He is the enemy agent you had to meet?'

Nod.

'He is the man who tried to kill you?'

Nod.

'Did you give him the secret information he was after?'

Wragby shook his head so violently in spite of his weakness that the doctor interposed, laying his fingers on the Professor's pulse. 'Take it easy, old man . . . All right, Superintendent, go ahead.'

'This agent contacted you by letter to arrange the rendezvous?'

Nod.

'Did your wife know you decided to keep the rendezvous?'

Shake.

'Your idea, Professor, was to make a bargain with him? If he took you to where Lucy is being kept, and released her, you would then hand over the information?'

An agonised expression came over Wragby's face. He tried to speak, but only a whispering croak came out.

'Wait a minute. I see I'm distressing you. Would I be putting it better if I said your plan was that he should take you to Lucy, on that understanding, and let her go, but you would then refuse the information?'

Wragby nodded.

'Good for you, sir. Just one more question. In your talk with this agent, did you get any inkling where Lucy is to be found?'

Nod. But Wragby's expression was unutterably sad.

'Where?—sorry—London?'

Shake.

'In this county?'

Wragby gave a little shrug of the shoulders.

'Somewhere to the west?' Sparkes asked at a venture.

Wragby nodded. The doctor, who had been watching his patient carefully, intervened. 'He's had enough. I'll ring you as soon as he's fit to talk, Mr Sparkes.'

Poor chap, thought the Superintendent, finding his way out. So near to making contact with his little girl, and then frustrated. Still, it bears out Strangeways' theory that Lucy is somewhere in the Longport area.

Back at the station he received further confirmation. One of the soldiers who had escorted the three gangsters volunteered that he had seen a large man, answering to the café-owner's description of the enemy agent, get into a car and drive off westwards along the main road: the road that passed through Longport. He had not noticed the car's registration number, but it was a Morris Oxford, black or dark maroon under the travel-stains and patches of snow. Messages went out to the patrol cars. The net was beginning to close.

Sparkes's inspector told him the three men under custody had at first refused to talk. Finally one of them was persuaded to admit that they had been hired on Saturday by a man called Peters to drive their van down from London yesterday, meet up with him at the café, and do a little job. They'd be told later what the job was. No, never seen Peters before—a contact brought him along.

145

Sparkes had a pretty good idea what they'd been hired for: to act as strong-arm for 'Peters', and to convey Lucy—alive or dead—in their van out of a neighbourhood that was growing too hot for the kidnappers.

'All right,' he said to the inspector. 'Charge them with malicious wounding—anything you bloody well like, they're bound to have done it. Fingerprints. Get their records from Scotland Yard. I'll have a go at them myself later.'

The vexing problem remained, though. How was it that no policeman in Longport and district had turned up, during his search, the pseudo-Ivan or got to hear about the real Ivan who had been living in the same house? Then Sparkes remembered that Bert Hardman, the Eggarswell chum, was off-duty, in hospital. Eggarswell, only a few miles from Longport: a small and remote village in a wild part of the country. Hardman wasn't too well equipped in the upper storey, but——

Sparkes seized the telephone, demanded to speak to the matron in person. No, this formidable lady replied, it was quite out of the question to talk to the patient: Bert Hardman was on the danger list and delirious.

He put the receiver back, his face heavy with defeat. Almost at once the telephone rang.

'Sparkes here.'

'Strangeways. I've discovered where she is. Lucy. If she's still there.'

'Good God! Are you—is it Eggarswell?'

'Never heard of it. I've got a description of the house and the view from the front windows.'

'What the devil are you talking about? How did you——?'

'Lucy wrote it. Reached here this morning. You could say she threw it here. Longport postmark. Must be one of the villages round about—a small one: letters collected, brought in to Longport, postmarked there.'

'But look here, Strangeways——'

'Stop chattering, old boy. Wastes time. I'm driving in straightaway.' Nigel sounded positively manic. 'Have an expeditionary force ready. Get hold of someone who knows that area. We're looking for a remote cottage on a hillside, with a farm near by. Gothic-shaped windows, an extensive view in front and a conical

146

hill with a clump of trees on it in the middle distance to the left. It should be easy: oh yes, and the photograph of a bearded academic gentleman in one of the bedrooms. Be seeing you.'

Nigel rang off before Sparkes had time to tell him that the Professor had been found. . . .

The post-van had arrived at the Guest House while they were breakfasting. The proprietor distributed the letters to the other guests, but left the Wragbys' mail on the hall table for another half hour. Clare and Elena were having breakfast in the latter's room. Nigel, who expected a call from the Superintendent, told a servant where he could be found and went out to the garage. Snow had drifted against its doors again during the night, and the yard itself was a foot deep. The sooner they could get Elena into Belcaster, the better. Nigel found a spade, and set to work digging the snow away from the doors. It had become stiff yet friable, like icing sugar: his spade hurled it aside in chunks. The doors opening at last, he started up his Citroën, let the engine warm, then backed out. The drive-in to the yard sloped upwards, and here, with front-wheel traction, the car's rear wheels could get no grip on the surface: the car slewed sideways and the engine stalled. Nigel restarted it and drove back into the yard. Another ten minutes was spent in digging out two wheel-tracks along the drive-in. He backed out again, the engine pushed the car up the slope until he was able to turn it and leave it ready for departure.

Entering the Guest House again, he found the Wragbys' letters on the hall table. One of them was addressed to the Professor in the childish capitals which Nigel associated with anonymous letters. Some crack-pot writing to abuse him for not taking better care of his daughter, probably: other people's tragedies always brought out the filth from poison-pen types and neurotic or officious busy-bodies.

Nigel's first impulse was to destroy the letter, but he restrained it and went upstairs with the mail. Elena was dressed. She had even managed to eat a little breakfast. Nigel sent the plain-clothes man down to have his. Clare gave Nigel an anxious look.

'No word from Sparkes yet,' he said. 'Elena, here are some letters for your husband. I'm going to open this one myself.'

She nodded apathetically.

Nigel stared at the foolscap sheet. He read:

Will the finder please post this to Professor Alfred Wragby, F.R.S., *The Guest House, Downcombe. It is a scientific experiment.* REWARD OF £5.

Nigel turned the sheet over. He grew tense as his eyes read along the lines written there.

'Who's Cinders?'

'Why, that's an old nickname of Lucy's,' said Elena.

'I thought so. It's *not* a hoax. Look!'

The two women were reading over his shoulder.

CHAPTER II. WHERE AM I?

Next morning, the madwoman, who Cinders had to call Aunt Annie, took her into a room at the front of the house. She let Cinders, who she called Evan for some loopy reason, look out of the window. Down below was a man called Jim. He had brought some milk. There was another man, but Cinders could only see the top of his head standing in the doorway. 'I expect he lives in the house and is Annie's keeper,' thought Cinders. Jim waved to her, and she waved back. He had on Wellingtons, an old Army great-coat, and a red woolly hat with a bobbel on top. 'Don't you dare call for help,' hissed the madwoman, 'or I'll stick this hipodurmic sirynge into you.' So Cinders didn't. She hates pricks, ever since she was so ill when she was a kid.

The pannerama from the window was truly spectaculer. Snow-covered hills lay like frozen waves of a bumpy sea. One hill, to the left of the picture, attracted her attention. It was connical, with a clump of trees four or five of them on its top. The cottage stood on the side of a hill, at least the ground went down into a valley beneath it. Cinders's observant eye noticed some farm buildings quite near on the right, I expect it was where the milk came from. It was the only house in sight. The window she looked out of had a sort of arched top and white wooden bars on it, which cut up the view. Cinders could see no more now, because the mainiak closed the curtain and with a fowl othe bade her begone to her own appartment. Cinders bewent, but not before she had seen a photograph of a bearded man in a cap and gown like her father wears hanging on the wall.

'Seven out of ten for spelling, ten out of ten for composition,'

148

said Nigel, thinking, 'a hundred out of ten for resource.'

'How on earth did it get here?' asked Clare.

'Look. See these faint fold-lines? She made a dart of it, and threw it from that window.'

'But——'

'And some children picked it up, I guess—no grown-up would pay attention to it—and saw about the reward and posted it. Unfortunately, in their excitement they forgot to write their own address, where we should send the reward to.'

'But the envelope has a Longport postmark,' said Clare.

'Quick!' Elena cried, 'Let us go there at once!'

But Nigel was out of the room, running downstairs to ring Sparkes. Waiting for the call, he reflected on one name in the missive. 'Evan'—they called Lucy 'Evan' to keep up the pretence that it was still Ivan in the cottage: no doubt they had called him Evan too.

Five minutes later they were whirling out of Downcombe on the Belcaster road, Clare driving, Nigel beside her, the plain-clothes man—who had been dragged from the breakfast table—in the back with Elena Wragby . . .

Petrov was plodding down the lane that led to Eggarswell. He was in a very wicked temper; but with Petrov temper did not rage in a vacuum, it smouldered until he found someone to vent it upon. Two miles back, rounding a bend, he had run his car into a drift from which he wasted ten minutes extricating it. The drift, as he proved by walking through it, stretched for some twelve yards ahead and at one point came half-way up his thighs. There was a spade in the car, but it would take him far longer than he could afford to dig a passage through; besides, even on this lonely road another motorist might turn up, and ask awkward questions.

Petrov dug out his front wheels and reversed along the road. A hundred yards back, a track led off it into a little wood. He got out again and tested this track. Under the trees, the snow lay less thickly. Petrov drove the car in reverse along the track, then into a clear space screened by trees, where it would not be noticed by anyone passing along the road.

He sat in the car for a few minutes, studying the map and adjusting his plans. He must not be seen in Eggarswell—what outlandish names the English gave their villages! That meant leaving the road quarter of a mile short of it, and striking across the fields. He must also avoid being seen by the people in the farm near Smugglers' Cottage, which would involve a wider detour.

Pieces of snow fell on the car roof from a wind-shaken branch, with the sound of fingertips gently tapping a door.

Petrov calculated times and distances. It was now some fifty minutes since he had killed the Professor. Quite conceivably one of his hired yobs would at first be suspected of it. No attempt had been made to prevent him leaving the café. Sooner or later, of course, one of the dumb English policemen would start asking questions about the man who had been talking so long with the Professor in the café last night, and a description of him would go out. But, Petrov calculated, he still had several hours to play with, at least.

It was a nuisance that he had lost the three men and the van in which he had intended them to remove the Professor and his little girl, dead or alive according to whether the Professor coughed up his information quickly or not. However, there was Paul Cunningham's car, which he would be unlikely to need much longer. Petrov could take that as far as the wood, drop Cunningham and Lucy here, and drive on with Annie. There might or might not be time to bury the bodies of Paul and Lucy in the wood: even unburied, they might with any luck not be discovered for weeks, months even.

Petrov got out, locked the car doors, patted the revolver in his overcoat, and whistling tunelessly went on his way. . . .

At Smugglers' Cottage, Annie and Paul awaited him, with varying degrees of eagerness. They had heard on the radio last night the news of Wragby's disappearance. They had waited up till 1 a.m. for Petrov to arrive, either with the Professor's secret or with the Professor himself: this was the plan which Petrov had conveyed to Annie over the short-wave set on Sunday. Something presumably had gone wrong with it: perhaps the road from the rendezvous to Eggarswell was now snowbound.

They had also heard about the discovery of Evan's body. This brought Annie down on Paul like a fury and sent him into a panic. She was still nagging at him this morning.

'If I'd had any sense,' he was saying, 'I'd have cleared out last night.'

'Sense! You didn't clear out because you were afraid of you own skin—afraid of getting caught by another blizzard and dying in it, like that wretched boy you left to die.'

Peevishly, Paul reflected how even the most unwomanly woman shares her sex's attibute of making a point endlessly and indefatigably, returning to it over and over and over again, like drops of water wearing a hole in stone.

'You're like the Chinese water torture,' he said.

'How far from the station *did* you leave him?'

'I've told you a dozen times, and why. A few hundred yards. He must have got lost and wandered round in circles. I didn't *leave* him to die.'

'Have it your own way. You left him *and* he died, if that suits your conscience better.'

'Oh for Christ's sake pack it up! Don't you see the point? This'll bring the police swarming all over the district. We've simply got to clear out while we have the chance.'

'We're waiting here till Petrov comes, or rings us up.'

'Petrov will have heard the radio news last night too. He'll be making tracks back to London. That's why he's not come here. Like any good Communist, my poor Annie, he's taught to save his own skin and leave his subordinate comrades holding the baby.'

Annie Stott did not take up this provocation. She was thinking of the baby they held. Annie had been brought up in a hard school: she admired toughness and courage, and during the last day or two, since Lucy's attempted escape, had come to respect these qualities in the little girl. Lucy seldom whined: she kept herself amused and made the best of the unnatural life she was living.

Paul too was favourably inclined towards the child, but only because she gave him no trouble. All he wanted now was to get her off his hands. If he could do this without further imperilling himself, he would do it. Tonight, when Annie was asleep, he'd smuggle her out into his car, drop her off in some village where she could knock up a householder, and drive away. Beyond this, he could see nothing: his was the brute reaction of the murderer who feels that, if he can get the blood off his hands, what he had done will vanish like a bad dream.

151

Upstairs, Lucy put the skipping-rope back in the cupboard. The first day after she'd tried to escape, she'd had to skip on one foot only; but now the ankle she'd twisted was much better and she could manage both. It was important, her father had once told her, if you were a prisoner of war, to keep as physically fit as possible: then, when the moment came to escape, you stood a better chance. Papa knew. He had been one, and he had escaped. Lucy had absolute confidence in him. She knew he would come to rescue her. It was now a matter of waiting patiently and keeping fit so that she would not be a drag on him when he and she ran away together. The prisoners of war who survived best, he had also told her, were the ones who kept their minds occupied too. No use sitting around on your boo-boo, brooding. Flushed with the exercise, Lucy got out paper and pencil, and began writing down all the animals she could remember beginning with the letter A. From them, she turned to towns beginning with L. She was sucking her pencil, gazing out of the window in thought, when the extraordinary thing happened.

Over the vertical cliff close outside, its top level with the window, appeared the head of a man, then his body, then his legs. Standing there, he loomed as huge as a statue. He was the first living thing Lucy had seen out of this window. He paused a moment, then moved along the bank out of sight, scuffing up the snow in little puffs with his boots, walking with a lumbering gait that reminded Lucy of a bear's. This must be the friend Annie was expecting. It was funny he should approach the cottage in this roundabout way, instead of walking up the track past the farm. I expect he's a gangster, she thought, though he doesn't look like one any more than Paul or Annie. Of course, he could be a policeman in plain clothes, searching for me. But she had been too surprised by this bulky apparition to bang at the window and attract his attention.

Petrov kicked the snow off his boots and went in at the front door. The footsteps in the hall were the first intimation Paul had of his arrival. Annie hurried out to receive Petrov. Paul Cunningham shrank in his chair by the log fire: he had made himself believe that Petrov would never come, but the rumbling voice outside was unmistakable.

'So here you are, all nice and cosy.' Petrov stood close to the fire, drying his trousers. 'I've had a long walk. I'm hungry.'

Paul started up—to get food, to get out of the room which the massive figure dwarfed.

'No, no, sit down. Talk first, then food.'

'You've got it?' asked Annie eagerly.

'The information? No.'

'But—but isn't Wragby with you, then?'

'Professor Wragby is with his fathers.'

'I don't——'

'I had to dispose of him. He tried to set another trap for me. I strangled him. Are you cold, Mr Cunningham?'

'No. Why?'

'You are shivering.'

Paul became aware that Petrov was raging with anger, for all his ice-calm exterior, and shivered still more uncontrollably.

He licked his lips, and ventured, 'So we've got to pack it in?'

'*Shut up!*' Petrov turned to Annie. 'Why did you not return the boy to London as you were ordered? Is he still in this house?'

'He's dead. His body was found yesterday. Didn't you hear the radio news last night, comrade?'

'So? Explain, please.'

'Cunningham can tell you all about it,' said the woman maliciously.

'Indeed? Let me hear from him then. Are you too hot, Cunningham? Better move away from the fire. You're sweating.'

'It wasn't my fault!' Paul's voice went up to falsetto.

'That is for me to judge. Get on with it.'

Paul told the story of the journey through the blizzard. In Petrov's formidable presence, the conclusion of it sounded more humiliating to him than ever.

'I see. You lost your nerve.' The eyes, small and dangerous as a boar's, drilled into Paul's. 'I made an error of judgment choosing you. The error must be corrected. Have you lost the other child too, Annie?'

'No, of course not. She's upstairs. You can hear her skipping.'

And Lucy was, having put on shoes—skipping as loudly as she could in case the visitor was indeed a policeman searching. To call out was more than she dared, with memories of the hypodermic.

'I hope you've enjoyed her company,' said Petrov. 'You won't have it much longer.'

'You're taking her away?' asked the woman uncertainly.

'We shall all be leaving soon, for various destinations.'

'I should hope so,' muttered Paul.

'Hope, Mr Cunningham, as your poet says, springs eternal in the human breast. Unfortunately, your bungling makes me alter my plans. That dead boy is going to put the idea of a substitution into some policeman's fat head.'

'We took in the local chap,' said Paul obsequiously, 'when he came round looking for Lucy.'

'You wouldn't take him in a second time, my dear sir—not after a description of the dead boy has gone out.'

'We needn't worry about him for a bit,' said Annie. 'Jim—that's the man from the farm—told me this constable is in hospital, on the danger list.'

'So. What dramatic lives you all live in these parts.'

'Is the Professor really dead?' she jerked out.

'Dear me, yes. When I kill someone, he does not come to life again.' Petrov grinned at his own joke. To Paul, it was like a crocodile's grin. 'Never mind, Annie, *you* have made no mistakes. The Party will not forget you.' He snapped his fingers at Paul. 'Food now. Look sharp. And plenty of black coffee.'

When they were alone, he sat down and spoke confidentially to Annie Stott. 'If anyone interrupts us, I am Evan's father, come to take him home. Now, here is my plan. You will pack your things, dismantle the transmitter, put everything in the back of Cunningham's car. The four of us will drive to where I left my own, in a wood about two miles away. We cannot afford to wait till dark: we must leave in half an hour's time. Can the car get down the track to the village?'

'Yes. The snow's been beaten down by a tractor.'

'Good. And after that the road is passable—I've walked along most of it—till we come to the drift where my car stuck. We drive ours as deep into the drift as we can. We walk through it, get into my own, and beat it for the main road west. I have contacts in Plymouth. If necessary, we ditch the car and take a train there.' He rubbed his hands vigorously. 'With a bit of luck, we can make it. What's the matter? Have you a better plan?'

'No. But we can't bring—what do we do about Lucy, and Paul?'

'Ah, but that is simple. We leave them in Paul's car.'

'But——'

'I'd thought at first of leaving them in the wood, where my car is. But, walking here, I had a better idea. Just before we leave, we have a little stirrup cup, the four of us. In two of the cups you will put the knock-out drops. By the time we get to that drift, two of us are asleep. Very good. We drive the car at the drift, if necessary shovel some more snow against the exhaust pipe, and leave the engine running. Soon the fumes will put them quite to sleep. It will certainly snow again soon. The car may be entirely covered with it, and it's a lonely road—I met nothing as I walked here.'

'I see.'

'The beauty of this is that it will confuse the trail. You see? The missing child is found dead in a car, with the kidnapper who was trying to take her out of the district. He has a dismantled transmitter in the car, too. The police find one criminal. They do not look so hard after that for his associates. . . . You have doubts still, comrade?'

Annie flushed, her eyes cast down. 'Is it necessary to k— to liquidate them?'

'Why should *you* worry?' Petrov jerked his head towards the kitchen. 'That piece of shit in there—what loss is he to anyone? His cowardice and stupidity have wrecked my plans. Have you fallen for him?'

'Don't be ridiculous! It's Lucy I'm thinking of. What's the point of killing *her*?'

'What do you suggest we do with her? Leave her in the locked room to starve? Take her with us and hand her politely over to a cop? The child knows too much. You always knew the child was expendable.'

How it happened, Annie Stott never knew. She was not a woman who prided herself on female sensibility or intuition, nor had she much of these qualities to pride herself on. But she suddenly felt a falseness in Petrov's words, a flooding conviction that he had a relish for killing and would enjoy killing a small girl. She began to wonder about the Professor's death: when everything depended upon keeping him alive to yield up his secret, it was strange that Petrov should have killed him. She watched him devour like an animal the food Paul had brought in. He'd said the Professor had laid a trap for him at the rendezvous: police presumably, perhaps soldiers too: was it conceivable that, in order to escape it, Petrov should have had to strangle Wragby—a slow business, surely, when every second counted and he had a revolver?

Annie asked Petrov about the trap. What he said, with his mouth full, was enough to confirm her suspicion. He even boasted a little about the fight, the marks of which were some of them visible on him. He wants to kill Lucy, she thought, because the anger and violence of that struggle are not exhausted. It is a piece of personal vindictiveness. Petrov is not reliable.

Unreliability is a deadly sin in the political circles where Annie moved. That Petrov should be unreliable—she felt it absolved her from the implicit obedience with which she would normally follow a superior Party member's instructions.

'I must go and dismantle that set,' she said abruptly. She slipped quietly upstairs and entering Lucy's room, put a finger to her lips. 'We're leaving soon. Put on all the clothes you can. Before we go, we're having a drink with our friend who's just come.'

'I saw him——!'

'Ssh! Pretend to drink it, but pour it away somewhere. Soon after we drive off, pretend to go to sleep.'

'Oh, am I coming with you?'

'Yes. And *don't* wake up till—till the car's stopped and we've left you.'

'But I don't——'

'Promise, Lucy! If you don't do exactly what I say, it'll be very dangerous for you.'

'Oh, all right, I promise.'

'Good girl.' Annie bent down and gave her an awkward kiss on the top of the head.

Petrov was at the bottom of the stairs as she came down. 'What are you doing up there?' he suspiciously asked.

'Lav. The set's in that cupboard down there. Won't take me long.'

'Don't you ever pull the plug?' Petrov took a step or two upstairs.

'Look. I'm in a hurry. We've got to get off soon. Hadn't you better see that Paul warms up his engine?'

156

'I guess you're right.'

'And don't let him out of your sight or he'll drive off without us.'

'Trust me, Comrade Stott,' he replied jovially. . . .

Half an hour before Lucy saw the figure of a man emerge from the snow-line outside her window, Nigel and his companions were sitting in Superintendent Sparkes's office at Belcaster.

Elena Wragby, unaware how much Sparkes had done since breakfast, was visibly fretting with impatience at his deliberation. 'Have you found the house?'

'Yes. We have also found your husband.'

Elena's cheeks blanched. 'Oh, I'm glad. Is he here?'

'He's in our hospital. Very dangerously injured, but they think he'll pull through.'

'Oh, thank God! May I see him? No, that must wait. We've got to rescue Lucy first.'

'I must remind you, Mrs Wragby, that you are under arrest. You are here to make a statement.'

'Yes, yes, I will do that presently. There are things more important.'

Sparkes was secretly tickled, impressed even, by the imperious manner of this white-haired woman, but he replied stiffly, 'I must be the judge of that, ma'am.'

She beat a fist on her knee. 'Oh, this passion for legality you British have. Don't you realise that Lucy is in dreadful danger?'

'It was you who put her there in the first instance,' said Sparkes formidably. 'And you are responsible for your husband's grave condition too. He was attacked and left for dead by the enemy agent he went to meet.'

Elena buried her head in her hands. 'Where is this man now—this agent?' she muttered in a choked voice.

'He was last seen driving away westwards, in the direction of Longport. The house where your step-daughter was imprisoned is a few miles to the south, on a hillside above Eggarswell.'

'He has gone to kill her. I know it. I feel it here.'

Elena struck her heart in a gesture both histrionic and utterly sincere.

'That is possible.'

'Then *why* are you sitting here, doing nothing?' she cried. 'Do you *know* she is already dead?'

'Calm yourself, madam. We have it in hand. I shall go myself in a few minutes.'

'And I shall go with you.'

'I'm afraid that's not possible.'

Caught by an imploring look from Elena, Nigel interposed. 'Just a minute, Mr Sparkes. Have you got the place surrounded?'

'Not yet. But the village is under observation.'

The Superintendent pointed a pencil at the large-scale map spread on his desk. 'Here's the village. The house—it's called Smugglers' Cottage—is up here. There's the farm Lucy mentioned. If the man who attacked Professor Wragby is trying to get to the cottage, he'll drive along this road and be intercepted by a patrol car on the edge of the village.'

'And suppose he gets out and walks across country?'

'I can't cover every eventuality. I haven't got an army at my disposal,' said Sparkes huffily. 'The sergeant in the patrol car has put one of his men in Thwaite's farm here to keep an eye on the cottage.'

'That's fine. The last thing we want is for the kidnappers to realise we're on to them, till we can move in. The point is, this X is a killer. If he goes to the cottage and then finds he's hemmed in there, his instinct will be to kill Lucy and shoot his way out with the others.'

'He'd not get far.'

'Probably not. But——'

'Look. To drive from Eggarswell to one of the two main roads you'd have to travel north or south. When I've got through to the village, I'm having snow-ploughs get to work on those two roads, just short of the main ones. Here and here.'

'To clear a path for the fugitives?'

'To push snow *on to* the roads—artificial drifts. It's a better block than any patrol cars could make, and the men in my car aren't armed.'

'Who says our police aren't resourceful? But the problem is, getting into Smugglers' Cottage and nabbing X and his accomplices before they kill their hostage. We need a surprise tactic.'

'It's not possible.'

'Oh yes it is. There's one person they wouldn't suspect.'

'I'm not with you.'

'I understand,' said Elena. 'You mean me?'

'Yes.'

'But Mrs Wragby is under arrest. It's out of the question.'

'To hell with the formalities, my dear chap. Let her walk up to the cottage alone, and try to divert their attention—hold them long enough for us to make our dispositions and move in.'

'Well, it's an idea,' said Sparkes doubtfully. 'But how is she to account for her arrival there without rousing suspicion?'

'I shall show them what Lucy wrote—tell them it reached me this morning and I came right over. I shall pretend I am still on their side, and have come to warn them.'

'I think you should let her do it, Mrs Sparkes,' said Clare. 'She wants to make some reparation, don't you see?'

Sparkes pondered for a few moments, then rose to his feet decisively. 'Very well,' he said.

CHAPTER 13

Paid on All Sides

JANUARY 1

Clare Massinger was at the wheel of the Citroën, following the two cars of armed police. On the back seat, Elena bit her nails and Sergeant Deacon offered up silent prayers as Clare executed hair-raising but controlled skids round the corners of the snowy road. Beside her, Nigel studied a large-scale map. Eggarswell was now four miles away. They were to approach it from the south— the opposite point from which Petrov had driven towards the village. To their left, as they rushed along the switch-backing coast road, lay the sea. The police cars ahead stopped for a moment while Sparkes had a word with the driver of a yellow snow-plough. Then they turned off this road, due north, into the minor one which led to the village. When the three cars had passed, the plough began making its snow-block.

Nigel studied the map. Smugglers' Cottage, ringed in red ink, was half-way up the contour lines above Eggarswell to the east. A winding dotted line represented the track which connected the cottage and adjacent farm with the village: Nigel was trying to calculate from the contours how far they could drive up this track and still be in dead ground, invisible to any watcher from the cottage. Three or four hundred yards, he estimated. Not enough.

'How did the Super get on to this place?' he asked, turning round to the sergeant.

'Easy, sir. I was born in Eggarswell. Recognised the cottage at once from the description you telephoned. Those pointed windows on the first floor the little girl mentioned. And there's the conical hill with a tree clump on it—see? We'll skirt round that in a minute. My God!' he ejaculated as the car sidled and slewed under them, hitting a deeper patch of snow.

Clare stamped on the accelerator, and the car clawed its way through and straightened up.

'Who owns it?'

'An Oxford gentleman; doesn't use it very often now, I believe. A week or two in the summer perhaps. Lends it to friends, or rents it. Lonely sort of place. Not my idea of a holiday. Used by smugglers once, they say: two hundred years ago maybe. They brought the stuff in from the sea on carts and stored it in a cellar there till the coast was clear to distribute it.'

'The cottage was well-placed strategically for that, I suppose.'

'That's right, sir. Good field of fire from it, if needs be, though I never did hear there was any battles went on.'

'Could one approach it from the hill at the back?'

'On foot, yes. Depends how deep the snow is lying. The Super's going to send a couple of chaps round that way if he can, just in case they try to escape up the hillside. Bloody fools if they do—begging your pardon, madam.'

'Oh, hurry! please hurry!' muttered Elena, twisting her long fingers together. They had passed the conical hill and were driving through broken, choppy country, with patches of snow-covered scrub, copses, bramble-bushes to their left and rough pasture-land mounting gradually on the other side.

'That's Tom Blodgett's stack. Only a mile now. Jesus!'

Rounding a corner, Clare saw the back of a police car stationary thirty yards ahead. If she braked hard she would infallibly skid or collide. In the narrow lane there was no chance of passing. She did a racing change down and let the accelerator up, braking gently: the Citroën slowed as if it had run into a wall of feathers. Clare changed down again, came to a stop six feet behind the police car, from which men were now jumping.

Nigel got out and ran forward. The road in front of the Super's car was blocked by a heavy van, with whose driver Sparkes was having a heated altercation.

'Who the hell d'you think you are? Stirling Moss?' yelled the driver from his cab.

'None of your lip. Get out of our way. We're on an urgent call.'

'You expect me to back this bloody thing for a mile? Use your loaf.'

'That's just what you are going to do, my lad. After we've searched it. Open up the rear door, and look sharp about it.'

The driver got down, grumbling, and unlocked the back of the van. Sparkes climbed in.

'What 'cher looking for? Stolen goods?'

'Yes,' shouted Sparkes from inside.

'That's defamation of character, that is,' remarked the driver with misguided relish. 'You wait till my boss hears about it.'

'All right,' said Sparkes, jumping out. 'Now back this bloody object till we can get past.'

'Pig's arse,' muttered the man, climbing into the driver's seat.

It was one of those tall vans, with no view to the rear unless the driver held the door open and craned his head out. This one took his time about it. First, his rear wheels revolving rapidly got no grip and merely beat the snow into a harder, more slippery surface. It took eight policemen, shoving like demons, to get the heavy van off this ice-patch. The driver reversed, slowly as a maimed snail, for some thirty yards. Here, there was another sharp bend in the road. And at this bend, whether from bloody-mindedness or the awkward configuration of the road, keeping too far from the ditch on his left and unable to see the one on his right, the driver put a rear wheel into the latter. There was a sullen crack. The van canted over, its ancient back axle broken. The road to Eggarswell was irremediably blocked now. . . .

In the garage at Smugglers' Cottage, Petrov fumed while Paul Cunningham tried to start his car. He had placed the luggage in the boot five minutes ago. But the self-starter ground away, and there was no spark of life from the engine—not even an apologetic cough.

'When did you run this goddammed heap last?' Petrov angrily inquired.

'Oh, a day or two ago. It was all right then.'

'Didn't you have orders to warm up the engine *every* day?'

His words were lost in another clanking outburst from the starter. He got into the driver's seat, thrusting Paul aside. 'Look, you've over-choked it, you stupid bastard.'

'All right, start the bloody thing yourself,' Paul muttered sulkily.

'Don't you talk to me like that. Open up the bonnet: you'll have to clean the plugs.'

'I don't know how to do that,' Paul faltered.

'You don't seem to know anything but how to screw your boy-friends.'

'Look here! I——'

'Shut up, and show me where your tool-kit is. I suppose you've got a box-spanner, or did you lose that as well as your head?'

Paul handed him the kit, and opened the bonnet. Petrov started detaching the leads, his head bowed over the engine. Paul stealthily took a large spanner from the kit lying on the floor. He had never hated a man so much as this cruel giant. He marked the spot on the back of the thick neck where he would strike the first blow, and raised the spanner.

The next instant he was sent flying at the garage wall. One powerful hand gripped his lapels, and the other struck him savagely three times, fracturing a cheek-bone. Paul slumped against the wall, writhing and whimpering.

Petrov did not even bother to look up again. Neatly, he began to remove the plugs and clean them. His movements were as unhurried as if he had the whole morning for it: he whistled through his teeth, every now and then taking a cautious look from inside the garage door. No one was approaching along the track. A man drove a tractor from the farm down towards the village. Icicles hung from the garage eaves like the teeth of a huge broken comb.

In five minutes the plugs were replaced. Petrov pressed the starter. The engine turned, broke into life. He let it warm up for a couple of minutes. The gauge showed that the petrol tank was three-quarters full. Petrov switched off and got out. He inspected the chains on the rear wheels: they were secure. He inspected Paul Cunningham, sitting against the wall nursing his cheek, meditated whether to finish him on the spot, and finally, opening the rear door, slung him into the car instead.

'You stay there. We'll be out soon.'

The young man, utterly cowed, gave a sickly smile and nodded. Petrov took the ignition key and walked back into the cottage. . . .

'Road's blocked good and tight,' said Nigel, returning to the Citroën.

'What the hell do we do now?' Clare asked.

'Sparkes's men'll have to walk the rest of the way. We'd better do the same. Wait a minute, though.' He turned to the sergeant. 'You know this bit of earth well. Can we do it cross-country?'

'Walk? Well yes, sir, but——'

'No, drive. Through that gate. Could we cross a field and get back on to the road ahead of the block?'

'She'd never make it.'

'This car,' said Clare, 'will go over anything except a river or a house.'

The sergeant's eye lit up. 'It'd be a matter of several fields, I reckon, and old Tom's farmyard.'

'O.K., tumble in. Hey, Sparkes!' he shouted. The Superintendent came pounding back along the road. 'We're going to try through this gate. Open it up, will you?'

'You must be crazy.'

'The blizzards have blown a lot of the snow off the slopes into the lanes. Fields mayn't be too deep with it.'

Sparkes flung the field gate open. Clare put into its top notch the lever beneath the dashboard which raised the body of the car from the ground, paused a minute while the Citroën elevated till its passengers felt as if they were sitting in an elephant's howdah, then bumped over the ditch, shallower here, into the field.

'Wait a minute, I'm coming with you.' Sparkes bellowed at his men up the road. One crew was to double along to the village on foot; the other he ordered to reverse their car and follow the Citroën.

Nigel's sergeant, sitting by Clare now, had a good memory or an X-ray eye. 'Follow the track, missus,' he said.

'What track?'

'Goes diagonally across the field. Gate at far corner.'

In bottom gear they bumped and bucked over the pasture. Yes, there was a gate. Sparkes leapt out from the back and opened it.

'Now you can see Tom's farm. Beyond the next hedge. Make for the hedge just below that chimney. Another gate there.'

Looking back before he jumped in again, Sparkes saw the police car stuck in the middle of the field. It had followed in their track, but with its low clearance had been arrested by a snow-deep little hollow through which the Citroën had clawed its way.

'If you can't get it out, follow on foot,' he shouted to the crew.

Clare reached the gap in the hedge. Another gate was opened, and she drove through it, the car shaking like an ague-patient as it negotiated the bit of ground where cart ruts and the pock-marks of hooves had hardened to iron under the snow.

'Round the corner of the barn there, miss. Keep to the edge of the yard, it's Tom's midden. That'll bring you on to the drive, and we're back on the road in fifty yards.'

As they turned past the barn, disturbing a drift of hens and geese, and sending five piglets flying before them, an aged red-faced man bellowed at them, inarticulate with shock and rage. He looked as if he might charge the car with his pitch-fork and toss it into the ripe-smelling midden.

His gaping mouth at last managed to frame words—'What the bloody hell you'm doing here? Get off my land!'

The sergeant stuck his head out of the window. 'Morning, Tom. Sorry you've been disturbed. Had to take a short cut. Police business.'

'Well, I'll be buggered! Young Charlie Deacon, isn't it? Haven't seen you for a tidy long time.' The farmer advanced towards the car, lowering his pitch-fork. 'Who's the young lady?'

'My chauffeur. Got Superintendent Sparkes in the back. Load of V.I.P.'s.'

The farmer stood in front of the bonnet, struggling to get some mental grip upon this extraordinary visitation.

'We're in a hurry, Tom. Can't stop. Drive on, miss.'

Clare put the car in gear and crawled towards the immobile farmer, who at the last moment stepped out of the way into the midden. As they passed him, the sergeant, who was showing signs of acute euphoria, stuck his head out of the window and remarked, 'See you later, Tom. We're off to blow up Smugglers' Cottage.'

'Don't make sense,' said the farmer to his wife a few minutes later. 'Young Charlie didn't have no cannons in the car.' But by this time, the Citroën was entering Eggarswell.

'Where's that bloody patrol car?' asked Sparkes.

'Far end of the village, sir. You told Enticott to wait there.'

Outside the village shop a huge tractor stood, drumming quietly away to itself: as they approached, the driver emerged from the shop—a man wearing Wellingtons, an old army great-coat, and a red knitted hat with a bobble.

'Stop!' Nigel ordered.

Clare executed a long, dead-straight glissade, skating the Citroën to a halt a few feet from the tractor while the sergeant averted his eyes and went pale.

'Are you Jim?' asked Nigel, leaping out.

'That's right.'

'We want your tractor.'

'Mebbe you do. But you're not getting her,' said Jim eyeing this tall, thin maniac cautiously.

The sergeant got out and explanations were soon made, while Sparkes hurried down the village street to find his patrol car. Yes, Jim was the chap Lucy had described: he worked at Mr Thwaite's farm. No, he had not seen the child at Smugglers' Cottage for the last day or two. At this information, Nigel's heart sank. He told Jim rapidly how Lucy had been substituted for the boy 'Evan'. Jim told him that this supposed boy had run into his employer's farm the other night and had been taken back by the 'uncle' and 'aunt', who said he was delirious.

'It was you who picked up a paper dart thrown from the window.'

'That's right.'

'And posted it?'

'No, mister. Shoved it in my pocket and thought no more of it. My own kids started playing with it, I remember. They must have read the message and put it in the post, without telling me or their ma.'

'They'll get a reward for that.'

By this time every woman and child in the village was standing at the cottage doors, obscurely aware that something momentous was afoot: to have had a police patrol car in the village for two hours, filled with grim-looking and uninformative men, was sensation enough. Now they saw the heavily-built man in dark overcoat and felt hat pounding back down the street.

Rumour grew wings and flew round the village uttering an ever weirder selection of gossip—Jim had been arrested for murdering his employer; the squire had been caught red-handed taking part in an orgy with four beautiful Russian spies.

'Sparkes, Jim here will take us up to the farm on his tractor,' said Nigel.

The Superintendent, breathing heavily, stared at him. Then he got the point. 'Good for you. The only vehicle they won't suspect if they're on the lookout.'

Jim climbed into the driving-seat. Nigel got on at the back. Sparkes rattled off a series of instructions to his sergeant, telling him what to do when the reinforcements arrived, then climbed up, gave a hand to Elena Wragby and hauled her after him on to the narrow platform at the rear of the tractor, an area already congested enough with iron stanchions, the apparatus of the winch, two oil lamps, several containers of milk, and other miscellaneous fixtures and cargo.

'Standing room only,' remarked the Superintendent.

Nigel looked down at Clare. 'You stay here. Shan't be long,' he shouted above the thumping of the engine.

Her lips formed the words, 'Good luck. Be careful. Darling.' She was wearing the secretive, charmingly sly look Nigel knew so well: he doubted if she would stay put here, but there was no time to argue about it.

The great tractor rolled down the street, followed—it seemed— by the whole of Eggarswell (*Pop.* 532).

'The bodyguard's awkward,' said Nigel.

Sparkes made gestures at them, like swatting a cloud of flies, and received a ragged cheer in response.

'Try making a speech instead.'

'Bah!'

The procession was halted a hundred yards on by the crew of the patrol car who, letting the tractor past, lined across the road and shooed the population of Eggarswell back towards their houses. Jim at once turned sharp right on to the track that led to the farm.

In the car and in the village it had been sheltered. Now, high up on the huge machine, unprotected, they felt the north-east wind tearing and chewing at their faces like a wild beast. The tractor reeled slowly uphill, with its enormous tyres scrabbling on patches of ice, lurching sideways like a small boat struck by a wave, when a wheel went in and out of one of the deep, bone-hard ruts.

Nigel, his foot painfully jammed between two iron fixtures, put his arm round Elena to steady her. He could feel her body shivering: her face was white and set. She gripped his hand, her rings digging into it. 'If only she's alive,' Elena kept muttering, like a prayer.

Half-way up the track, Nigel said, 'This is where we become invisible. Let's hope.'

The roof of a cottage began to appear above the bleak skyline ahead. The passengers bent low as they could behind the stalwart frame of their driver. If anyone was on the lookout, he would see the familiar sight of Jim returning to the farm on his tractor.

Jim turned right into the farmyard, stopping behind an outbuilding that cut them off from view of Smugglers' Cottage. They got down and hurried into the farmhouse, where they were met by the patrol-car man who had been ordered to keep the cottage under observation.

'Anything moving?' asked Sparkes.

'No, sir. But you're only just in time. A big chap—I reckon he's the one whose description you circulated—came out with another man, fifteen or twenty minutes ago. They went into the garage. Trouble starting their car, maybe. The big chap's only just gone back into the house. The other one must be in the car or the garage still.'

'Good. That's two of them. Did you see any others?'

'No, sir.'

'No sign of the child?'

'Afraid not, sir.'

'Right. Back to your post.'

The constable ran upstairs.

Sparkes turned to Nigel. 'Looks as if they don't suspect anything yet. We can't do anything till my chaps get here. That'll be ten minutes, maybe. We don't know how many of them there are in the cottage. All we know is they're going to make a break for it any minute. If the child's alive——'

'The child *is* alive. We've got to act on that assumption.'

'Right. They'll try to take her out with them. They can't get very far, but I daren't risk her being involved in a gun battle. On the other hand, if they saw us moving in on them now, I'd be equally afraid for her life.' He turned to Elena. 'Mrs Wragby, it's all yours now. Try to keep them talking as long as you can. And try to keep them away from the windows. We'll be with you as quickly——'

'Don't worry. I understand you.'

Sparkes hesitated a moment, then shook his prisoner's hand, wished her good luck and let her free.

From a bedroom window they watched her walk unfaltering up the track, knock at the cottage door . . .

'Go and answer it,' Petrov ordered Annie. 'I must keep out of sight.' He had not seen the figure of the woman pass the sitting-room window: Annie had, and assumed it to be some visitor from the village come to inquire about 'Evan's' health. So, when she opened the door and the visitor said, 'Good morning, I've come to ask about——' Annie interrupted fulsomely, 'Oh, that's very kind of you. Evan's better. His father's come to take him back to London. We're just off. I'm afraid I must ask——'

Annie's voice trailed off, for the visitor's pale face froze into an expression so formidable, so fierce that it might have been the Medusa confronting her.

'Ivan's father? Ivan's father has been dead for years. I am Ivan's mother.'

Annie stared at her in bewilderment. Petrov had never told her the exact provenance of the boy. But she recognised now the visitor's voice: it was the voice of the woman who had telephoned to her from the Guest House—Mrs Wragby.

She tried to shut the door, but Elena thrust her aside and stepped into the hall. 'It's Lucy I've come for. Where is she?'

Annie's face turned a sicklier yellow. Before she could speak, Elena flung open a door and made an entrance grander and more dramatic than ever she had made on the stage.

'So it's you,' she said to Petrov.

'How the hell did you get here, Mrs Wragby?'

Elena crossed to the window-seat—thank God there's only one window, she thought—and sat down. 'I drove to the village, inquired for this house, then walked up.'

'And how did you know about this house?' Petrov's voice was a silky rumble.

Elena explained about the message Lucy had managed to smuggle out. 'The letter reached me this morning. It was addressed to my husband. I opened it.'

'*You* opened it?'

'My husband could hardly do so, being in hospital.'

'Hospital?'

'You did not quite succeed in killing him,' said Elena in a cold, matter-of-fact voice. She glanced at Petrov contemptuously. 'You need not look so alarmed. He is unconscious still. He has told the police nothing. I don't understand why you thought it'd be necessary to kill him, once you'd got the information from him.'

Petrov's little, wild-boar eyes probed at her. 'That is none of your affair,' he said at last. 'You informed the police about this letter from Lucy, no doubt?'

'*Informed* them? *I?*' Elena's voice was weary and exasperated: she did not make the mistake of sounding indignant. 'What on earth do you take me for? I'm in this too deep to go running to the police.'

'Then how did you find your way here alone?'

'The envelope had a Longport postmark. I remembered seeing a cottage, like the one Lucy described, while my husband and I were motoring around here last year.'

'Well, go on.'

'I was allowed to go into Belcaster this morning. I said I wanted to visit my husband in hospital. I was not allowed to see him—he's too ill. Then I drove over here.'

'With the police following you. That was a stupid thing to do. Stupid, or worse.'

'I made quite sure there were no police cars behind me. I'm quite used to throwing off shadowers—from the old days.'

'When you tried to betray the People's government.'

Elena shrugged. 'I've paid enough for that, haven't I?'

'You may yet have to pay more. And I'm still asking, what have you come here for? Make it snappy. We've got to get off.'

Elena reached for the handbag on the window-seat beside her. Petrov pounced, with fantastic alacrity for so cumbrous a man, tore it from her hands, opened it, shook out the contents on the floor.

'No revolver. What a nervous man you are, my poor Petrov,' said Elena pityingly. 'Perhaps you should take off your overcoat. You're in a muck-sweat, as the English say.'

'I asked you a question.'

'What have I come here for? To ask *you* two questions. First, where is Lucy? Is she alive?' Elena raised her magnificent, carrying voice on these last six words. Upstairs, Lucy faintly heard them, recognised her step-mother's voice. The past week had taught her caution. She repressed the impulse to call out, and reached for her skipping rope.

'Lucy?' babbled Annie, who had been listening to all this with hypnotised attention. 'Oh, she's not here any longer. She was moved elsewhere last night, she tried to run away, and we thought——'

'Shut up!' said Petrov.

The faint thump of feet skipping could be heard from some-where overhead.

'That answers my first question,' said Elena. Her impassive face gave not the slightest inkling of the joy that flooded her heart. Lucy is here, and alive. But somehow I must keep her alive. Time, time, play for time. She dared not even glance out of the window to see if the police were closing in. 'My second question is, why did you kill Ivan?'

'I did not kill Ivan.'

Elena gave him a look that would have made anyone but a Petrov quail. 'Do not add futile lying to your other despicable qualities.'

'Annie, we must be off in five minutes. You were going to get us a drink. Bring one for Mrs Wragby too.' When the woman had gone out, he turned to Elena. 'Ivan's death was a mistake. I regret it very much.'

'You regret it!' she said in a searing tone.

'Yes. A stupid young man, who was helping Annie over this affair, took him to the station. There was a blizzard, it seems: the car stuck in a drift, quite near Longport, and this young fool lost his head and told Ivan to walk the rest of the way.'

Elena's face, white and hard as marble, gave no hint of her feelings.

'We made a bargain,' she said quietly. 'In return for my help, you were going to give me Ivan and get us back safely to our country. I see I was a fool to trust a man like you.' She added two words in Hungarian that brought sparks of fury into Petrov's eyes.

'I had every intention of keeping the bargain,' he angrily protested.

'But the bargain was not kept. Why should I believe this story of yours? You are incapable of the truth. You have told so many lies in your life that you have forgotten what truth is. I pity you.'

'And what about the lies you told your husband? You to talk about lying—a woman who could betray her husband and his little girl!'

'I am not proud of it.' Elena's voice became broken and appealing. 'I have nothing left to live for. That is why I offer *you* a bargain. Let Lucy go, and you can do whatever you like with me. Kill me, make me your mistress, anything.'

'Well, well, well. Why should I want a stringy, dried-up old bitch like you for a mistress?'

'Perhaps not. But you love killing, don't you? Don't you, Petrov? Maybe you've never killed a *woman* before. You'd find it most enjoyable. And you'd be in no danger from me any more.'

This statement, made in Elena's most thrilling, intense voice, disconcerted Petrov: it turned their encounter into a kind of fantasy he could not cope with. Certainly this woman must be disposed of; but that she should encourage him to do it made him feel, for a moment, profoundly uneasy. His immediate reaction was to think she must have some card in her hand ready to trump him. He moved to the window, pushing her aside: no, the farm away to his right seemed quiet as ever.

Annie came in with a tray of drinks. Brandy, soda, a glass of

171

lemonade. A silent look passed between them. Annie nodded slightly, reassuring Petrov that the lemonade and one of the brandies were doped. 'Where's Paul?' she asked.

'Waiting outside.'

Petrov handed Elena the brandy glass Annie indicated. His mind was working fast again, its animal cunning restored. Let her drink the doped brandy. They'd have to make room for her in the car. She'd asked him to kill her. Very well, she too should die the death he had planned for Paul and Lucy.

'Cheers,' he said, raising his glass. 'Come on, Mrs Wragby, drink up: you must be cold, and we're in a hurry.'

'I do not drink with pigs. I offered you a bargain. Do you accept it?'

Petrov glared at her. 'Fetch the child,' he commanded Annie. . . .

The armed police from the stranded cars had arrived in Eggarswell five minutes before. Charlie Deacon, whom Sparkes had told to wait for them, sent two on a detour to approach Smugglers' Cottage from the back and prevent any escape that way. The rest he had led up the hillside to the right of the track, keeping the farmhouse between them and the cottage—six armed men panting after their mile run, and himself. From boyhood escapades, he remembered every fold in the ground, every gap in a hedge. Silently they filed through the farm's paddock gate and in at a side door.

'The Super's upstairs,' said Mr Thwaite. 'I'll take you.'

'All present and correct, sir,' said Charlie. 'I've got two of them working their way round to the back. They should be in position in three or four minutes.'

'Good lad. I want the two best shots up here with the rifles. Halford and Bright. If the big chap tries to get away, they're to nail him.'

Charlie ran down and fetched the two men upstairs.

'Hallo,' said Sparkes, still peering through the window. 'There's a chap coming out of the garage. That's the other one, eh? Wambling about a bit.'

The figure of Paul Cunningham disappeared through the front door.

'Right,' said Sparkes. 'The rest will come with me.' He ran

downstairs, Nigel and Charlie following. 'We're going to move in,' he told the four men. 'Hope Charlie's lads are in position. Any of you want a medal?'

The policemen grinned uncertainly.

'You may get one today. There's a man in the cottage who's a killer. There may be others. We've got to jump them before he harms the little girl. The cottage has no windows at this end. So unless someone's getting a crick in his neck watching sideways out of a front window, they won't see us till we're close. We're going to move out of the farmyard, cross the track, walk up along the grass on its left-hand side. That way, we'll soon have the garage between us and the cottage. When we get there, *if* we get there, we can have a cosy chat about the next move. And now put these on.'

Sparkes handed out four milkmen's overalls he had borrowed from Mr Thwaite. 'Won't catch the eye so much in those against the snow. Keep your weapons hidden underneath them.' He stood back to admire the effect. 'Lumme, what a shower you look! They'll take you for a deputation of cricket umpires.'

The men laughed. Charlie protested:

'What about me, sir?'

'You can set up a first-aid post here, Sergeant.'

The men laughed again.

'Haven't you got a white coat yourself, sir?'

'Don't fuss, Charlie boy. I'm going to lead this shower from behind. Off we go.'

Annie Stott pushed Lucy into the room. For a few moments Elena failed to recognise her, and Lucy didn't see Elena, sitting with her back to the window through which the snow-glare dazzled the child.

'Hallo, darling,' said Elena gently. 'What *have* they done to you?'

Lucy's eyes widened. Then she ran into Elena's arms.

'I *knew* you'd find me! Have you come to ransom me? Where's Papa?'

'He's in hospital. Don't worry, he had an accident, but he'll soon be well again. He's sorry he couldn't come with me.'

'When he's well, we can all go tobogganing, can't we?'

'Yes, darling,' said Elena, wincing.

'Will my hair grow again?'

'Of course it will. *And* go back to its natural colour.'

Lucy beamed at her. 'You're a super mother, Elena.'

Elena hid her face a moment in the child's shoulder. Oh God, why don't they come? I can't keep this up any longer.

Lucy turned in her arms. 'Who's that man?'

'Don't point, darling. He's a friend of this lady here.'

'Aunt Annie's friend. She said he was coming. But I don't understand——'

'So this is Lucy,' said Petrov, coming over and putting his hand on the back of her thin neck. 'A pretty little girl. Well, Lucy, we're all leaving now. Here's a nice glass of lemonade. Drink it up quickly, and we'll start.'

Lucy took the glass, remembering what Annie had told her. Annie sat tense, hardly daring to breathe. She felt confused and helpless: she could not think what Petrov had in mind—did he intend to take Mrs Wragby to the same death as he'd planned for Paul and Lucy, or was he going to accept her bargain? A sense of failure and foreboding overcame Annie: the mission she had so proudly accepted and so efficiently carried out was lost in a fog of unreality, which had been thickening during the last few days, blotting out any possible shape of the future.

She saw Lucy pretending to sip the drink, wandering across the room towards a potted plant in one corner. She must distract Petrov while Lucy poured it away. For that plucky kid to die now would be a pointless waste, serving no purpose but Petrov's ruling passion. Annie got to her feet, moving to put herself between Petrov and Lucy. Then she stopped, thinking it might be better if Petrov forced the child to drink—better if she were asleep when Petrov killed her.

Elena Wragby sat silent, passive, withdrawn: as though, Annie thought, she was praying or waiting for something—an issue which was now taken out of her hands.

'Haven't you finished that lemonade yet?' barked Petrov, moving over to the child.

The door flew open and Paul Cunningham staggered in. He had got out of the car a few minutes before. Though the farm buildings blocked out from the cottage any view of men approaching it up the fields from Eggarswell, the garage, thirty yards to the right of the

174

cottage, gave a different angle of vision. Glancing through the garage window, Paul noticed the tail-end of the file of policemen moving into the farm paddock: their caps and the muzzles of rifles showed above the hedge.

For a minute or two, Paul was paralysed with despair and indecision. This was the end of everything. Disgrace, long imprisonment. It could be less long if he went straight over to the farm and told the police everything. But Petrov might see him walking away; and he feared Petrov far more than the police. Feared him, hated him, but in a perverse way felt bound to him, as an adolescent is bound to a harsh father infinitely stronger and more resourceful than himself. Petrov's contempt for him rankled, like the pain of his cheekbone. The contempt would change to gratitude, admiration even, if he stood by Petrov, went in and told him what he'd seen, like a loyal son. Perhaps Petrov, with his ruthless cunning, could even now fight his way out of the trap and take Paul with him. He started the engine, then hurried towards the cottage, staggering in the snow.

'I told you to stay in the car,' Petrov shouted.

'Police! I saw them going into the farm. The engine's running. They've got guns,' Paul gasped.

Petrov swung round on Elena, looming above her like a cliff about to fall. 'You treacherous bitch!' He drew the revolver from his overcoat pocket and clamped a hand on Lucy's neck. He would run to the garage, holding the child as a shield between him and the armed police, and make a break for it.

'Don't you touch the child!' Elena leapt to her feet, but he thrust her back on to the window-seat.

'Back door,' said Paul. 'They'll have the front covered.'

Elena made another rush at him, but he swung Lucy between them. 'Get out of my way, or I'll shoot you both.'

He backed into the passage, through the scullery, and with the hand that held the gun felt for the door-knob behind him. Elena was after him like a tigress. As he pulled the back door open, she snatched Lucy from him. 'Run!' she cried. She was between Lucy now and Petrov, who stood on the threshold.

Petrov shot her in the body. With her last strength she slammed the door in his face and locked him out.

Nigel, from the bedroom window of the farmhouse, heard the

shot and went pelting downstairs, out into the yard. The tractor was there, its engine turning, Jim in the iron saddle. 'Wait there!' Nigel shouted, and ran to peer over thé low hedge between farmyard and track. Sparkes and his file of men had only just gone out: they were moving along the grass verge to the left of the track. Charlie's two men were stumbling down the hillside at the back of the cottage, still fifty yards away from it.

Petrov slunk along the deep passage behind the cottage, invisible to them, reached the garage and slipped inside before the riflemen in the farmhouse could fire. Sparkes, leading his men from in front, broke into a run; but he was still twenty yards from the garage door when the car shot out of it, skidded on to the track and accelerated.

Sparkes's detachment desperately tried to get out the weapons they were carrying under their milkmen's overcoats, but while they were still fumbling, Petrov was almost past. Sparkes leapt at the running board, and was flung back sprawling on to the snow. His men began to fire at the receding car, and one of the farmhouse riflemen shattered its windscreen. But the driver was apparently unhurt.

Nigel had seen the car plunge out of the garage. He gesticulated and yelled to Jim, 'Drive out! Block the track!'

Jim was not in time to do that, for the tractor stalled at the first, over-excited acceleration. But he started it again instantly, and began trundling out of the farmyard towards the track. He could hear the crack of rifle-shots. From his high seat he saw over the hedge the roof of a car speeding downhill, ten yards away. He accelerated. The tractor hit the car amidships, flung it on its side over the verge of the track, and continuing its impetus struck the shattered car again. The front wheels mounted. The tractor came to a stop, like a great blue and red heraldic beast rampant over its prey.

'Rammed the bugger,' Jim remarked to himself with satisfaction. It was worth the pain of the sprained wrist and the bruises he had received from the collision, desperately gripping the wheel so as not to be flung out of his seat.

Sparkes and Nigel, running up now, saw a terrible thing. With the huge weight of the tractor recumbent upon it, the body of the car, already weakened by the first impact, began to cave in, slowly crushing the driver. Through the torn metal and shattered glass they saw Petrov's excruciated face and heard him screaming, like an animal trapped.

There was nothing they could do. The tractor was immovably couched upon the wreckage beneath.

A man came running back from the cottage. 'Kid's all right, sir. Mrs Wragby's dead. She tried to stop him taking the kid away, and he shot her. We've got two others under guard.'

'Thank God for that,' came Clare's voice from behind them. She had walked up the track, unnoticed in the confusion. If Petrov had got away, thought Nigel, he might well have run her down in his berserk career.

'Go to Lucy!' he said.

Petrov had stopped screaming at last. It seemed to leave a hole in the air. Everything was hushed again, silent as the expanses of snow that stretched into the distance all round. Gradually this silence filled up the jagged hole left by Petrov's screaming.

From the cottage, as Clare approached it, a man and a woman emerged, handcuffed, policemen on either side. Their faces were drained of all emotion. They moved like puppets.

In the sitting-room a sergeant had Lucy on his lap, trying to comfort her. Men were coming from the farm with a hurdle on which to carry Elena's body away.

When she saw Clare, Lucy began to cry again. Clare took her from the sergeant.

'He tried to shoot me,' Lucy sobbed.

'That's all over, darling. You're quite safe now. Nigel and I are taking you back to your papa. He'll be so proud of you—to hear what a brave girl you've been. It was a marvellous idea, writing that story about Cinders and making a dart with the paper.'

'Well, I thought it was rather a super idea myself; but I never thought you'd get the letter.' Lucy gave only a stifled sob now.

'We did. I'll tell you how, later. There's a nice sergeant called Charlie who used to live in the village, and he recognised this house from your description. So we all piled into cars and drove here at blinding speed, through drifts and fields and farmyards——'

'You *didn't*!' Lucy's eyes began to shine.

'We did. Two fields and one farmyard anyway. Scattering ducks and hens and pigs before us. It was a great lark.'

'And Elena came with you?'

'Yes. She was the one who really rescued you.'

Lucy fell silent for a moment, puzzling out something in her mind. Two men passed the window, but the body they carried on a hurdle was invisible below the level of the sill.

'Were they really spies?' asked Lucy.

'Oh yes. They kidnapped you: they wanted to exchange you for an important scientific secret your father has.'

'I see. But he didn't give them the secret.'

'No.'

'That big man—he was the chief spy?'

'Yes. Your papa had a fight with him. That's why he's in hospital. He put up a splendid fight, but Petrov was much stronger.'

'Poor Papa.'

Clare judged it was now the right moment. 'You'll have to be extra nice and loving with him for a bit.'

'And Elena too.'

'You'll have to make up for Elena, darling.'

Lucy took Clare's hand, bracing herself. 'You mean she's dead?'

'Yes. Petrov shot her. She died saving you.' Clare went on quickly, 'He would have tried to take you away with him, but Elena stopped him. She——'

'I know. She snatched me from him and told me to run, and I ran into this room. There was an awful bang.' Lucy gulped.

'Elena was a real heroine. Never forget that. She wasn't sorry to die, because she knew you were safe.'

Lucy was quiet, digesting this. Then she trembled. 'He won't be coming back?'

'Petrov? No fear! He was trying to escape in the car, and your Jim drove into it with his tractor. There was quite a battle before that. I expect you heard the rifle-shots.'

'Yes, I did . . . You mean, Jim killed him?'

'Yes. The tractor squashed the car flat, with Petrov inside it.'

'Good,' said Lucy, her grey eyes sparkling. 'Sardined him.'

'Sardined him is right.' Clare was relieved that her instinct had been correct. Lucy was only a child, with a child's ignorant and wholesome delight in gory detail. Soon, with any luck, the last week would seem no more than a fairy-tale to her—a tale in which the ogre came to a sticky and satisfying end.

'Can we go and see Papa soon?' Lucy asked.

'Let's go now.'

THE END